a novel

FRONT RANGE BRIDES
BOOK 1

DAVALYNN SPENCER

To the one

who found me.

Whoso findeth a wife findeth a good thing,

and obtaineth favour of the LORD.

Proverbs 18:22

CHAPTER 1

Olin Springs, Colorado, 1880

The shooter did not flinch.

Neither did Henry Reiker. He merely slammed to the bank lobby floor with a hole in his chest.

Mae Ann dropped to her knees, ears ringing from the close gunshot. She lifted Henry's head, and his blue eyes teared at her touch. Her first.

"I'm sorry," he whispered. "I . . . " Blood trickled from the corner of his mouth as he fought for a gurgling breath.

His last.

Mae Ann gently lowered his head and stood to face his murderer. Her fingers clenched into tight balls at her sides, lest she claw the smirk from the gunman's face. Surely he would dispatch her to join her betrothed. Such a fate would be ten times better than what awaited her in this treacherous town. For she had no family, no means, no friends. Nothing—other than Henry's offer of marriage.

Gun smoke veiled the lobby, stinging her nose and shrouding the robber and the other patrons too frightened to move. That had been Henry's mistake. He'd moved in front of her when the gunman reached for the cameo at her throat.

She tore the brooch from her collar and threw it in the shooter's face. The pin pricked his cheek and bounced to the floor, clanking against the hardwood. A red dot rose on the man's face.

He stepped over Henry's body with a threat in his cold eyes. No, a promise.

"Tuck!"

The harsh reprimand jerked him to a halt, but not before his tobacco-fouled breath washed Mae Ann's face.

Stuffing money bags with coins and stacks of bills, his partner cursed from behind the counter. "Get over here and help me carry this. We ain't got all day."

The gunman's disrobing glare swept her from neck to skirt hem before he spit on Henry's coat and turned away. Only after the animal joined his companion did she dare look down at the shiny black spot marring the worn and faded fabric. Right next to a seeping hole.

A slight sound drew her to a tall man by the darkened window. He slid a finger behind the shade the robbers had hastily pulled when they entered. His dark eyes moved but his head did not, and he watched the bandits as he leaned toward the glass for a quick glance outside.

"You better go out the back." His voice sent shivers up her spine. Deep and gravelly as if dug from a dark pit.

A hammer cocked. The murderer raised his weapon and pointed through the teller's gate. "You tellin' us how to do our job, cowboy?"

The man lowered his hand and met the gunman's threat straight-on, neither fear nor contempt on his face. "I'm telling you the sheriff is headed this way, and your lookout is danglin' over the hitching rail."

The hammer slid back.

"Come on." The leader yanked the gunman's arm. "I told you no shootin'. Now we got the law on us." He rushed into the back room and jiggled the doorknob until the door gave way.

The gunman paused at the counter, a gorged bag under each arm, his foul glare resting on Mae Ann. "This ain't over, missy."

The back door did not close, though she knew they were gone, as did the others, who all began talking at once. A woman fainted into her husband's arms—a bit after the fact.

The man at the window raised the blinds and opened the front door but did not leave. Instead, he spoke with each patron, giving a firm handshake to the men and reassuring words and a tip of his wide-brimmed hat to their wives. Mae Ann remained the only woman alone.

Again kneeling beside Henry, she pulled a hankie from her sleeve and wiped the spittle from his clothing. Her hand shook, but no grief weighed on her heart other than pity for an innocent man slain. She knew little of Henry Reiker. Only what he had shared in his letters—that he was weary of loneliness and longed for someone to help him on his meager farm. He'd promised hard work but faithfulness as well, and joy in the small things of life. Could a woman in Mae Ann's position ask for more?

She looked for a basket or spittoon to deposit her hankie in. Two dusty boots stopped beside her, and her gaze followed long trouser-clad legs to a belt, a chambray shirt, and a calloused hand offering assistance. The man from the window.

She accepted, and stood to look *up* into dark eyes. A rare occurrence for a woman as unfashionably tall as she.

"My condolences, ma'am." He doffed his hat and glanced at Henry. "I'll take him to the undertaker for you."

She'd not thought that far ahead. Oh, Lord, what should she do? Only the wedding had been on her mind since meeting Henry at the train station, not a burial. She clasped her hands tightly. "Thank you, sir. I—uh—I appreciate your help." Her hands trembled in spite of gripping them until her fingers ached. "If you could just tell me where that might be, I can make arrangements." How she would pay for those arrangements, she had no idea.

Traitorous tears fought to escape. Blinking rapidly, she looked away, toward the counter where the teller leaned, ashen and shaken. In that time, another patron had come to help carry Henry's body. The first stranger caught her eye and tipped his head slightly to his right. She followed them out the door.

A man did indeed lie over the hitching rail near Henry's farm wagon. With his hands cuffed beneath him, he hung there like a sack of corn, crying.

Tugging at her velvet jacket, she disdained its snuggly tailored fit, much too warm for the afternoon. But it held her together and upright, kept her from crumbling, as if it were emotional armor. She lifted her skirt at the alley and followed Henry's bearers, who mounted the next boardwalk and continued on, unceremoniously carrying her future to its end.

She reached for her reticule, forgetting it had been snagged by the gunman's greedy paws. Her fingers habitually felt for the brooch, the cause of poor Henry's death, and she could not remember if the murderer had stooped to pick it up or if it still lay on the bank floor. Everything of value was gone, other than her trunk in Henry's buckboard. She glanced back but could not see the wagon for the people rushing in and out of the bank.

When she looked ahead again, the men were gone. She stopped and pressed a hand against her waist and the rising fear within. Never had she felt so alone, so abandoned. Not even after her mother's consumptive death at the rooming house. Why had Henry insisted they stop at the bank before going to the church? That singular decision changed everything. It cost her a husband, a home, and all the money she had scrimped and saved. It cost her—yet again—a small hope of joy, snatched away at the last moment like her little dog, Percy.

And it cost a gentle and innocent man his life. *Oh, Henry, why did you have to defend me?*

Across the street, storefronts advertised a saddle shop and livery, a small bakery, and the mercantile, but no undertaker. Just ahead, a shingle hanging above the boardwalk said *Hardware.* She bent slightly to read the one beyond it. *Barber.* In smaller script below, *Undertaker.*

Oh dear.

The stranger's head and shoulders popped into view from the doorway, and he motioned her inside.

She hurried to the threshold, but halted at the sight of Henry lying on a table inside. A spectacled man in a barber's apron stretched a measuring tape alongside him, then scribbled something on a small paper and applied the measure to Henry's shoulders.

Mae Ann gripped the door frame, afraid she might lose what little breakfast she'd had before boarding the train in Denver that morning. The stranger came to her, took her elbow, and pointed to a settee, a small table, and an old ladder-back chair across the room—the undertaker's efforts to dress up his sorrowful establishment.

Mumbling her thanks, she chose the hard chair. Comfort seemed inappropriate for such a time and place.

He took a knee before her, a most unexpected gesture regardless of her situation. His warm eyes posed no threat, nor did his strong jaw, and he removed his hat to reveal dark hair dented from its constant presence. A man accustomed to hard work, she presumed, consistent with the calloused hand that had helped her earlier.

He did not smile, but sympathy tinged his expression. "Can I help you in any other way, ma'am?"

The thought came suddenly and clear, as if it were the most logical and well-suited idea. She weighed her options—which were nonexistent—squared her shoulders and met his unwavering regard. "Do you have a wife?"

He glanced away and his mouth worked as if sorting through possible replies. "No, ma'am, I do not."

She schooled her features as best she could, feigning confidence. "Would you like one?"

~

Mrs. Reiker's question shot Cade Parker to both feet. He set his hat and regarded her openly. Was this offer for herself or for another mail-order bride? An acquaintance or a sister? He knew of her expected arrival—the whole town did. For the last two months, Reiker had talked of nothing else every time Cade saw him at the church house or the mercantile.

He cleared his throat. "Thank you kindly, ma'am, but I'm not looking for a wife."

She cut a look to her dead husband, then back to Cade as if he hadn't given an answer. "I am a woman alone. As are you."

He swallowed a smart reply. "Beg pardon, ma'am, but I do believe that is not what you intended to say. Last time I checked . . ." He left off.

Her brow furrowed and realization smoothed it, painting her cheeks a becoming pink. Not only was she bold, she was a handsome woman to boot. Not too thin. Eyes and hair the color of coffee, a fair neck beneath her torn collar. She bit her lower lip and its color deepened. Reiker's gamble on a mail-order bride had paid off.

During the holdup, Cade had expected her to fly into the bandit, and had thought what a loss if the rough killed her as he'd killed her husband.

She let out a breath, impatience insinuated. "I *meant* if you have no wife, as you say, then you are also alone. As am I." Her eyes shot suddenly to his. "Unless you have family."

"None here." Not counting Deacon, his dog, and his horse.

"Well then." Her bearing relaxed. "In light of your bravery and kindness, I would like to make a business proposition."

Bold, handsome, and quick to judge. He'd been called a lot of things, but never brave or kind. *Pigheaded* flitted by on a memory, but he swatted it down with a dozen other titles he didn't care to face. "I'd have to say your husband qualified on both counts you mention, and it got him killed. Shouldn't you be mourning him instead of making business deals?"

She interlocked her fingers, squeezing them until her knuckles whitened. Not the hands of a pampered woman, but neither were they red or cracked. In a low voice she answered his question. "He was not yet my husband."

Full of dandies, this one. He folded his arms across his chest and darkened his tone. "You know nothing about me. I could be a hornswoggler, an outlaw. A gambler."

Unmoved by his words, she raised her chin a notch. "On the contrary, sir, I know as much about you as I did my betrothed." Her eyes strayed to the undertaker, who continued to measure and mark. Returning her attention to Cade, she met him brace for brace. No whimpering female, she.

"I know you are not a self-centered man, or you would have fled the bank at the first opportunity. I know you are brave but thoughtful, based upon how you spoke to the robbers. I know you are gentle by the way you regarded each woman in the bank after the robbery—and Henry's murder—and I know you to be respected by the men impacted by the situation, for each spoke to you with goodwill and friendliness."

She paused and studied her hands, then looked him in the eye. "And I know you are kind, for you are the only one of ten who offered to help me with Henry."

Where was she last fall when he was dickering with the cattle buyers?

"Nor are you a gambler, for your hands and attire speak of a man acquainted with hard, honest work." She sighed and glanced again toward her dead intended. "But if you are employed as Henry was, a farmer, then you may well indeed be a gambler."

A wittier woman he'd never met. She'd be a hard match for any man not up to snuff. But she'd picked a cold trail, and he'd already told her so.

He'd considered a wife once. Thought he couldn't make it in this country without someone beside him, the way his ma was for his pa. But he'd chosen poorly when he settled on the fair and flirtatious Alexandra Hemphill, who'd sashayed under his nose at a church social, hobbled his good sense, and then taken up with a flashier man. They'd left for parts unknown. San Francisco, he'd heard later.

But Cade and his cows had done all right.

"Well?" The widow, or whatever she was, queried him from her seat, ramrod straight, not a begging bone in her body.

He must be out of his mind, though he had been thinking about hiring a housekeeper. This gal's throat-choking riggin' and air of respectability spoke to sound morals. And if she could cook, well, so much the better.

He shifted his weight and stood squarely. "A business proposition, you say."

Hope glimmered in her eyes before she masked them by considering the plank floor. "Yes, a *business* proposition. I am quite a good cook, I'll mince no words. And I keep a clean house. Wash, mend, tend to a garden."

The offer became more appealing as she tallied all the things he did himself besides work the ranch.

"Can you ride?"

She blinked up at him. Then again.

His answer, but he asked again anyway. "Can you horseback?"

Her chin rose higher. "I can learn."

He held in a snort. She'd not answered him directly, but she'd not lied either. "This business proposition—what's in it for you?"

At that she stood, and he noticed for the first time that she had no lady's handbag. No satchel. Her hands smoothed the sides of her suit, dark brown like his bay gelding tied near

Reiker's old wagon. A rip in her collar bore witness to the brooch she'd thrown at the gunman.

He saw it now—her desperation.

"A home and respectability. Safety." Her color heightened and she lowered her gaze and her voice. "I have seen my twentieth birthday—plus a few—so if I do not appeal to you, we can live as man and wife in name only."

Plus a few? He'd wager one, maybe two. Nearly a decade stood between them, a surprising discovery since Reiker had been closer to forty.

"I have no expectations other than that if you are not satisfied with my help and companionship, you send me away with enough funds for lodging until I can find employment elsewhere. You have my word that I shall repay you every penny."

Shame nicked his conscience for forcing such an admission from her. But taking on a wife—before God and man—was no small thing. He removed his hat, plowed his hair back, caught her eye. "I'll put you up at the hotel tonight and cover your fare home on the next train."

Her steel melted and she sank to the chair.

"Mrs. Reiker." The undertaking barber lifted his hand. "A word, please?"

Before should could rise, Cade crossed the room and pulled a silver coin from his vest pocket. "Will this cover a decent burial in the town cemetery?"

The barber nodded and accepted the offer. "It will. Thank you, Mr. Parker."

Cade returned to the woman who'd also made an offer—herself, as a matter of business. A risk he'd not take if the roles were reversed. But if offers were being made here today, why couldn't he accept hers? It wouldn't be the first time a couple married sight unseen. Under different circumstances, he might have been the letter writer requesting a bride rather than Henry Reiker.

He took in her squared shoulders, her tight jaw, and the absence of Alexandra-like mewling. She'd faced down a gunman, been cheated out of a husband and probably all her money, and considered him trustworthy. Was he? Or was he plumb loco?

"Ma'am?"

She regarded him mutely, dark eyes clouded, back straight. A fighter to the finish.

"We're done here." He offered his hand as he had at the bank.

She accepted and stood, but did not cling to him and withdrew her fingers.

He stepped in closer than acceptable, but hang it all, not one thing yet today had been acceptable. Moving closer still, he caught her hair's flowery scent and the fading traces of fear. He lowered his voice. "Were you and Reiker to be married this afternoon?"

Pain flickered across her lovely face, but she settled on his eyes. "Yes." A whisper.

He turned slightly and offered his arm. "Then if you wouldn't mind becoming Mrs. Cade Parker, I'd like to see if the preacher is still available."

She stiffened, no hint of relief or gratitude. "I am not in need of your sympathy, sir."

Ah, pride. He smiled to himself. "But you are in need of a husband, as you so aptly stated a moment ago."

She hesitated, then placed her hand in the crook of his arm.

He covered it with his. "Your name?"

11

"Mae Ann. Mae Ann Remington."

"Well, then, Miss Remington. Shall we be on our way?"

Lord, help him. *Loco* didn't even come close.

CHAPTER 2

W ho had asked whom?

Mae Ann still stung from Mr. Parker's earlier refusal, yet here she was, on his arm, headed for a white clapboard church at the end of Main Street.

Had male pride insisted he reject her offer and then make his own for the very same thing? *Humph.* She regarded him from the corner of her eye. He could be the sort of man who must be in control at all times, at any cost. A penchant for domination was a characteristic not so easily observed during a bank robbery when others held the guns.

But if he *were* that sort, theirs would be a tenuous arrangement at best. Submission was one thing. Kowtowing quite another.

Regardless, she was about to be bound to Cade Parker in lieu of poor Henry Reiker. After months of praying and fretting in equal parts over the risks associated with becoming a mail-order bride, she would forever think of her original groom as *poor* Henry—a man shot for his ill-placed chivalry.

At least she'd had Henry's letters alerting her to what she was getting herself into, or so she had thought. Now— and she stole another glance at her escort—she knew only what she had surmised in the bank. At her conjecture that he might be a farmer, he had neither assured nor corrected her, but merely given an odd twitch to his mouth that suggested humor.

She rolled her lips. If he were the type of man to make light of a woman and ridicule her ways, then he was indeed a gambler with no idea of what was about to befall him.

On the other hand, certain things suggested he was not a farmer, at least not in the sense that Henry had been. His bearing was not bent from following the plow. He carried himself with a hint of dignity, and his hat bore a thin braided band that looked to be made of horsehair.

But more than anything, the *thud-clink* of his angled boot heels informed her. A jingle of sorts. The man wore spurs.

And the shooter had called him *cowboy*.

She'd read about cowboys, but Mr. Parker did not have the swagger associated with the dime-novel breed.

In spite of the odd looks she encountered from passersby, Mae Ann held her head high, taking in the late-afternoon shadows that stretched low along the storefronts. The church stood mutely in its fenced yard, its front door ajar as if waiting to announce her arrival.

The train whistle called from a distant canyon, such a lonesome sound trailing its passage to the next town. The hopefulness that had accompanied it as the train delivered her to the station earlier had departed long ago. Had she accepted Mr. Parker's charity, she could be on that train at its next passing, but headed where? She'd left St. Louis for good, and nothing there bade her return. Better to face the fate of her own choosing than the unknown.

Besides, she'd not take anyone's charity, especially Mr. Parker's. She would pay her own way with a fair trade of her talents, just as she had done in St. Louis.

She glanced his way again, but this time he caught her eye and worked his lips in that jerking fashion. A spark lit his expression—a spark of what, she could not tell, though she suspected she would soon enough know.

Her neck warmed and again she fingered the torn collar. Earlier she'd wished for a photograph of her wedding day, but she now felt great relief that no such record would mark her sudden decision and scandalous appearance. No wonder the few women they passed looked askance at her. She'd had no opportunity to freshen herself after alighting from the train mere hours before. She must look a sight.

She reached to adjust her hat, though without both hands and the benefit of a mirror or window glass, it was a useless gesture. But she dare not stop and preen in a storefront window. The thought sent flame into her cheeks, just what she did not want—an unseemly flush at the moment of her marriage to an even more peculiar man than her earlier intended.

What had she been thinking?

They stepped from the boardwalk into the street. Closer now, she saw a figure standing inside the open church door. The preacher, judging by his frock coat. Henry said the minister had agreed to marry them that afternoon after arrangements at the bank. Her breath snagged and she reached again for her torn collar, an irritating reflex. Snatching her hand away, she attracted Mr. Parker's concerned frown, and he turned aside at the low fence framing the churchyard and drew her behind a large cottonwood tree.

Her heart pounded beneath his pointed scrutiny. First her hat, then her face. Her throat, her jacket—dusty from her trip. Her skirt, blotted with dirt from crossing the street. She'd not held it high enough. Finally, her shoes, which she tucked beneath her hem, the only part of herself she could truly hide.

Without a word, he drew a knife from his pocket, opened it, and reached for her.

A gasp stuck in her throat and all the blood rushed to her feet. Would he murder her here in the shadow of the church steeple?

He stopped, and his lips twitched in that curious way. "Do not fear me, Miss Remington. I'm after that torn piece at your throat." His brows drew down. "Your neck." Farther down, until a scowl marred his otherwise pleasant features. "I mean, let me cut away the flap that troubles you. Later you can mend it. Or add lace. Or do whatever it is womenfolk do."

He appeared flustered by his small speech, and she froze like one of the silent shadows, risking that perhaps he spoke truthfully. If not, what had she to lose other than her lifeblood on the roadside as Henry had lost his to the bank floor?

Mr. Parker moved closer, his back to the street, shielding her from onlookers. His molasses-brown eyes were clear and quick as the blade that sliced the fabric dangling at her throat. He closed the knife, slipped it into his pocket, and took her hand, into which he placed the remnant and folded her fingers upon it.

Warmth and strength seeped into her from his touch and slight smile.

"Keep this for later repair."

He stepped back, tugged on his brown vest, and adjusted the silk neckerchief that hung low about his neck. "I apologize for not being dressed more appropriately, Miss Remington, but I did not expect to attend a wedding today. Especially my own."

Again, that spark of something in his eyes. She glanced at her traveling suit and brushed a spot high on her skirt.

"But you." He took both her hands in his. "You make a most becoming bride."

Her pulse fluttered at his words. Unaccustomed to compliments, she scarcely knew how to respond.

With a light pressure to her fingers, he released them and offered his elbow again. "Shall we?"

Shall we what? Take vows before God that she fully intended to break if this man were a ruffian? Was that what it meant to pledge her troth—to keep a promise if it suited her? Troubled by doubt and his flattering words, she took Mr. Parker's arm and focused on the duty at hand. And right now marrying Cade Parker was the only duty she could find.

~

Cade had not attended many weddings. Out here, shoved up against Colorado's imposing mountain wall, such affairs were mostly private and among family. With no family nearby for his own spur-of-the-moment ceremony, he figured it'd be just the parson and Mrs. Bittman.

The church door opened farther, and the couple stepped out. Clearly in the family way, Mrs. Bittman greeted them with a smile. A puzzled frown marred the parson's face.

"Cade." Bittman extended his hand. "I heard the commotion at the bank took Henry Reiker's . . ." He flashed a regretful look at Miss Remington. "My apologies, miss." In a pastorly way, he reached for her hand. "I take it you are, or were, the bride from St. Louis."

She met the question straight-on. "Mae Ann Remington."

That's my girl. Cade's gut clenched at his reaction. *Whoa there.*

Mrs. Bittman led her inside the church, and the tightness in his chest let up. He breathed a mite easier.

"So why are you here, Cade?"

He was asking himself the very same thing. Clearing his throat, he took off his hat. "We'd like you to go ahead with the wedding."

The preacher's brows steepled and he pulled his chin back. "She wants to marry a dead man?"

What kind of fool question was that? Cade cleared his throat again. "No, she wants to marry me." He met the parson's dumbfounded stare. "Or rather, I want to marry her. I mean, we have agreed to marry each other. That it's for the best."

Any fair-minded man would understand the situation. Any fair-minded man who didn't stand gawking with his mouth hanging open like an empty bucket.

The parson's jaw clapped shut. "I see. Well, this is a bit out of the ordinary." He looked over his shoulder into the church. If the man dallied much longer, daylight would be gone and they'd have to light the lamps so he could see who he was marrying.

"If you don't mind, we'd like to do this today. Before tonight."

Bittman stroked his chin and looked Cade up and down. "Well, you are an upstanding citizen. And both of you are of legal age."

That last part was the only thing Cade knew for certain. That and the fact that Reiker was dead. Mae Ann Remington could be lying through her teeth about her name and everything else. Though there wasn't much else.

The parson drew himself up and stepped aside. "Then a wedding it is." He indicated the door and waited for Cade to pass through.

"Nothing long or drawn out. I'd like to get back to the ranch before dark." Wishful thinking if ever there was.

Bittman nodded. "I understand."

The women sat in the first pew. Cade followed the preacher, doubt nipping at his heels. He'd gotten himself into some fine fixes in his day, but this pretty much beat 'em all. The first bride he'd picked turned out to be the wrong one. Now he was hitching up with one who picked him. The closer he got to the front of the church, the crazier he felt. But what else should he have done—left her in the barbershop alone and penniless?

He stopped next to the front pew and fumbled with his hat. If he backed out now, it'd be worse than if he hadn't agreed to this fool idea in the first place. He wouldn't humiliate any woman like that.

"Millie, dear." Bittman helped his wife to her feet and steered her to a spot at the head of the aisle. "You and Miss Remington stand here, please." Then he looked at Cade. "And you here, to Miss Remington's right."

Cade swallowed what felt like a horseshoe and set his hat on the pew. Then he took his place next to the woman he was about to marry and prayed that the good Lord wouldn't let him buck and run.

Bittman stayed true to his word and kept things short, but when he got to the part about the ring, he paused. Cade gave a slight shake of his head. Miss Remington gripped her folded hands even tighter.

"Very well. Cade, will you please take the bride's right hand in yours."

He'd already touched her, but this was different. She placed her trembling fingers in his, an act of faith that shot him through with dread over the future but also a strange desire to protect her. Could he make a solemn vow that, on pain of shame and dishonor, must not be broken?

The parson placed his hand atop theirs and offered a final word on the matter. "'The Lord bless thee, and keep thee: The Lord make his face shine upon thee, and be gracious unto thee: The Lord lift up his countenance upon thee, and give thee peace.' Amen."

Smiling as if pleased with himself, Bittman completed the brief ceremony. "I now pronounce you man and wife. You may—"

Miss Remington withdrew her hand and dropped her head. A clear sign she had no desire to seal their business arrangement with a nuptial kiss.

Tamping down sudden disappointment, Cade offered his arm. She took it and again he covered her hand with his own. He'd done more handholding in the last hour than he had in the last five years.

The four of them exited the church house into the last dregs of daylight.

Mrs. Bittman linked arms with his new bride and led her away with a flurry of female camaraderie.

His bride. Words he hadn't expected to ever use after his close shave with Alexandra. They made his collar tight and it wasn't even buttoned.

Mae Ann smiled briefly at Millie Bittman, her posture as unyielding as the gatepost ahead of her. Lord, would the woman not relax? She'd be stiff as a barrel band in the morning if she slept . . .

His collar tightened again. He wouldn't put her in his old room. He'd take it, and give her his parents' room, where he'd been sleeping the last five years. It was only right. He couldn't ask her to take anything less than the best he had when she was willing to work and cook and—

"Cade?"

He turned from his worries and faced the parson, who tapped his head. "You forget something?"

"Right." He hurried inside and returned with his hat. "I'll square up with you next time I'm in town."

"About that." Bittman lowered his voice and turned his back to the women. "They'll be burying Henry Reiker tomorrow, and since he has no kin around here, do you think he should be buried in the town cemetery or out on his farm?"

Cade shoved his hat on and tugged down the brim. He'd told the undertaker to bury Reiker in the cemetery, but Mae Ann might want him on the farm. He glanced at her standing next to the road. "I suppose we should come back for the funeral. Or drive in to pick him up, if that's what she wants."

Bittman nodded slowly. "She's the next thing to family that he's got. Would be fitting, though awkward for her, I imagine."

Cade rubbed the back of his neck. Of all the blasted predicaments, this beat everything. Asking a woman on her wedding night where she wanted to bury her intended. Cade didn't know about Reiker's private affairs other than the fact that all his scrape-by outfit had going for it was water that Reiker apparently didn't know what to do with. Cade sure did, but richer men than he had tried to buy Reiker out, namely that scoundrel Sean MacGrath. In his refusal to sell, Reiker had bitten down like a coyote on a chicken neck.

"I'll talk to her. Either way, I'll be back tomorrow. Still have affairs at the bank to take care of."

Bittman's wife did her best to draw Mae Ann out, chattering away. But his new bride stood resistant and rigid. If that was her natural way, he'd as soon sleep in the barn. His chest cinched. He wasn't ready for a woman. Neither was his house. He ran a finger under his collar and found it unchanged—open, but still choking him.

When had he last scrubbed the sideboard and table? Or changed the tick as his ma used to? Or cleared boot dirt away from the door?

He held his hand out to the preacher. "Thank you for helping us. Her. I mean Miss, er, Mrs.—"

Bittman shook his hand and gripped his shoulder. "You did an honorable thing today." He paused but didn't release Cade's hand, suggesting more than the surface value of his words.

"A very wise man once said, 'Whoso findeth a wife findeth a good thing, and obtaineth favour of the LORD.'"

Cade held in a snort. Trouble was he hadn't been looking for a wife, a fact he'd mentioned earlier at the undertaker's.

With a quick nod, he broke free and covered the cobbled path to the fence, where he closed the gate behind him. No, he hadn't been looking for a wife, and he'd argue the honorable part with the preacher on another day. But if the Lord's favor was part of this harebrained deal, Cade would sure enough take his share.

CHAPTER 3

"Wasn't that Henry's rig in front of the bank?" Mae Ann flinched at the sound of her near-husband's name on her new husband's lips. His deep tone sent shivers over her skin and she wondered if his voice would forever take her back to the bank lobby and the holdup. Her former confidence had fled the moment she said "I do" and she flicked a look at Mr. Parker. "Yes. My trunk is in it."

"I'll tie my horse to the back, and we'll take the wagon to the ranch."

Ranch? She nodded and turned away.

"Wait." He touched her arm.

She flinched, then tried to relax. He must think her a nervous twit.

"It's near dark. Stay close to me, Miss—"

"Mae Ann," she interrupted. "You should call me by my given name now. Mae Ann."

"As you wish."

She slipped her fingers into the crook of his arm again, the only familiar thing from the entire day. Drawing comfort from it, she allowed a semblance of security to seep into her hunger-weakened constitution. Far be it from her to ask him for food.

Again, his hand covered hers, and its warmth reinforced her resolve. Dare she hope that her so-called business arrangement might result in a pleasant situation? She took her skirt in her left hand as they stepped into the street, clenching the heavy fabric as well as her jaw.

The entire thoroughfare lay in shadow. Daylight had fled the town and skulked low along the mountain ridge like light beneath a drawn shade. She would not see her new home from afar, nor have opportunity to spin daydreams as they approached the house. Or shack. Or campfire. She'd no idea what awaited her as a rancher's wife and no way of knowing until she stepped from Henry's wagon. Without Henry.

Mr. Parker stopped by the shadowy contraption and handed her up. She arranged her skirts on the narrow bench as he walked to the other side. He checked the harness, patted the horse's neck, and mumbled something at its ear.

His mount waited ahead of them, and he led it to the back of the wagon, where Mae Ann assumed he was tying the reins. She refused to follow his every move as if she were a frightened child, and instead focused on the bench. A rather narrow bench for a wagon seat, now that she considered it.

When he took his place beside her, she tensed. The length of his leg rested against hers and pinned down the folds of her skirt. Was she trapped or held securely? Perspective made all the difference, her mother had often told her. She determined to believe the latter.

With a light hand, he snapped the reins on the old mare's backside, and the wagon jerked ahead, nearly pushing Mae Ann over backward. Her reflexive reach landed squarely on his leg, but she quickly regained her balance and modesty, folding her wayward hand into the other. Suspecting the odd tug of his mouth, she discounted the notion and blamed it on the lack of light.

"Do you know the horse's name?"

She looked at him.

He returned her regard with eyes even darker than before. "Well?"

"No." She refocused on the mare's undulating rump as it reached forward with one back leg and then the other. The steady *clop, clop* hit every other beat of her running heart. At this rate she might faint before they reached their destination.

At least she wouldn't fall out of the wagon.

He flicked the reins again, and the nag picked up her pace. Ahead, a light winked on, easing Mae Ann's disdain for the dirt-street town. Too bad the lamplighter couldn't run ahead of the wagon and light their way.

"Cold?"

His introduction of the possibility made her shiver. "No."

He chuckled under his breath and reached around her with his right arm, tugging her against him. A hitherto unspoken longing urged her to lay her head against his shoulder, but she suppressed the sensation. He would think her fast—a lightskirt—and that would never do. But she willed her body to loosen its grip on her nerves and soak up his offered warmth. Perhaps he was truly as kind as she had determined him to be in the bank.

That seemed a lifetime ago. Had it truly been mere hours since she waited for the completion of business Henry had found so pressing? If only he hadn't.

A sigh escaped, and she relaxed somewhat against her companion, blaming the odd lulling of wagon and horse hooves. Every muscle in her body begged for rest, as did her eyes. The unexpected swirl of cedar and sage filling the night air did not help. The pure scent compared quite favorably to that of the cramped rooming house in St. Louis and the pinch of coal dust on the train. Breathing deeply, she nestled in the shelter of a strong and warm embrace. Sleep called like a siren.

A barking dog nipped at the edges of her dream. Percy? Could it be that he'd survived that pack of mongrels in the alley? Again and again the dog yapped, excitement drawing a near whine from its throat.

"Mae Ann." Deep tones rumbled against her ear. A warm breath brushed her neck, but the dog persisted. She must find him. The strength that had encircled her receded, and once more the voice came. "We're home."

Memory shot her upright, and immediately she regretted the move. Her neck was as tight as her corset and she squinted, focusing on the man beside her. "How long did I sleep?"

His mouth tugged sideways, revealing even teeth. Almost a smile. Warm, not mocking, but edged with laughter. "All the way from Olin Springs. More than an hour."

He stepped to the ground and turned to hand her down, or so she thought. Instead, he encircled her waist with strong hands, lifted her from the wagon, and set her lightly on her feet. His hands lingered just above her hips and he watched her closely, his protectiveness nearly tangible. And foreign. She would decide later whether she liked it or not.

At the moment, she must attend the dog that whined around her skirts, sniffing the very color from her suit.

"Blue!"

The dog dropped back at Mr. Parker's scolding and lifted pleading eyes his way.

"Go on now."

That was exactly what Mae Ann wanted—to go on and lie in a soft bed. Preferably not her husband's, though such accommodation was unlikely. She'd suggested this *business proposition* with her eyes wide open, yet had already denied his kiss, and in front of the minister and his wife. Shameless.

Common courtesy forced her attention to him. "Thank you for your help."

"It's been a long day, and it's not over. Let's get you inside and then I'll see what I can do about supper."

She stared, concentrating on keeping her mouth from gaping. Men did not talk like that. Rubbing her temples with both hands, she closed her eyes and reopened them, assuring herself it was not all a dream.

"I'll get your trunk later. Come on."

With his hand low on her back, she took in her surroundings, for she could see surprisingly well. Oil lamps hung on pegs at each side of a wide door set in the two-story log house, and a stone walkway led to a wide flagstone porch marking the entrance. The pressure of his fingers urged her forward, and she gathered her skirt and walked past the mare, lathered beneath the harness and flicking her ears at sights and smells no doubt as unfamiliar to her as they were to Mae Ann.

At the door, Mr. Parker reached ahead and pushed it open, then stepped back for her to enter. But the ground beneath her shifted. The threshold pitched beyond her vision. She touched her brow and closed her eyes, and her pounding pulse drowned out the deep voice that spoke her name.

~

Cade caught her as she tumbled backward, lifting her into his arms and through the doorway to one of the wingback chairs before the hearth. Her face was as pale as new canvas, and his heart threatened to break from his chest.

Was she ill? Hungry? When had she last eaten? He'd not asked, and he berated himself for his ignorance. After settling her against one high-backed wing, he pulled the footstool closer and lifted her feet to it, not at all happy with the slight rise and fall of her chest. Fear overrode propriety, and he fumbled with the small, tight buttons of her fitted jacket, tempted to tear them open. But if she woke during his frenzied efforts to help her breathe, she'd call him anything but kind and brave.

With his fingers against one of her wrists, he held his breath, waiting for life to beat beneath her white flesh. Faint but steady it came, and relief routed fear. At least she wouldn't die in his home on her first night there.

He went to the kitchen to stoke the fire in the cookstove. Somewhere he had tea, old tea he'd not thrown out after his parents' death. Women preferred tea, didn't they? Rummaging through the stores on his shelves, he knocked a baking powder tin to the floor. It rang like gunfire in his ears. Just what she needed. He picked it up and peeked around the wall into the room where she lay in his chair as still as he'd left her.

What have I gotten myself into?

Maybe he should loosen those high-top shoes. He always felt better after taking off his boots. But Lord have mercy, he wouldn't be taking them off in her presence. She'd likely pass out again once he revived her.

He pumped water into the kettle and set it on the stove, then returned to work on the shoes. More buttons. Even smaller than those on her jacket. His ma had something she'd used on her Sunday shoes. As quietly as he could, he scaled the stairs two at a time, then burst into his darkened room. He lit a lamp on the chest of drawers, opened the top one, and pulled out a small walnut box. The last he'd seen the long, hook-ended piece was five years before when he gathered all his ma's things and stashed the smaller items with her other keepsakes.

Lifting the hand-carved lid, he stopped short—even though he knew it would be there, gleaming like yellow silk in the lamplight. He slid his mother's gold wedding band aside and poked through the doodads and bobbles until he found what he sought.

At the top of the stairs, he paused to see if his guest had roused. The hiss of water popping off the stove sent him down, past her unconscious form, and into the kitchen, where he grabbed the kettle handle without benefit of a towel. The clatter of the dropped kettle and his bad judgment would wake the dead, not to mention Mae Ann.

What was he in such an all-fired hurry for? He stopped, realizing he still wore his hat, and hung it on a chair. Then he plowed his fingers across his scalp and filled his lungs. Tea. Hot water. A cup. Surely he could handle those three little things.

And food. He spun around, taking in his kitchen and the remains of his last meal. Dirty dishes. Coffee. Day-old biscuits on the table. Cold beans and bacon in a pan.

He set the pan over the fire, gave it a stir, and put two biscuits on a tin plate with a mug of tea. Leafy, but he didn't know the whereabouts of the silver ball his ma had used. He picked up the plate, took another deep breath, and walked into the main room. Mae Ann Remington—*Parker*—sat straight up in his leather chair, staring at the cold hearth.

She was beautiful.

She'd removed her hat, and a splotch of color marked her cheeks. As he approached, she turned her head, dark eyes watching him like a deer in a thicket sensing death. He swallowed and forced what he hoped was a smile that would hide his relief and ease the tension in her shoulders.

She took the cup he offered and held it close as she breathed in the steam. Her eyes never left his face. Was she checking for liquor or laudanum?

He set the plate on a small table beside her. "You gave me a scare. How do you feel?"

She blinked twice, as she had when he asked if she could horseback. Possibly her *tell* when avoiding a direct answer. She'd lose at poker.

"What happened?" She sipped the tea and grimaced.

"I have sugar." He fled the room, angry at himself for being so spineless when she had more starch than most men he'd met. At the back of a cupboard he found the silver bowl his ma had always left on the table. Hunger nipped at his innards, and he grabbed himself a biscuit, thought again, and put it on a plate. Poured himself some tea and found a spoon for the sugar.

She hadn't moved a hair.

He set the sugar on the side table and his plate on the hearth, then laid a fire from wood stacked by the fireplace. Shielding the match, he nursed the feeble glow until yellow flames licked up into the split logs. He pulled the other chair near the hearth to face her and balanced the plate on his leg. Heat from his mug warmed the tin and seeped through his trousers.

Mae Ann relaxed, leaning toward the fire as she'd leaned into him on the ride home.

His chest burned with the memory of her pulled close against him, and he gulped the bitter tea. Another task for tomorrow while he was in town—more stores. More tea.

"What happened?" she asked the fire.

"You fainted at the door."

Her cheeks flushed deeper and she pushed at a wave of hair tumbling toward her brow. If she were truly his wife, he'd set if free of its pins and let it fall across her shoulders.

Another gulp of the leafy brew.

"My apologies, Mr. Parker. I—"

"No."

A startled look.

"Call me Cade."

She stared at him.

"If you wouldn't mind."

She glanced at the hearth. "Very well. Cade. I suppose it is only right, since we are . . . married."

"Yes. About that—"

The door burst open and the old man blustered in to hang his hat on the tree by the door, then stopped dead in his tracks. His mustache twitched. A sure sign he was conjuring up a smart remark.

Cade beat him to the draw and stood. "Mae Ann, I'd like you to meet the ranch foreman, Deacon Jewett." He turned to his lifelong friend. "Deacon, Mae Ann Parker. My wife."

Not much in Deacon's many days had given him pause, but Cade's introduction obviously did. He choked, no doubt on a chaw. It'd serve the old codger right if he swallowed it. He knew Cade didn't allow spitting in the house.

Deacon gawked first at Cade and then at Mae Ann. She tugged at her unbuttoned jacket and tucked her feet beneath the chair.

Cade joined Deacon at the door and lowered his voice. "If you've got nothing peaceable to say, it can wait until morning."

Deacon worked his tongue around the inside of his cheek, adjusting his chaw. He drew himself up and aimed around Cade's shoulder. "Nice to make your acquaintance, ma'am."

To her credit, Mae Ann stood, but she remained by the fire. "And yours." She dipped her head in a short nod.

Cade stepped closer. "I meant to thank you for lighting the lamps tonight." He shoved both hands in his pockets and spread his stance, refusing to invite Deacon to stay. No telling how long he'd make himself at home, and Mae Ann was worn. So was Cade. The tension rubbed him rawer than any weeklong branding he could bring to mind.

"No need." Deacon's blue squint darted from Cade and Mae Ann to the crackling fire.

Cade knew that look. He also knew Deacon had his own pile of wood and a stove in his cabin.

"Well, seein' as how you was late gettin' back, I wanted to make sure you didn't have trouble in town." His ancient eyes snapped, and Cade could hear the wheels turning. "Someone's cuttin' wire on the Rei—"

Cade gripped his foreman by the arm and turned him toward the door. "We'll talk tomorrow." He handed Deacon his hat. "Thanks for checking."

The old cowboy was suffering something terrible, holding back both his chaw and a joke. He plopped his hat on, gave Cade a wink, and nearly shouted, "Sleep tight. And don't let them bed—"

Cade shoved the door closed and waited long enough for Mae Ann to finish blushing—certain that she was.

"I understood you to say that you were alone."

So it began. "Not entirely."

He added two logs to the fire before taking his seat. "Deacon has a cabin next to the barn. He's been on this spread since before I was born. As to your question about a family, I clearly replied, 'None here.'"

Her chin came up, and he smiled to himself. Her challenge somehow set him at ease.

"So am I to assume you have a wife, children, or siblings elsewhere?"

She could drop and gut an elk with that look, and he shoved the biscuit in his mouth to keep from laughing. He knew little to nothing about womenfolk other than he did not want a mad one in his house so near to the fire poker.

She waited while he chewed and chased the dry bread with the rest of his unforgiveable brew.

He leaned forward, arms on his knees. "It means that you can take me at my word." To drive his intent home, he met her eyes straight-on. "You are the first and only woman I have ever married. I have no children or brothers. A sister lives in Denver. Our parents lie at the top of the hill beneath a ponderosa pine, the result of a buggy accident." *That I could have prevented.*

His aim found its mark. Mute for the moment, she gripped her hands tightly on her lap. The rise and fall of her blouse went beyond what he'd seen in her unconscious state.

A log snapped through, and she jumped. "I see."

"Good."

Sparks fled up the chimney.

"Well then." She flicked a glance his way, then back to the fire.

He drew a breath through his nose. Things had been going fine until Deacon blew in. Cade had been about to tell her their sleeping arrangements and mention Henry's burial tomorrow and ask where she thought it should be.

Should he apologize? He shifted in his chair. For what? Confounded woman.

She turned toward him with a frown and sniffed. "Are you cooking something?"

He shot from his chair to the kitchen, where the beans had charred in the pot. This time he grabbed a towel and pulled the pan to the side. If she was hungry, he'd give her canned peaches. If he had any.

She appeared at the doorway. "Let me help you. I did say I would cook and clean and such."

Her face pleaded more than her voice, and he sensed her need to clear the air between them and not just from the smell of scorched food.

"Well, I imagine you're better at all this than I am anyway." He stepped back as she approached the stove.

She picked up the towel he'd used, doubled it around the handle, and took the pot to the sink, where she pumped in water until the hissing stopped, set the pot aside, and laid the towel on the counter.

Then she faced him. "Thank you for the biscuits and tea." Looking down at her jacket, she fingered the cloth-covered buttons. "And for . . . making me more comfortable."

"When you fainted, I was afraid you couldn't breathe." What kind of fool thing was that to say? He didn't need to make excuses. But he did need to make plans. "I was about to discuss something with you before Deacon arrived."

"Yes?" She laced her fingers together.

Indicating the fire and chairs, he let her precede him while he stared at the floorboards rather than the gentle sway of her skirt.

He scrubbed one hand hard down his face to clear his vision and thoughts. This arrangement might be more difficult than he had anticipated. He must *not* think of her as his wife.

They each took a chair and studied the hearth for a full minute before he found words to say what needed saying. "Where do you want to bury Henry?"

CHAPTER 4

M ae Ann heard the air leave her body, and for a moment she forgot how to get it back. She gripped the chair arm, and the smooth leather gave beneath her fingers. *Breathe.* How did one breathe?

She closed her eyes and a band tightened around her brow. Cade touched her arm and she gasped. Ah yes. Inhale.

"Are you all right?" Concern tinted the question. His voice changed like the play of light across a lake. Dark and cold one moment, warm and caring the next.

"I am not usually given to such displays." Frowning into the fire, she ordered her brain to function, reminding herself that a kindhearted man sat before her with worry darkening his features. "You were saying?"

Cade Parker let a groan escape, stretched his long legs out, and combed both hands through his thick hair. Fatigue pulled at his eyes. How well she knew the feeling.

"I told the barber—er, undertaker—to bury Henry in the town cemetery. Parson Bittman said that would happen tomorrow since he had no kin." He slid her a scant glance. "Except you, that is."

But she was not. "I hardly qualify as kin." She was only *almost* his bride, now married to another man.

"He asked if you would prefer Henry be buried on his farm, since that farm could now be yours."

The idea fired through her veins, bittersweet. "Mine?"

He pulled his feet in and leaned on his knees. "Do you know what business Henry had at the bank when—" He averted his gaze.

Mae Ann refused to dance around the subject. She was not a fainting flower . . . well, not with a dry biscuit in her belly and her mind made up about facing things head-on. "When he was shot, you mean."

Cade flinched at the word. Quite a different man than the one who had come so bravely to her rescue. Her heart softened toward him, and she could imagine drawing him close and offering a wife's comfort.

She doused the tender image, unnerved that it should appear at all, considering the situation. "He did not discuss it with me. He merely insisted he file some papers with the clerk, make a payment on something, and withdraw a modest amount for household things I might need." The admission planted a barb of sadness in her heart.

"Do you know what happened to those papers?"

"I never saw them." She rubbed her forehead, attempting to draw a clear picture from her memory. "They were not in his hand. They may have been in his coat."

At that, Cade leaned back in the chair, expelling a long sigh. He was as weary as she, but he had not yet mentioned their sleeping situation. If she looked at her state of affairs from a practical standpoint, she was in a new home with a stranger for a husband. As far as her original plans and expectations went, nothing had really changed other than the husband.

"Well, what do you want to do?"

She hiccupped.

"About the burial."

"Oh." Heat flooded her neck, and she pushed at her hair. She must look disgraceful. "I, um—let me think a moment."

He watched her, the fingers of his left hand tapping his chair arm.

Serious decisions must not be rushed. Where would Henry prefer to be laid to rest? His letters had never mentioned such a topic.

The tapping quickened. Cade continued to regard her, willing her to speak, it seemed.

"The farm." There. She'd decided. "Henry wrote often of his farm, as if it meant more to him than anything."

Cade huffed. "That it did. More than once he'd been offered a nice sum for the place, but he wouldn't sell."

"Why? Is it rich and productive land with fertile soil and good possibilities?" She'd often imagined a warm home with chintz curtains at the windows and hearty meals on a large kitchen table.

"The only possibility on that place is the spring snow-melt that floods the west edge of the property. The ground is rocky and poor in most places, but Reiker was determined to farm it rather than run cattle in the drainage where there's good grass." He snorted. "Range wars have started over less."

"Oh dear."

"I tried to buy it from him myself."

She waited for the telltale ripple indicating humor but it never came. "I see."

He slapped both hands on the arms of his chair and pushed to his feet. "It's settled, then. I'll drive in tomorrow with the buckboard and bring him out to the farm. It's a few miles farther north from here, a wedge-shaped piece that cuts between this ranch and the next."

She stood. "I will go with you."

This time, his mouth ticked and his tired eyes sparked. "I figured you would."

He went to the open staircase that cut up against the wall to the second floor, and stopped with his hand on the railing. "I'll get your trunk, but I need to fix a few things in your room first." Without waiting for her reply, he mounted the stairs.

Her room? Did he already find her unappealing? Her hand strayed to her collar, but she jerked it down. In accordance with her earlier wish for her own bed, relief washed against one side of her heart. Shame against the other.

Emotional fatigue clenched her stomach the same way she clenched the folds of her skirt. A new town. A holdup. A murder, a wedding. She sank to the chair. It was almost too much—running the gamut of emotions from expectation to horror to hope of refuge, all in a single afternoon. She leaned her head back, discovered her slipping hair combs, and attempted to reassemble the mass.

Idleness was not part of the arrangement. Clinging to her word of making a pleasant home, she laid her jacket over the chair arm, gathered the tinware, and took it to the kitchen.

A pump perched by the sink—a blessing indeed. Running water was one thing she'd specifically prayed for. She'd heard stories of families in the West who still hauled water. At least she'd have one less chore in that regard.

The window above the sink hung black with night, limp curtains framing four panes of glass that offered a view of what, she could not imagine. Mountains? Cattle? Horses? Cade had used the term *ranch*, and several cowhides covered the floor of the main room in the absence of carpet or braided rugs. Mounted horns hung above the rock fireplace, particularly long and curving up at the tips. Clearly a man's abode.

But the kitchen bore a woman's forethought. Perhaps his mother had instructed in the building of this room, for it was a comfortable size with ample space for working. A solid table and four chairs anchored the open area, with walls of cupboards on two sides, and a baker's cabinet with bird's-eye maple doors at one end. Even a pie safe.

She opened a door at the opposite end to find a closet-like space with a copper bathing tub that wooed her to soak away her weariness. Another nearby door offered a small-paned window that looked out onto a wide covered porch.

Choosing busyness as respite from a painfully remarkable day, she set a kettle to boil.

The pastor's blessing hummed through her mind like a familiar tune as she rolled up her sleeves, found a length of toweling for an apron, and shaved soap into a large wash pan. In spite of nothing going according to plan, the Lord had blessed and kept her. He had rescued her from a dreadful situation at the bank, placed her in a comfortable home with a man she'd judged to be kind, and given her a room of her own. Her mother would have rejoiced at such riches, and Mae Ann's mind stumbled over a stone of grief.

After washing the dishes and stacking them on the board, she scrubbed the table, the stove top, and the area around the sink, grateful for the activity.

She pulled the towel from her waist, folded it neatly to lay on the counter, and slowed at the distinct sense of being watched. Turning, she was tempted to ask how long he had been standing there.

His mouth quirked. "It's ready. First door on the right at the top of the stairs."

With that, he left her again. The latch on the heavy front door spoke of his exit.

Mae Anne returned to the large chair for her jacket and climbed the stairs. Three doors greeted her at the top. One to her right, opened. One at the end of the brief hallway, closed, and another across from her, also closed. Which was his?

Tentatively, she pushed the open door farther and stepped into a room warmed by a large braided rug beneath a bed with an intricately carved headboard. A lit lamp welcomed her from atop a chest of drawers, reflecting its light in the mirror of a handsome dressing table next to a long window. A washstand occupied the far corner.

Behind her stood an armoire, also beautifully carved, and she ran one hand along its lovely finish. The size and beauty of the furnishings took her breath away. Not at all what she had anticipated in a cowboy's home.

Heavy steps sounded on the stairway, and she pulled the door back. Cade met her eyes momentarily, then entered the room and set her trunk beneath the window as easily as if it were a basket. Henry had needed her assistance lifting it to his wagon.

She studied the man before her, lean but broad-shouldered with hands she knew to be calloused yet caring. The lamplight drew shadows across his face and into her heart.

"The bed clothes are clean."

She glanced at the ornate headboard once more, noted the smoothed coverlet and the quilt folded at its foot. "It's beautiful. Everything in here is so beautiful."

"Yes, it is." His eyes swept her brow and cheeks and mouth, much the same way he had assessed her outside the church.

Fever burned up through her from her belly to the tingling tips of her fingers. The sensation was not at all what she had expected on her wedding night. But neither was the man she had married.

"I'll be across the hall if you need me."

He stood like an oak, unmoving, waiting for what? For her to dismiss him from his own room? She was certain this was where he normally slept. Or for her to voice the frightful longing that so closely resembled the need he mentioned?

Yes, she needed him. She needed him to accept her. Approve of her. But she would never reveal such things. She folded her hands. "Thank you for bringing my trunk."

Almost imperceptibly, his shoulders fell a notch, anticipation slipping from them. He nodded curtly, turned on his boot heel, and gently shut the door behind him.

She crossed to her trunk and knelt to release the bands and open the lock, but she had no key. Realization landed like the proverbial straw on the camel's back, crushing her beneath one more blow of an inconceivable day. The key was in her reticule, which was in the thieving hands of the man who had murdered her *first* husband. Her *almost* husband.

Giving way to the mounting grief and tension, she leaned against the locked trunk, dropped her head to her arms, and wept.

~

Cade stood in the hall, his pulse pounding in his ears. Under different circumstances, he would not be standing outside his own bedroom alone.

He entered the room that would again be his, closed the door, sat on the edge of the narrow bed, and pulled off his boots with less ease than usual. One bootjack was downstairs and another across the hall where he usually did the deed. He'd fetch it tomorrow.

As he hung his vest on a chair and pulled his shirttail free, a shy knock on the door shot his heart to his throat and stilled his hand before it reached for his belt.

It sure enough wasn't Deacon in the hall.

He swallowed what tasted like fear and opened the door. Mae Ann stood as stiff as a board in her traveling clothes, the lamp in one hand, the other arm across her waist. Eyes moist, face damp in the kerosene glow.

"I have no key." Her voice was thick.

He frowned. *Key?*

"For my trunk. I cannot open it."

"Where's your key?"

"In my reticule."

"And where is that?"

"The bank robber took it."

Could he not talk to her without bringing up her predicament every time? "I'll get my gun."

A quick breath parted her lips, and her free hand shot to her throat.

"I'm not going to shoot off the lock, if that's what you're thinking."

He hurried downstairs to the gun rack and reached behind the Winchesters and shotgun for his holstered Colt. He popped the cylinder, emptied it of its shells, and returned to find Mae Ann waiting in the hall. She remained there after he entered the room and stopped at the trunk. Two ticks, and still she hadn't joined him. Was she afraid of him?

"I need the light."

"Oh. Yes." She came to stand beside the trunk, the lamp held low.

One good blow with the butt of his gun broke the lock, and he slipped it from the pad and handed it to her.

Her fingers grazed his as she took it. "Thank you."

She was even more beautiful in the lamplight. Vulnerable, fragile-looking. The discovery knotted his gut and cinched his lungs. "All right then."

"Good night."

He closed her door behind him again and uttered a silent prayer for help.

As quick as the words cut loose from his soul, a soft whimper slipped under the door. He leaned closer to listen. No rage, no despair. Just the quiet sobbing of a woman alone. A woman who, for some unexplained reason, he'd vowed to protect and cherish above all others.

CHAPTER 5

Feather tick swaddled Mae Ann, a downy cloud that eased her weariness. She burrowed deeper, relishing the soft warmth and clean scent of fresh linens.

Turning toward the window, she panicked and threw back the quilt. Dawn pinked the horizon.

He'd let her sleep. That would never do.

No water at the basin. Her own fault. And her hair—what a sight! The dressing table mirror revealed what her new husband would surely define as unruly. *Unattractive.*

Hastily she chose stockings, a petticoat, and the nicer of her two housedresses, a muted blue stripe, then brushed and coiled her hair into a knot at her neck, praying it would hold in its combs. With a whisk at her skirt and a deep breath, she peeked into the hall.

The door facing her was ajar, the room's furnishings in a softer light. Hers must front the east.

Curiosity drew her closer to spy a side table and chair. A low, narrow bed hugged one wall, similar to her cot in the rooming house. She grimaced. He had relinquished his comfort for her.

At voices from downstairs, she turned resolutely toward the landing. Another deep breath steeled her, and she drew on long-practiced composure to mask her misgivings.

The sweet lure of pan-fried bacon met her halfway down the staircase, and her stomach surged to life, watering her mouth in turn. Such strong reactions this morning to such simple pleasures as a soft bed and good food.

The great room welcomed her as she entered from above, noticing things she'd not seen the night before. A large desk occupied one corner, bookshelves spreading like wings along each wall—another surprise for a rancher's home. Near the front door, a wide window offered a view of the barn and out buildings.

Ashes lay cold in the hearth, a silent reminder of a most unusual evening.

The aroma of a hearty breakfast drew her around the dividing wall and into the kitchen. Cade and Deacon sat at the table, bent over their tin plates of bacon and hotcakes. A coffeepot posed between them, and an extra plate and cup awaited.

Deacon saw her first, and his oversized mustache tipped up on one side. "Mornin', ma'am."

Cade rose and stared, his fork still in hand. Had she forgotten something? Her shoes? No. A wiggle of her toes confirmed their presence without looking down.

He pulled out the chair to his left. "Mae Ann. Please join us."

He was clean-shaven, his face smoothed from its formerly shadowed appearance. He reclaimed his seat at the head, a fresh shirt pulling across his broad shoulders. The brown vest and silk scarf were the same.

She tapped the coffeepot's handle to find it not too hot, and lifted it toward Cade's half-empty cup. "More coffee?"

He dipped his head in a universal *yes*, his mouth full of meat.

"Deacon?" She paused.

"Don't mind if I do." He met her halfway across the table with his cup and what she assumed was a smile. It was difficult to tell with his bush-covered mouth, but his blue eyes crinkled at their edges. She returned the pleasantry.

A quick glance at the stove located a small pitcher and an iron griddle, and she rose to pour more cakes.

"In the oven."

Cade's tone was brusque, but how could she blame him? The morning half over and his wife just now making an appearance? With the folded towel from the evening before, she reached in for the tin plate stacked several cakes high and brought it to the table.

Deacon gulped his coffee and stood as Mae Ann sat. "Best be gettin' back to work. Thank you kindly." He bobbed his white head and topped it with the old hat from the back of his chair. "See you this evenin'."

Cade raised his hand in a near salute and continued eating. Judging by his silence, he must be starved. Mae Ann was not far behind him.

He pushed the syrup tin her way without looking up.

She surveyed the counter and sideboard for butter but found none. Not surprising. She could picture neither Cade nor Deacon churning butter, and the question popped from her mouth without permission. "Have you a milk cow?"

His attention sufficiently caught, Cade looked in her general direction but avoided her eyes. "No."

"So you have no butter, cream, or milk."

He frowned, and went back to his cakes. "I used the last of the milk for the hotcakes. Neighbors have a cow, and I buy what I need from them. Their boy should be riding over in a day or so."

Neighbor? Hope sprang, whether eternal she would decide later. But the possibility of another woman this side of Olin Springs encouraged her immensely.

"And how far away are those neighbors?" She placed two cakes on her plate and topped them with syrup.

"Three miles, give or take." He mopped up the remains of his breakfast, gulped his coffee, and took his plate to the sink. "We need to leave soon. I'll harness the horse and have the buckboard waiting out front."

Alone at the table, she flinched when the front door banged shut. Appetite fled, but she'd not spend another ride faint from hunger, so she forced herself to the food. A small bite. Chew. Swallow. Repeat. She might as well eat the towel for all the flavor she enjoyed. Her vision blurred and a tear plopped on the edge of her plate. Others joined it when she squeezed her eyes against the isolation.

The new was already tarnished, and she'd not been in the house twenty-four hours. She swiped a hand across her face. So be it. Companionship was evidently not part of their arrangement.

However, there was much to be said for a roof over one's head and food in one's stomach. She washed the breakfast dishes in cold water and hurried upstairs for her shawl and bonnet. It was bad enough she'd be going to town in her housedress, but Cade seemed upset about getting a late start. Or maybe he was simply upset about having a wife.

Things often looked different by the light of day. Usually better. Perhaps for him, this time they looked worse.

Cade stood by the buckboard, looking toward the mountains. At the door's click, he turned to her with worried eyes that he quickly shuttered. He handed her up to a much broader bench and followed as she adjusted her skirts. A gray horse stood in the harness, heavier than Henry's mare. With a slap and a jerk, they set off down an unfamiliar road.

Weariness and the monotony of a moonless night had swept her from her senses on the trip from town, but not so much that she didn't recall the strength of Cade's embrace and his protective warmth. This morning he was so different, so distant. No smile teased his mouth. No light filled his eyes. Only . . . avoidance. He was avoiding her. Avoiding looking at her, speaking to her.

Like a third person, silence perched between them on the sturdy bench.

Rather than pick at him with idle chatter, she chronicled her surroundings, noted the way the grassland rolled up against pine-draped mountains blotched with lighter, brighter green. She'd not seen such blue sky in all her days, and it put her dress to shame. Topaz, saffron, and amethyst wildflowers winked along the roadway, encouraging her to breathe deeply of the clean, unfouled air.

After miles of creaking wagon, clomping hooves, and occasional bright birdsong, houses began to dot the landscape, appearing closer together as they neared a town sprouting from the horizon. Riders and other wagons passed, and drivers lifted a hand or nodded in passing. Cade stared straight ahead as if going to a funeral.

Oh dear. That was exactly what he was doing. Taking her to gather the remains of her betrothed. How could she have forgotten?

~

Cade drove down Main Street for the second day in a row. A first in his memory for coming to town more than once in a month.

If he hadn't ridden in yesterday, his life would be as it had been for the last thirty years—routine, predictable. Now it was anything but, and he still hadn't completed his business at the bank. He turned at the alley and came to a stop behind the barbershop. "Wait here."

His conscience barked, clearly audible over his churning gut and his ma's voice telling him kindness never killed anybody. He seemed to have used up all he had the day before. Never had he been in such a fix, and it was costing him his manners. Leave it to a woman to work a kink in his rope.

He looped the reins on the brake handle and jumped down without looking at Mae Ann. He couldn't look at her and keep his wits. In her simple bonnet and blue dress, she stole the breath right out of his lungs and the good sense from what little brain he had left. It wasn't so bad yesterday in the bank with tension running high as a flooded creek. Even at the church, when he still felt he was doing right by her, he hadn't had a good view of what lay ahead. But now, in clear daylight, he had to work at not making a fool of himself. How was he going to *live* with her?

He entered the building to find Reiker's coffin propped against a wall in the back room as he'd expected. The doorknob pushed against his hand when he attempted to close the door, and he gave way. Mae Ann.

She looked him square in the eye, daring him to deny her. So much for doing what he'd told her. If not listening to him was her idea of a manageable arrangement, then she was in for a surprise. As he understood it, they were business partners. And he ran the outfit.

"Mornin'." Ward came from the front with his barber's apron on, smelling of shaving soap and tonic. "The preacher stopped by and said you'd be in." He looked to Mae Ann with a slight nod. "Ma'am. My condolences."

"Thank you, Mr. . . ."

"Ward. Bartholomew Ward." He pulled his apron off and dropped it on a desk chair. "I have something for you that I found inside Henry's coat."

From the top desk drawer, he withdrew two darkly stained envelopes and handed them to her. Each was shot through the middle with a neat hole. Cade's chest tightened.

Mae Ann's breath caught in that little gasping way, and her hand trembled as she reached for the papers.

Ward couldn't keep from pointing out the obvious. "You'll see he labeled them. His will and a payment."

One thick. One sealed. Both discolored with Henry's blood. She turned them over in her hands, and Cade turned away from watching her.

He gripped the top of the coffin. "We'll be taking him to the farm."

The barber bent for the bottom. "Ma'am, if you could get the door, please?"

She looked at Cade, dragging his heart out of his chest with her dark, shining eyes. He held her gaze a moment, then stepped to the door and pushed it open before returning to the rough-finished pine.

The coffin slid easily to the head of the wagon, and Cade latched the back board. If someone had told him he'd be hauling Henry Reiker's body to his farm after taking the man's bride as his own, he'd have cuffed them hard.

Mae Ann didn't wait for help, but climbed to the seat. She had more spine than most, he'd give her that. Yet she had an air about her that made him want to be a better man.

That was the part that hobbled him.

He joined her on the bench and drew in as much air as he could hold. "You might want to read those before we leave town. If that really is a land payment, we can take care of it on our way out. I have to stop at the bank anyway."

She stared at the envelopes, tracing the hole in the top one with her finger. "You are right."

He gathered the reins and clucked Smoke down the alley to the corner, where he turned back to Main Street and pulled up in front of the bank. She still hadn't read the papers. He set the brake and leaned forward on his knees to give her the time she needed. Lord knew he hadn't given her much else this morning.

From the corner of his eye, he saw her thumb through several bills in the thicker envelope. She laid it in her lap and ran a finger under the other envelope's sealed flap. It gave way easily, and she withdrew a folded paper covered in dark script, much of it blurred. He looked across the street and studied Reynolds Mercantile.

Fred Reynolds's wife usually had butter and cheese in the storeroom that she sold to bachelors like himself. It wasn't yet warm enough that it'd melt before they got to the ranch.

Paper rustled and he leaned back.

She returned the letter to its envelope and tucked it in a pocket in her skirt. "I'd like to make the land payment."

"Before you see the farm?" She didn't know what it was like. Neither did he, but he felt obligated to warn her before she handed over money that could pay her way back to St. Louis if she decided to leave. The possibility that she might do just that made him uneasy.

"It was Henry's wish, and as his heir, I intend to carry it through."

His heir. That beat all. He'd signed the land over to her before he even married her. That'd chap Sean MacGrath's hide for sure, a woman getting the land he'd tried to buy from Reiker. "Suit yourself."

He jumped down and reached for her, gripping her about the waist as he had before. But this time she laid her hands on his shoulders. She held on a mite past what she needed and searched his face as if she were looking for gold.

"Thank you." A hint of maple syrup brushed by on the words. She'd eaten alone. He should have been there.

Releasing her, he stepped back and opened the door for her.

The bank was as crowded as the day before. Mae Ann looked down and stopped, rigid as a new rope. Her breath came short and quick. The floor had been scrubbed, but Henry Reiker's blood stained the wood. Only time would erase it, and then maybe not completely.

Cade moved in close and linked an arm around her waist. Hang what people thought. She was his responsibility, and he'd brought her back to the scene of Reiker's death.

For the life of him, he couldn't shake the idea that she was promised to Henry first. Made him feel as if he'd run under the man whether the fella was dead or not.

Just barely, she leaned into him but maintained her set jaw. *That's my girl.* He'd thought the same thing yesterday, but today it was true. At least as far as the parson was concerned.

The teller coughed politely. "Mr. Parker."

Cade moved forward, still with a hold on Mae Ann. "Busy today, aren't you?"

The man shuddered. "I'm afraid so. Yesterday's robbery delayed several transactions." His attention drifted to Mae Ann. "I'm so sorry, Miss . . ."

"Mrs. Parker," Cade replied. "My wife, Mae Ann Parker."

The teller's widened eyes flicked between the two of them, and he stumbled over his tongue. "Uh, well, yes. How can I help you?"

She slid the thick envelope through the window. "I'd like to make the next payment on Henry Reiker's land note."

More adept at business than small talk, the teller opened a ledger. "According to this, there is only one more payment and it isn't due until the end of July." His fingertip inched the envelope his way. "But I'd be happy to complete the transaction for you today."

Cade bit the inside of his cheek to keep from speaking his mind.

Mae Ann stuck her hand through the window, palm up. "Very well. I will wait."

The teller glanced at Cade, then returned the envelope.

"However, I should like to deposit this on account until the note is due."

The man reached for the money, and Mae Ann pulled it closer to her. Cade choked back a laugh.

"A personal account, please. In my name."

The teller stared. "That is highly unusual, Miss—er, ma'am. Women do not normally open accounts of their own. But if you'd like to make a deposit to Mr. Parker's account . . ."

Cade opened his mouth, but she beat him to the draw.

"Normality has nothing to do with this situation, sir. I have in my pocket Henry Reiker's last will and testament, written by his own hand, which declares me as his sole heir. That means the money is mine, not Mr. Parker's or anyone else's."

Silence turned Cade's glance toward other patrons, who had halted their conversations to hear how the Olin Springs Bank would care for its newest customer.

"If you will excuse me one moment, please." The teller held up a finger to indicate that moment and scuttled to the bank president's desk in the far corner. Cade would wager that every eye in the lobby followed him.

Mae Ann's shoulders hardened and she stretched herself to her full height. If Cade was a bettin' man, his money'd be on her.

The president leaned around the teller and peered over his spectacles at Mae Ann, and with a flick of his hand, sent the teller back with his decision.

"As you wish, Mrs. Parker." The poor man's face reddened like a late apple in fall, and bonnets bobbed as women whispered their hearty approval.

Pride edged under Cade's rib cage until he realized that her same steely determination would be riding home with him and fixing his meals for the next—well, forever.

Mae Ann handed over the money. The teller counted it out and gave her a receipt. She stepped aside yet stayed close enough for Cade to sense her body trembling like a colt new to the halter. But she stood on her own two feet.

He thumbed his hat up a notch. "I need fifty dollars from my account."

"It will have to be in bills today. They took all the— well, you already know about that." The teller opened the drawer where he'd just deposited Mae Ann's cash, and withdrew the fifty from her payment.

Ironic that the robbers hadn't checked Henry for money.

Cade nodded his thanks.

Mae Ann stepped in front of him and leaned near the window, her voice a whisper. "Did you—did anyone—happen to find a brooch from—from yesterday's . . ."

The man's expression softened and he shook his head. "I'm sorry, Mrs. Parker."

Her shoulders fell.

Cade laid his hand against her waist and ushered her to the door.

On the boardwalk, he drew her aside. "Reynolds Mercantile has just about everything you might need, and if not, I know Fred's wife has a Montgomery Ward catalogue." He peeled off a twenty-dollar bill and pressed it into her warm hand. "You can order another brooch."

Mae Ann's eyes glistened and she stared at the mercantile across the street, refusing to look at him. A muscle in her jaw flexed, and her voice came even softer than it had with the teller. "It was my mother's."

Cade rarely came to town armed, but sudden regret at not having his gun yesterday left a bitter taste in his mouth. "I'm sorry."

Her eyes met his. "It's not your fault."

He swallowed and reset his hat with no clear idea of what to say next other than the obvious. "I've got business at the telegraph office. Go ahead and get what you need. Butter, cheese, and anything else you want."

He paused for her response. It didn't come. "Do you feel up to waiting at the mercantile until I get back?"

She drew herself up, and he squelched a holler, relieved that her fire had returned so quickly.

"I am not a dolt."

"I didn't say you were. I was only trying to make it easier on you."

She cut him a look that thanked him and insulted him at the same time, and he walked away before that holler broke loose.

At the corner, he checked to see she'd made it across the street unharmed, and caught her stepping through the door. Tugging his hat down, he continued to the telegraph office to wire the money he'd promised his sister, the other woman in his life who kept him twisting like a bronc.

Between the two of them, he'd have no hair on his hide at all by the time the fall roundup came.

CHAPTER 6

M ae Ann hadn't had so much money to spend at one time in all her life. She folded the bill and tucked it into her pocket next to Henry's will. Thank God she at least had a pocket.

A cheerful bell clanked above her as she stepped inside the mercantile, and an equally cheerful voice greeted her from the left, but no one was there.

"Hello?" Easing the door closed, she took in the wall of canned goods. Notions and dishes filled glass-front cases, and barrels of pickles and dried beans and crackers crowded the narrow aisles. Aromatic spices blended with the tang of lye soap and leather goods. Nearly everything a person could want filled the cramped establishment. On the counter, distinctive yellow-and-red Arbuckle's packages and a coffee grinder caught her eye. She headed that way but stopped short when a broom-thin woman popped up behind them like a jack-in-the-box.

"Good morning!" Both hands patted silvered hair and then brushed a neat apron as she stepped from behind the counter. "Just rearranging, making room for catalogues and such. I don't believe I know you." She extended her hand. "I'm Wilhelmina Reynolds and so happy to see a new face in town. Please, call me Willa."

Mae Ann returned the greeting, unaccustomed to such an open welcome to strangers. "I'm Mae Ann Rem—*Parker*. I'm pleased to make your acquaintance."

The woman's eyes skipped to Mae Ann's left hand and back to her face. "Parker, you say? As in *Cade* Parker of Parker Land and Cattle Company?"

Heat climbed Mae Ann's throat and she tucked her ringless hand into her pocket, masking her discomfort with a polite smile. "We were married yesterday by Parson Bittman." She braced herself for raised-brow judgment and tsking disdain and was, therefore, ill-prepared for Willa's exuberant response.

The woman threw her arms around Mae Ann in a quick embrace and kissed her cheek. "Welcome, welcome! Finally, someone has captured that cowboy's heart. How he needed it after that little hussy treated him so poorly a few years back. But do tell me all about the wedding and your trip here, since I know you're not from these parts. Did you come on the train? Oh, what a journey that must have been from . . . Where did you say you were from."

Hussy? Mae Ann found herself holding her breath as much from surprise as gratitude. "I didn't say, but St. Louis." She inhaled deeply and the tightness in her shoulders eased somewhat. "I arrived yesterday on the train from Denver."

Praying the woman wouldn't bring up the bank robbery, she reached for a package of Arbuckle's. "I'd like ten pounds of coffee, please. And I need to see what else you have that I may need at the ranch."

Willa skittered back behind the counter and pulled out an empty Arbuckle's crate. "Well, if you ask me, you'll be needing everything from flour and sugar to lard and licorice. And if I were you, I'd choose some garden seeds too. I know for a fact he hasn't kept the garden up. Travine Price told me and she's as good as gold. Her son, Todd, rides over to the Parkers' now and again with fresh milk."

"Cade did mention a neighbor with a milk cow."

"Good thing too. Honestly, those men live on bacon and beans."

Men?

"And that Deacon." She huffed. "Old coot needs to trim that bush on his face, if you ask me."

Mae Ann laughed. Men. Of course. "He is a sight, isn't he?"

"At least Mr. Parker does not let him influence *his* appearance. How did you meet, if you don't mind my asking?"

Mae Ann turned away, searching for some necessary item to draw the woman's interest from yesterday's events. "You mentioned butter. That would be lovely. We have no milk cow for cream, but you already knew that."

"Oh yes, butter, cheese. All those things that bachelors can't do for themselves. And I have Eagle Brand milk to tide you over until Todd rides out. You'll have to water it down, you know. I imagine those cowboys are short on canned fruit as well."

With twenty dollars, Mae Ann felt she could buy half the store, but she wanted to prove herself frugal. If only she'd had more time to look through the larder and see what they needed. Surely Cade had a smokehouse and root cellar. And beef. It was a ranch, after all. She worked her way toward the back, mentally compiling a list and distancing herself from the inquisitive owner.

She had not lost her sewing kit or linens packed safely in her trunk. And she had two dresses in addition to her suit, with petticoats and stockings and an extra pair of stout shoes—precious purchases she'd made before leaving St. Louis for life on a farm. A barb snagged behind her breastbone, and she remembered Henry's coffin in the wagon bed.

Willa swept by in a rush of words. "I'll fetch another box for you dear."

A muffled question floated from behind the curtain where she disappeared. "Has Mr. Parker told you about his family?"

Mae Ann ignored the query and picked through a collection of seed packets, then perused showcases and shelves. Cade's family matters were not any of her business, at least not yet.

"It was a tragic buggy accident, about five years ago, if I recall."

Curiosity strained Mae Ann's ears toward the warbling words, and her Christian training warned of gossip. Cade would tell her what she needed to know in good time. Perhaps if he cared for her one day, he would share his family's history.

Reality brought her up short. Affection—another item that was *not* part of their business arrangement.

The barb twisted. She had hoped love might blossom with Henry after time, though she had prepared herself to settle for mere companionship. No matter, Colorado offered a fresh start away from the city that had stifled her for so long and taken her mother's life.

The bell rang quietly, and Mae Ann glanced toward the door, expecting another woman. A man entered, wearing tall black boots and a blacker countenance. She shivered involuntarily.

"Worst winter we ever had." Willa returned through the curtain, chattering from behind two stacked crates as she continued to the front. "The accident took both Colonel Parker and his wife, Madeline. And Betsy was never the same after that, poor girl. Up and ran off to Denver with a no-account."

The man moved without sound to the window as if watching for someone.

"I hear he sends her money every now and again. Mr. Parker—Cade, that is—"

The crates dropped against the countertop, and Willa's cheerful demeanor soured as she addressed the stranger. "Can I help you find something?"

The man gave Willa a dismissive shake of his head, then fixed his scrutiny on Mae Ann.

She stiffened.

With a slow hand and what appeared as more sneer than smile, he touched his hat brim. "Mrs. Parker."

How did he know? Willa had said nothing revealing since his arrival, and he certainly wasn't at yesterday's brief ceremony at the church. The back of Mae Ann's neck crawled, but manners pressed her into a curt nod. She joined Willa at the counter and continued her conversation in more hushed tones.

"You mentioned a Betsy?"

Willa watched the man like a snake watching its prey, never taking her eyes off him as she lowered her voice. "Truth be told, I'm surprised Mr. Parker didn't go after his sister and that shyster. He does love Betsy. They were close as children."

Mae Ann forced her concentration to this tidbit. A man who loved his sister could be as kind and thoughtful as she had judged Cade to be. She pinched the twenty-dollar bill between her fingers. "Is there a millinery in town, where I might find a reticule and other such things?"

"We are not quite that civilized yet." Willa's defiant glare bored into the stranger's back. "But I do have several catalogues, and I keep a few items on hand just in case."

She bent behind the counter and came up with a tray of lady's items.

Blooming from the center like a morning glory was a blue silk bag that dashed all Mae Ann's frugal planning.

How beautiful! And oh, how tempting.

Mae Ann picked up the reticule and fingered the embroidery, calculating what she'd already spent filling three crates with necessities. "Do you have anything less . . . not quite so fine?"

The bell rang a second time, and she turned as Cade halted in the doorway, eyeing the black-booted man in a less-than-friendly manner.

The stranger again tipped his hat in her direction. "Good day, ladies." Then he stepped toward the door and locked glares with Cade. "Parker."

"What do you want, MacGrath?"

This time the man's sneer was heartfelt. "Other than the Reiker place?" He glanced at Mae Ann.

Cade's hands fisted, but he stepped aside and watched the man walk across the street and into the saloon before closing the door.

Willa heaved a great sigh. "That fella makes me nervous every time he comes in here, which, thank the Lord, isn't all that often."

Concern marred Cade's expression as he strode to Mae Ann and took hold of her arm. "Did he give you any trouble?"

"No."

Cade's stare cut through her, demanding the truth.

"He just seemed . . . he seemed so *dark*. Why do you ask?"

Releasing her arm, he glanced through the window. "That was Sean MacGrath." Cade's eyes met hers again. "Remember? I told you he tried to buy Reiker's—your place—but Henry wouldn't sell."

Willa coughed and fluttered at what she'd just heard, failing miserably at pretending to not have figured everything out. "Mr. Parker. I must say, congratulations are in order. What a lovely bride you have. Wherever did you two meet?"

Mae Ann was certain Willa already knew and was simply fishing to feed the local gossip mill. She returned the reticule to the tray. "Perhaps next time. When you have something a little less costly."

Cade riffled through the crates, his frown deepening. "No tea?"

Surprised by his request, she scoured the tightly packed shelves behind the counter. Last night's bitter brew was certainly an odd choice for a man, but it might be improved if served with her favorite cake. "Have you any Baker's Chocolate?"

Willa whisked away down the length of wall.

Mae Ann turned to Cade. "What kind of tea do you like?"

He gave her a blank look. "Not for me, for you."

"I prefer coffee." The words fell from her lips before she could form a kinder remark.

One side of his mouth ticked.

Willa returned with a box of Grand Union tea and another of Baker's, and handed them both to Mae Ann for inspection. She set the tea aside and dropped the cocoa in the crate. "That should do for today." Rolling the pocketed bill between her fingers, she prayed she'd not overspent, especially with Cade standing there watching. "Can you please tally everything for me?"

Willa wrote out a ticket and offered it to Cade. Mae Ann snatched it before it touched his fingers, drawing a gasp from Willa and raised brows from her husband. She didn't care. She wanted to know the bill so she could put back the least-needed items if necessary. Like the chocolate.

To her great relief, she had a bit more than enough. Allowing her shoulders to relax, she unrolled the twenty-dollar note and gave it to Willa. Cade picked up the blue reticule, dwarfing it against his large hand. He turned it over, pulled at its cord, and dropped it in the crate with the Baker's.

"I didn't purchase that. I was just looking." Mae Ann reached for it, but Cade pulled the crate away and turned for the door.

"I did."

Struck dumb, she stared after him through the window as he loaded the box in his wagon.

Willa's thin face blushed with a smile as she counted out Mae Ann's change, then leaned across the counter with a whisper. "Here you are, dear. You've got yourself a fine man there. Surely you know it." She squeezed Mae Ann's hand, then straightened to address Cade when he returned for the other crates.

Arranging the Arbuckle's packages right under his nose, Willa added, "Next time you're in town, you'll have to check out my new jewelry collection, Mr. Parker. Brooches, tie tacks. Even wedding rings."

Mae Ann stared at the floor, willing it to open and swallow her on the spot.

Cade seemed not to have noticed the woman's unveiled insinuation and hefted a crate under each arm. "Give my regards to Fred."

Mae Ann opened the door for him and glanced back to find Willa beaming from behind the counter, having set all things right in the world.

"Cade," a man hailed from across the street. The sun glinted off a star on his vest as he approached the wagon.

Cade loaded the crates and locked the back board in place, then shook the man's hand and turned her way. "Mae Ann, this is Sheriff Wilson. Sheriff, my wife, Mae Ann."

The introduction flowed smoothly with no blunder or hesitation, and Mae Ann could almost believe Cade sounded, well, not resentful of her. At least he hadn't introduced her as his business partner.

"Sheriff." She nodded briefly.

He touched his hat brim. "Pleased to meet you, ma'am."

If surprised at Cade's sudden married state, he hid it well. Facing away from her, he lowered his voice, naively mumbling his news in the presence of a woman with perfect hearing.

"Neither hide nor hair of the bank robbers that killed Reiker yesterday, and their lookout's not talking. I've sent a couple men out following sign. We'll find 'em."

Cade reset his hat. "I know you will."

Mae Ann climbed to the seat, her breakfast turning in her stomach. She reached for her brooch that wasn't there, irritated by her reflexive habit and grieved anew by the sheriff's comment. Nothing was as it had been the day before, nor would it ever be again.

Cade drove for the ranch with tight hands and a tighter jaw, as tense as he'd been on the way in. No doubt the sheriff's remarks played into his morose withdrawal, as well as his encounter with Mr. MacGrath, whose mere presence had thrown Cade into a scowling storm.

Resolve steeled her spine despite the hard bench and jostling ride. Mr. MacGrath might be in the habit of intimidating people to get what he wanted, but it hadn't worked with Henry, and it wouldn't work with her. The farm was not for sale.

Forcing her thoughts away from the man's overbearing demeanor, she considered the clear spring sky that canopied the greening grassland. In the last dozen years, she'd seen so little of the earth's seasonal renewal that she gathered each spot of color and each birdsong and tucked them next to her childhood memories of happier times before her father left. Before the dank city and rooming house. Before her mother let loose the cords that bound her to her earthly suffering.

She and Cade had at least one thing in common.

A deep sigh escaped and drew his notice, reminding her of what he'd done. "Thank you for the reticule."

His posture eased a bit. His mouth ticked and he slid her a glance. "What makes you think I bought it for you?"

She stared straight ahead, humiliation flaring through her breast. Of course he hadn't bought it for her. How prideful she was. He'd known her one day. Surely there were other women in the area who might have caught his eye—

yet he'd *married* her. Oh, Lord, how would she ever make a pleasant home for a man who might love another?

Then again, perhaps he'd bought it for his sister. The tension in her neck eased somewhat. Surely he'd bought it for Betsy.

He huffed, and ire displaced her embarrassment. Dare he mock her? Perhaps she would forget to add sugar to the chocolate cake she'd planned for supper.

And then he looked right at her with a genuine smile. "You need it, don't you?"

She turned from his warm gaze, completely undone by his change of temper. She was unaccustomed to one who bantered or teased. Up to this point, life had not presented opportunity for playful speech. She studied the point between the horse's ear tips and deliberately softened her voice. "As I said, thank you."

"You're welcome." With that, he snapped the reins and the gray quickened its pace.

She folded her hands in her lap and prayed that someday she would indeed be welcome.

The parson's blessing threaded through her heart, inching further with each clop of the horse's hooves. *Be gracious.* What exactly did that mean? Pleasant? Kind? Conversational? She drew a deep breath. "How many cows do you have?"

Her question turned his head again, but this time no humor lit his features. Had she misspoken? Was it a secret?

He looked away, silently taking in the open land to his left until she decided he was ignoring her again. So much for pleasantries.

"Two hundred pairs, give or take." He huffed again. "Lately, there's been more taking."

"Who would take a pair of cows?"

He gave what sounded like a snort, completely mirthless. "A cow-calf pair. And who's stealing them is what I'd like to know."

Another sudden shift in his temper. Maintaining a gracious demeanor might be harder than she imagined if his mood continued to change with every wind.

A dark cluster of buildings sprouted near the mountain's base, and Mae Ann soon recognized the two-story log house. Coming upon the ranch in clear daylight gave her pause, so majestic was its simplicity. The house fronted a grove of white-barked trees with small fluttering leaves, and across the yard, a log barn—eaglelike with wings spread on each side and a peaked roof.

Corrals skirted one end, and beyond them squatted a small cabin with a porch across its length. That must be Deacon's. The mottled dog that had greeted them last night bounded toward the wagon, scattering chickens in its dash.

Cade stopped in front of the main house and set the brake. Mae Ann started to climb down.

"I'm unloading the stores and then heading on to the farm." His words pushed her against the seat, laden with shame. How could she have forgotten their day's mission again? A quick glance over her shoulder confirmed that Henry was still with them.

"You don't have to go along if you don't want to." He waited, watching her with no hint of judgment or scorn, then jumped down and went to the back of the wagon.

Deacon came from the barn and paused to scrub the dog's ears before hefting a crate. "Afternoon, ma'am. Nice day, ain't it?"

A nice day for what? Forgetting that the man who had defended her honor lay dead in a box behind her? She shuddered and crossed her arms, chilled by the thought.

Deacon followed Cade into the house, leaving her alone with Henry. She shuddered again, and her mother's teaching quickened in her spirit. It was not really Henry in the wagon bed, but his remains, as if he had shed an old suit of clothes for a new one. The illustration had once comforted Mae Ann in the wake of a boarder's death, and when her mother died, she'd wrapped it tight around her, swaddling her heart against the pain.

The sun warmed her back, and the chill melted as she drew upon Henry's letters. They were few, but she had committed them to memory and illustrated each one with fanciful dreams of the new life that awaited her. He'd sounded so hopeful to "make a go of it" and repeatedly expressed his delight that she agreed to join him on his "meager" farm. The word had cost her several hours of concern, but she eventually convinced herself he was simply being modest.

Cade returned to the wagon and gave her a glance as he picked up the reins. She released a long breath and quieted her thoughts for what lay ahead, for she was about to see what would have been her home had things gone as planned.

Deacon approached with two shovels and laid them in the wagon bed. "I'll meet you there."

Cade nodded and tugged his hat down, then turned out of the yard and back to the road.

Mae Ann had never felt more useless in her life.

CHAPTER 7

No surprise that Mae Ann stayed in the wagon. She was as determined a woman as Cade had ever met. But his taking that piece of fluff at the mercantile *did* surprise him. When he saw her holding it like a cherished treasure, the look on her face made him forget his good sense. And finding MacGrath in the same room with her nearly made him forget his upbringing.

The man went after what he wanted like a cougar after a fawn. He'd bought out every rancher who bordered his place, other than Reiker and Cade, and Cade suspected he was behind the rustling. He'd not heard about any of MacGrath's cattle gone missing. What better way to drive people off than by stealing their stock?

However, he'd have an easier time proving the sun rose in the west. Hard to catch a thief other than red-handed, and he didn't have time to lay wait on someone sneaking into his herd at night. Now he had even less time with a woman to look after, especially who just happened to have ties to what MacGrath wanted.

He cut her a look, a bit prideful of how she drank in the country as if it were worth it. Truth was, he didn't know what she'd seen or not seen, only that she was from St.

Louis. They hadn't talked much other than her asking about his cattle and him asking where to bury Henry.

It all came back to Henry.

Cade hadn't seen the Reiker place up close, just the outline of buildings from a distance. His ranch shared a stretch of boundary fence on the farm's south side, but the lay of the land swept down to a small valley with sweetgrass and a snowmelt lake in the summer.

Henry Reiker hadn't known what he had, but every other rancher around here did, especially MacGrath, whose acreage bordered Reiker on the north. Cade's pulse kicked up. The man knew about Reiker's mail-order bride, too. Everyone did. And he'd no doubt heard about the shooting and quick nuptials last evening. McGrath had eyes and ears everywhere, the cur. That had to be why he was at the mercantile this morning, hoping to get a look at Mae Ann.

Cade's blood heated and he strangled the reins.

Mae Ann's gasp broke into his brooding, and she covered her mouth with one hand as they drove into the yard. He couldn't blame her. It was worse than he'd expected.

A busted-up porch sloped off the front of a small, narrow-windowed house, and a half dozen chickens ran out the open front door. A tottering shed must have served as a barn, for a cow bawled from inside, begging to be relieved.

By the time he stopped in front of the rickety corrals, Mae Ann had both hands over her mouth. He wanted to pull her into his arms. Comfort her. But it was daylight, and Deacon had them in his sights.

"I'll scout a place for the—"

She cut him to the quick with the same look she'd had at Ward's when the barber asked her to hold the door.

He laid a hand on her shoulder and gentled his voice. "Wait here. Or get out and look around if you want." As if she needed his permission. She'd do what she well pleased. He jumped down and grabbed his work gloves and the shovels.

Deacon ground-tied his horse and they scouted a small rise behind the barn. Cade jammed the shovel blade in the earth and turned to survey the place. Mae Ann was already walking the yard, her arms clenched across her waist as if she was holding something inside. He'd known her less than twenty-four hours, but he couldn't imagine her living out here in this desolate spot.

Nor could he figure why Reiker let the place get so run down. Cade had always thought the man a decent sort. A greenhorn, but decent. Didn't know a cow from a cabbage, so he didn't realize his place was prime for grazing cattle. But it looked as though he'd put every dollar into the land payment rather than fix what needed repair. How could he bring a bride home to this tattered outfit?

At the bite of Deacon's blade through dirt, Cade returned to grave-digging, but kept Mae Ann in view, marking her slow, deliberate wandering. She disappeared into the house and must have shooed more chickens out, for they flapped and squawked through the door as if a fox were on 'em. The cow's urgent pleas never let up, and while Cade considered telling Deacon to go milk her on the ground just to shut her up, Mae Ann charged out of the house with a bucket.

He snorted. She'd likely never milked a cow. Could be interesting, though he sure enough didn't want her to get kicked. He stuck his shovel in the piled-up dirt and wiped his sleeve across his forehead. He or Deacon could milk the beast and set Mae Ann to picking eggs.

On second thought, a sudden recall of her earlier *dolt* comment changed his mind and he resumed his digging.

The cow stopped hollerin', and a smile crept across his face.

An hour later, he and Deacon lowered Henry's coffin with a rope and filled in the grave.

He cleaned up as best he could with his neckerchief, and found Mae Ann with a grain can trying to herd the chickens into a stall. He snorted a laugh, and she whirled with frustration furrowing her pretty brow.

A fist shoved against her hip. "You have a better idea?"

Yeah, he did. She was awful pretty all fired up like that, but he had no right thinking such a thing when he'd just buried her intended. He took his hat off and slapped it against his leg. It was time to say words over Henry. "We're finished."

"Oh." She paled a bit and set down the can to smooth her skirt, looking everywhere but at him. "Thank you."

"We picked a high spot with a good view of the place." Somehow that mattered.

She followed him to the small rise behind the barn where Deacon stood mopping his face and neck. He shoved his hat on and squared himself as Mae Ann stopped next to the dark mound of fresh dirt and folded her hands. A breeze danced around her skirt and played with her hair that had worked loose.

Cade removed his hat.

Deacon held his against his chest. "The Lord is my shepherd. I shall not want. He beds me down in green pastures with sweet water."

Cade cut a look at Mae Ann, but she showed no reaction to Deacon's loose interpretation of Scripture.

"He leads me on a good trail and stays with me in the tight places."

She raised her eyes to Deacon, taking in his cattleman's words that weren't exactly what the parson would say but sure enough painted a picture of these high mountain parks.

"And the Lord's spread will be my home forever." Deacon jerked a nod to punctuate the end of his piece and shoved his hat on. "Amen."

Mae Ann bowed her head. A sudden gust kicked over the rise and snagged her skirt like a flag. Cade eyed a thick gray band edging the horizon. They'd have just enough time to get home before the rain hit.

He stepped in close and touched her shoulder. "You all right?"

"Yes." She gave him a solemn but tearless look. "I appreciate you doing this."

He wanted to tell her she had a home for as long as she wanted and everything would be all right. Instead, he set his hat. "We should be going. Storm's a-comin'."

On their way to the wagon, Mae Ann retrieved the grain can from the barn and gave it to Deacon. "Can you catch the chickens for me? There's a coop in the barn that we can put in the wagon."

She wasn't asking, she was telling him, and he shot Cade a panicked look.

"We have chickens at the ranch." Cade saw the concern on her face before she voiced it.

"I know. But these will starve or be eaten by wolves."

Deacon said not a word, and Cade would pad this month's pay for the way the old man took the grain can and marched into the barn.

The resulting chase was a worthy theatrical performance, though unsuccessful. Deacon promised to return at the full moon and sneak up on the hens while they were roosting.

Disappointed but accepting of the situation, Mae Ann led the cow from its stall and gave Cade the rope. He tied it to the back of the wagon and then handed her up and climbed in beside her.

"We don't have wolves." He flicked the reins. "Just coyotes and lions."

She held him with widened coffee-colored eyes and breathed out the word. "Lions?"

"Cougars. Mountain lions." Her tension bled into Cade, and if the storm wasn't coming, he'd round up those hens himself. "The chickens'll get up on something. Don't worry." He didn't tell her a cat could get up on something too. She'd had enough death in the last day.

As they drove away, she turned to watch the ramshackle buildings slide past, and by the curve of her shoulders he knew she didn't hold out much hope. "How long until the full moon?"

"Not long," he said, dipping his hat against a chilly gust. The sky had grayed over while Deacon was trying to herd hens.

Mae Ann shivered and hugged her thin shawl closer, and Cade pulled her to him as he had the night before. Brittle beneath his arm at first, she soon enough relaxed. The woman had a lot to learn about life in this high country, like not leaving the house without a proper coat or cape regardless of how hot the sun was.

But Cade had as much to learn about her. Holding her close and feeling her go soft against him shamed him for trying to shut her out as he had that morning. But what in this windblown valley was he supposed to do? She nearly had him snubbed to the post and halter broke already.

~

If Cade hadn't sheltered her from the bluster, Mae Ann surely would have blown off the wagon. The force of the wind stung her eyes and stole her breath, and tiny hail pellets hit like buckshot as she lit from the wagon. Cade trotted the cow to the barn, and Mae Ann dashed inside the house. For a moment she doubted the windows would hold as the skies opened above them, shooting ice against the glass and piling it upon the sills.

Wasn't it May?

Chilled and hungry, she went to the kitchen and stoked the stove. Three crates sat on the table, the blue reticule gleaming atop the Arbuckle's packages like a satin jewel. Again she marveled at Cade's changing nature, as swift and unpredictable as Colorado's weather.

She laid the bag aside and stocked the open shelves in the kitchen, taking account of everything Cade already had, which was precious little. But she would make do, starting with a cake. If they had eggs.

Mae Ann didn't know whether to laugh or cry over Henry's chickens. Deacon had looked for all the world like a flapping stork chasing those frightened hens. They might never lay again. But with no one to feed them or pen them at night, she feared they would not survive until the full moon.

At least she'd remembered how to milk a cow and relieved the poor thing's misery, though she'd poured out the milk.

A small bare pantry off the kitchen offered ample room for her purchases. A can of molasses sat half-full on one shelf, as did a crock of jam, and a few potatoes huddled in a dark corner. The man had next to nothing, not counting a large sack of dried beans. Behind the door she found a slab of salt pork and a half bag of Arbuckle's. She lined up the new packages and took the opened one to the stove.

Fried potatoes, onions, and bacon didn't seem like much for dinner, but the aroma would be a comfort, so she cut chunks of pork into a skillet and set it over the fire. She added an extra spoonful of grease from a can on the stove, and sliced in onions and potatoes to cook while she finished unpacking the stores.

Opening the Arbuckle's, Mae Ann breathed in the rich fragrance that combined with dinner to fill the kitchen with a homey smell. No tea for her, thank you, though she'd not fault Cade's thoughtfulness the night before. Tea didn't have what it took to keep her going at the boardinghouse, and she'd come to prefer coffee's heavier flavor. She set out what she needed to make biscuits, picked up the reticule, and went upstairs for the aprons in her trunk.

Stunned by the view from her window, she surveyed the yard below, blanketed in solid white. Did Cade have a garden? If so, he likely did not have one anymore. She had so much to learn about him and his ways, how the ranch was run, the expectations he held for her. Some she could easily assume as those she mentioned at the undertaker's: cooking, baking, cleaning. But what did he *like*? What were his favorite desserts and meals? Did he have a preference in the way his shirts were laundered?

She laid a hand against the cold window glass and then against her cheek to squelch the heat rising there. She would be doing his wash.

Kneeling before her trunk, she leaned the lid against the wall and burrowed to the bottom for her kitchen linens. From her pocket she drew Henry's will and the coins left over from her purchases. She slid the envelope along one end of the trunk and dropped the coins into her new reticule and closed the lid.

As she'd planned, an enticing aroma filled the kitchen when she returned downstairs. She left her linens on the counter and tied on her apron, pulling the strings into an even bow at her back. A quick search located a baking pan, and in no time she slid it full of biscuits into a hot oven. The coffee was ready, the potatoes and bacon waited at the back of the stove, and she jumped when the front door blew open. She smoothed her apron and took three mugs from the cupboard to the table while feet stomped and hats and trousers collided in what she assumed to be a noisy dusting of snow and ice.

"Smell's mighty good in here, don't it?" Deacon's crusty voice tugged a smile from Mae Ann's heart.

"That it does."

"You done right by that little gal. Grub with a woman's touch'll do my old bones some good for a change."

Cade's voice answered closer, and the crisp snap of wood indicated he was laying a fire. "You never complained before."

"Never had a choice before."

The room fell silent, and Mae Ann stepped near the opening to listen. If they padded around in their stocking feet, she'd never track their movements. Inching closer, she leaned forward—and into Cade.

He caught her around one arm, a brow arched and his mouth cocked to match it. "Steady there, girl."

Girl? She squelched a sharp retort and waited until he released her, then brushed invisible crumbs from her apron. Humiliation was best countered with confidence, so she met his laughing tone with her most composed and completely-in-control expression. "I was just about to announce that dinner is nearly ready."

His smile bloomed full and he reached past her to the safe on the wall. "Need more matches. It's a mite chilly in the house, wouldn't you say?"

No, she would not say. She couldn't make any more words come out than she already had. They'd all tucked tail and run the way she wanted to, but she couldn't do that either.

He dropped a handful of matches into an old soda tin he must have had on the mantel, and his dark eyes danced with merriment. "About how long?"

She turned away, hoping he'd do the same, but she couldn't tell. "As soon as I set the table." Picking up an embroidered tablecloth from her stack of linens, she snapped it out with a sharp crack and laid three place settings of blue transferware she'd found in a cupboard. Most of the plates were chipped, as were many of the cups. The lovely dishes had suffered greatly at the hands of two men over the past— what had Willa said? Five years?

She sensed his absence and pressed the corner of her apron against her brow, not at all chilly with the warm stove and her blunder. This whole bride business was proving to be more awkward than she had imagined. For she had never imagined a strapping and handsome man like Cade Parker would be her husband.

CHAPTER 8

C ade turned his back to the fire and stretched his arms across his chest one at a time, pulling the cold-induced kinks out of his muscles. So much for the *sign* that Sheriff Wilson's man was following.

He looked down at his socks and wiggled his toes. For some inexplicable reason, he'd pulled his boots off on the jack by the door rather than traipse mud across the floor. His father used to do that for his ma, though he said it went against his grain to be without his feet covered and he'd gone to wearing moccasins.

"Just in the weather," his mother had said with a soft touch of her fingers to her husband's cheek. Cade clamped off the memory. Mae Ann wasn't Madeline Parker, and Cade wasn't the colonel.

Deacon dropped himself into one of the leather chairs near the hearth, his holey socks not a fetching sight.

"I know you've got a needle in your war bag," Cade groused. "You earn enough to either darn those socks or buy new ones."

"They're fine by me."

Cade indicated the kitchen. Deacon caught his meaning and bent to turn his socks over, bottom-side-up, as if that would make a difference.

Kitchen cupboards opened and closed. Pots scraped across the stovetop. Dishes clinked, and the aroma of a hearty meal dredged up images that Cade had shoved down for a long time. Restless, he bolted up the stairs two at a time and slid to a stop at Mae Ann's door. Pushing it open with a finger, as if it wasn't his own room, he slipped in and to the wardrobe.

Her suit and another dress hung inside. Several unmentionable items were folded neatly on the narrow shelves. A thin blue ribbon looped through the handwork on something white and soft-looking, and he quickly stooped and reached into the bottom shelf where he'd stashed his father's "inside shoes."

The smooth sheepskin that greeted his fingertips poked a sore spot in his chest. His parents hadn't been old when their buggy overturned in that blizzard. They'd just been in the wrong place at the wrong time. Like him.

He trotted downstairs and caught the envious look in Deacon's pale blue eyes. There was something to be said for keeping the peace with a woman and keeping your feet warm at the same time. He didn't know if Mae Ann cared about dirt on the floor, but if she was anything like his mother, he figured she did. He wiggled his toes again. The old sheepskin didn't feel half bad.

She appeared briefly in the doorway. "Dinner's ready."

Deacon gave Cade a once-over and huffed. "You're goin' soft and she ain't even been here two days."

"Get your own moccasins," he growled.

A big skillet of potatoes, bacon, and fried onions sat in the middle of the table right next to a pan of fluffy biscuits and mercantile butter. Hot coffee filled three cups, and a fork, knife, and spoon sided each plate. The sight gave his stomach notice that good food was on its way.

Mae Ann stood behind her chair. "I assume you men have washed?"

At her unrelenting stare, Deacon exchanged a look with Cade, and Cade nodded him on.

Cade didn't take kindly to being told how to come to his own table. She wasn't his mother. Though he did wonder how long it'd been since Deacon had bathed.

Mae Ann folded her arms across her middle and pinned him with a schoolmarm's glare. Was she staking out her territory? He picked up his coffee, took a sip, and held her challenge over the edge of the cup. Weak, but tolerable. The coffee—not her. She was anything but weak.

She studied him in return, as if reading his judgment of her and her coffee and finding it—what? He couldn't decipher what lay behind those dark, clear eyes.

Deacon dried his hands on the towel she had waiting by the sink and then pulled out his chair. Cade washed and returned to the table just as the old codger gulped his coffee and grimaced.

Mae Ann passed him the silver sugar bowl. "I have canned milk if you'd like."

"No, ma'am, thank you. I prefer my coffee horned and barefoot."

Her surprise was worth every dollar Cade had spent at the mercantile, but he swallowed his laughter and reminded himself that she was a city gal.

"That's what you get for not waitin' for grace," Cade told his foreman.

"Is something wrong with the coffee?" Her gaze shifted from Deacon to Cade and back again.

"A bit on the thin side is all, ma'am." Deacon took another gulp to show his gratitude.

"Thin? As in *weak*?" The way she said it made it sound like a forbidden word not to be uttered in polite company.

Cade bowed his head. "Thank you, Lord, for the moisture in the storm. And this food and the hands that prepared it. Amen." He glanced her way as he reached for the serving spoon, as surprised by the pink staining her cheeks as he was the fancy tablecloth and his ma's dishes instead of tinware. He hadn't calculated on such changes when he was at the undertaker's calculating the brave front Mae Ann put on.

He helped himself to a biscuit and butter. At least she wouldn't be tellin' him how to manage his herd.

"I'd like to see the ranch after dinner."

Her request stopped the biscuit halfway to his mouth, and butter slid down his fingers.

"I need to know where things are, like the root cellar. You do have a root cellar? And a smokehouse?"

"Got a garden patch too, but it's been weedin' up every summer for quite a spell." Deacon slabbed butter on a biscuit, shoved it in his mouth, and closed his eyes in delight.

His manners didn't ruffle Mae Ann's feathers at all, and she continued with her dainty, lady-sized bites, taking her time to swallow between each one.

"I bought seeds today," she said. "Just in case."

Cade wiped the butter from his fingers rather than lick it off. "I'll be happy to show you where things are. But it'll be sloppy after the storm. Do you have boots?"

She looked at him and blinked twice. He knew what that meant.

85

"I think I can find an old pair that will work until the next trip to the mercantile."

"Old beats new any day if you're askin' my opinion."

Cade cut Deacon a glare that said he wasn't.

"Won't rub blisters on your feet." Oblivious, the old man shoveled in a heaping bite of potatoes and leaned heavily on the table with his other arm.

Mae Ann refilled her coffee cup and lifted the pot toward Cade with the silent question in her eyes.

He picked up his cup. "Still have some." Deacon was right. Belly-wash weak, but Cade wasn't about to tell her that. Not at her first meal. She'd figure it out.

She added a spoon of sugar to her cup and stirred without clinking the sides of the china. Evidently, she wasn't one to make a racket about what she wanted, instead taking the gentler, more deadly approach. Like getting Deacon to wash before dinner.

Cade needed to remember the power of her quiet assault.

~

Mae Ann sipped her cooling coffee, keeping her elbow close to her side and her focus fixed on the daisy bouquets she had stitched so carefully into the white linen cloth. These men had gone far too long without a woman to sharpen their social skills.

Cade scooted back from the table. "Thank you for the fine meal."

She squelched a huff. It was anything but fine, but perhaps he'd not had fine in quite a while. "I'm glad you enjoyed it." She also stood and gathered his plate to set atop hers.

"Come to the barn when you're finished and I'll give you a tour of the outbuildings."

She met his eyes and tipped her head in the affirmative, relieved that she'd have opportunity for a bit of privacy to find the necessary and empty the chamber pot from her room.

"Good grub, ma'am." Deacon's mustache flicked sideways and his pale eyes sparkled. The man might as well wear a mask. "If'n you need someone to grind them beans for you, I'd be happy to."

Surprised by his offer and still bruised by his judgment of her coffee, she suspected his gesture had more to do with the peppermint stick in the Arbuckle's bag than with making amends. "Thank you, Deacon. If you have time right now, you can grind up a bag and pour it into the canister there on the counter. We'll use it this evening."

She retrieved a new unopened bag of beans from the pantry for him, then filled the dishpan with hot water from the stove and shaved in soap. With nothing left from their midday meal, she toweled out the cast-iron skillet and returned it to the stovetop.

The sharp aroma of freshly ground coffee beans made her mouth water even though she'd just eaten. The smell conjured memories of dark mornings in the boardinghouse kitchen preparing food before other residents had stirred. Come to think of it, she recalled several men who'd wrinkled their noses at her coffee. Sometimes she had to stretch the brew to ensure that everyone got at least one cup. Perhaps she had been stingy with the beans today.

Horned and barefoot, indeed. She snickered, dunked a plate in the rinse water, and set it on toweling on the counter.

From the corner of her eye she watched Deacon carefully pour the grounds into the canister as if pouring gold dust onto a scale. Then he clamped the lid on and rolled the empty bean packaging into a tight stick, similar to the peppermint that lay on the counter.

Mae Ann dunked another plate. "Why don't you take that peppermint for your troubles, Deacon? Come Christmastime I'll save them for cookies, but until then, consider it my thanks for your help."

He picked it up like a delicate flower. "Mighty kind of you, ma'am. I do have a sweet tooth." Rather than saunter toward the front door, he shuffled his feet and rolled the peppermint in his fingers.

Mae Ann dried her hands and faced him. "Is there something you'd like to say, Deacon?"

He shot her a quick look under his white brows, and the bush above his lip pulled sideways. "You truly fixin' to stay through Christmas?"

His question jarred her. Why wouldn't she? She had married Cade Parker in front of God and witnesses. Was there something she should know that he hadn't told her? She watched Deacon closely. If a horrid secret lay hidden, she preferred to know it now, not later. "Why would I not?"

The old cowboy shifted his weight and pulled at his whiskers, then glanced at the stove.

Her coffee. She tossed the towel aside, reached for the canister, and tempered her voice. It was best not to let hurt feelings peek around the edges. "Before you return to work, would you mind showing me how much coffee you use when making a fresh pot?"

The man's eyes lit and he bolted to the stove and snatched up the pot quicker than she thought he was capable of moving. But she stayed his hand when he tried to pour out the dregs.

"Don't throw those away. I'll use them in the garden."

His jaw unhinged, and she squelched a giggle as she took a small bowl from the cupboard.

"Pour them in here, please."

He complied and she rinsed the pot and set it on the counter to watch. With a gentle hand, he tipped the coffee canister over the pot and tapped it lightly until a steady dark stream filled the bottom of the pot. Heavens! He poured in nearly a cup of ground beans, but she held her tongue. At that rate of consumption, they'd go through ten pounds of coffee in a week.

With a peek inside and a tight nod, he replaced the lid on the canister and scooted it against the wall. "That'll do." He handed her the pot. "Just fill her up with water and set it on a hot stove."

His mustache made that little move again.

"Thank you Deacon," she answered with a smile.

"My pleasure, ma'am." And with that, he took himself and the peppermint stick out the front door.

She found the necessary close behind the house, and on her way to the barn met Cade halfway there. He set his fists at his waist and looked her up and down as he had at the church, then stopped at her feet and frowned. She hid them beneath her skirt. Her heavy shoes were in her trunk. She hadn't taken the time to put them on.

"I'm sure I've got some boots that will fit you. A snake'd bite right through those shoes." Without lifting his head, he raised his eyes and held her with them.

His was a most penetrating look, but she refused to weaken beneath it and instead put iron into her words. "I have heavier work shoes."

"Good." He continued to regard her, searching for her chinks, no doubt. "You'll need 'em if you plan on a garden." Without asking her to accompany him or indicating a change in direction, he strode off past the house toward a fenced-in area. She followed sedately, determined not to scuttle after him.

Hog wire cordoned off a large plot, and two strands of barbed wire stretched above it, anchored on tall posts as further discouragement for foraging animals.

Cade tugged at the lopsided gate. "It's been a few years since we've had a garden."

"I can see that." She walked into what she imagined had once been a fruitful area. Pieplant peeked through a thin layer of pea-sized hail not yet melted in one corner, and a few onion tops had sprouted. "I can work up the soil and plant what I bought at the mercantile."

When he made no remark, she caught him watching her. He yanked his attention away and pinned it on the gate, wrinkling his brow either in anger or in serious consideration. She didn't know him well enough to discern which.

"I take it you have a hoe and rake?"

"In the barn." He headed away from the garden and then stopped and pointed out the small wooden structure tucked discreetly into a cluster of stunted trees. "The privy's over there in the junipers."

At least he'd thought to tell her, though a little late. Judging by the way he avoided looking at her, it embarrassed him to do so. Apparently, he felt as uncomfortable about such things as she did.

She hitched her skirt and stepped gingerly through the weeds toward the gate, praying that none of those snakes he'd mentioned were sunning themselves after the storm. Few white patches remained, and the downpour had loosened the soil. Tomorrow she'd start on the garden.

He showed her the root cellar, the smokehouse, and the barn with a chicken coop attached at the rear and a small room where he kept tools. She rummaged through a few cans on a sturdy shelf and found seed corn. Choosing an empty pail for a temporary egg basket, she entered the coop and gathered a half dozen eggs.

A plump hen eyed her from atop a corner nesting box, and Mae Ann let her be, hoping for hatchlings beneath the glaring matron. On her way out, she latched the gate, much sturdier than the one at the garden.

Not far from the barn, a hand-hewn bench waited invitingly in the shade of a several slender trees like those from the grove beyond the house. A lovely place to rest and take in the orderly buildings Cade seemed so proud of. His countenance had relaxed somewhat, and confidence warmed his expression as he'd shown her each log structure, whether big or small. Everything was well built by someone who took pride in the property—completely unlike what they had discovered at Henry's farm. Did such pride come from the elder Parker or Cade? Perhaps he took after his father, for in all that she'd seen that afternoon, there was not one loose board or unpatched hole. Only one place lay in neglect and triggered a frown. The garden.

She left him to his chores and returned to the house. The garden had been abandoned because the men had not tended it, the women had, and they were gone—his sister and mother. The kitchen had fared somewhat better because men must eat. But the absence of a woman's touch was evident in the spare larder and the limp, dusty curtains.

The window framed a perfect view of the neglected patch. Had Cade's heart been left in similar condition after losing his mother, sister, and the—well, the woman Willa had mentioned?

An idea sparked in Mae Ann's breast. A tiny flare that hinted at purpose. Could God use her to break through Cade's wintered soil and stir life there again? Perhaps that was why she was here and not with—

No. God had not taken Henry's life. She had to believe that.

As soft as the parson's blessing had whispered earlier that morning, words she'd learned at her mother's side rippled through her like a silken thread. *All things work together for good to them that love God.*

She did love God, but did she love Him enough? He'd allowed her mother to die penniless and abandoned by Mae Ann's father, yet still the dear woman had insisted God was working all things together.

And He'd allowed Henry to be gunned down in cold blood—an act she would never understand. How did God plan to work that together?

Her fingers ached, and she looked down to see them clenched and white at the knuckles. Taking up her apron, she tied it on, then wiped the eggs clean and gathered other ingredients for the cake.

She sifted flour into a large crockery bowl, and its fine dust rose before her—a stifling threat if given enough. As she stirred in sugar and dark cocoa, the thought struck her that perhaps this was how God did it—threw everything in and then worked it all together until the outcome looked nothing like the original ingredients.

Cocoa without sugar was bitter and dry. Flour without eggs was merely dust. But together, they all made something beautiful and good.

The Parker ranch stood as a solid example of hard labor and diligence and a family's strength. Mae Ann was determined to do her part in continuing that heritage. This was her home now too, and with God's help, her marriage could become beautiful and good as well.

Even if love were not involved.

CHAPTER 9

The next morning, Cade studied Deacon across the table, determined to name what was different about the man. Mae Ann came near with a skillet of gravy, distracting him as she ladled it over the biscuits on his plate. Heat from the pan radiated through his work shirt, and the smell of sausage stirred his insides. But her presence unsettled him, waking a long-repressed need he thought he'd rooted out the same way he culled feeble stock from his herd.

He couldn't afford weakness.

Deacon lifted his coffee cup and took a swallow, his eyes closed. A slow nod and what looked to be a smile curved his silvered lip. That was it—the old man had trimmed his mustache and beard.

Cade reached for his coffee, and before it touched his lips the aroma told him Mae Ann had put iron in the pot. The strong hot brew hit his stomach with a jolt, and Deacon met his look across the table with a sly wink.

Other changes drew his attention, mainly in Mae Ann's appearance. She wore what must be her work shoes, and he held in a scoff. At least they were better than those fancy button-up things she'd had on yesterday. And her hair wasn't piled on top of her head, but pulled back with a ribbon that allowed it to ripple down her back. Reluctantly, he turned his focus to his plate and the mental list of chores he had planned for the day.

"Mighty fine coffee, ma'am," Deacon said. "Mighty fine."

"Thank you, Deacon." Her cheeks pinked and she kept her eyes down.

Cade took another biscuit, forked it into his remaining gravy, and shot Deacon a look. "I need you to check on the late heifers today. We've got at least three or four at the north end."

Deacon nodded and finished chewing. "If'n I recall correctly, we've lost a few first-year mamas and their calves from that section."

Cade's blood turned gravy-hot. That fence line bordered part of MacGrath's land and Henry Reiker's farm. Mae Ann's farm now. All that much more reason to keep a close watch. If it hadn't been for the storm, Deacon could have checked yesterday. And if the grass could bear it, Cade would move everything from up there onto another section. But he had to graze it off evenly.

He caught Deacon's cold eye. "You recall correctly."

"I'll take some tack with me and make a day of it. Check fence, unless you need me here."

"I can handle things for the time being."

Deacon cleared his throat and cut a look at Mae Ann, and his eyes grew soft. "Do you have any of that chocolate cake left from last night?"

"I do."

At her reflexive answer, she blushed full out. He'd heard her say those words two days ago. The reminder fogged his brain, and that was another problem he couldn't afford. He shoved back from the table. "Thanks."

Curt. Against his resolve to at least be kind. But she had too much of an effect on him and he had a ranch to run. His plate and cup clattered in the sink and he marched to the door.

He strode across the yard, sidestepping Blue, who trotted up like the faithful companion he was. A man could count on a dog to be predictable. Dependable. A woman was anything but, and Alexandra had proven that by dallying with him until someone more to her liking came along.

Since then, he'd cut a singular trail that didn't involve any heart-tangling females, which was part of the reason he'd agreed to a simple business arrangement. No entanglement. Just a straightforward agreement. She'd do her part, he'd do his.

But he hadn't counted on Mae Ann unsettling his well-balanced, female-free life with her fine cooking and gentle ways. He'd figured they could live their separate lives. That things would go on the same way they always had.

He'd figured wrong.

At the barn he reached for the pitchfork and stomped into the first stall that needed cleaning. The work would do him good, as would the smell. He couldn't clear his nostrils of her scent and the scents of her hands—chocolate cake, hot biscuits, sausage gravy. And her hair. She was filling him up in a way he hadn't expected. *Lord, what do I do now?*

The prayer gushed from his insides like a mountain spring set loose from winter's ice. He'd prayed more in the last two days than in the last two years. Leaning against the pitchfork handle, he stared out the stall window. A woman had turned his head once before, and it cost him everything that was dear. He knuckled a dull pain in the middle of his chest, allowing that the Lord's help was exactly what he needed. But he didn't want to be the kind of man who ran to God only when he needed something. Like his pa.

He must have stood a long while, for Mae Ann stepped into his view, heading his way with her determined stride. If he hurried, he could slip out the other end of the barn.

Or he could see what she wanted.

He stood his ground and waited.

Blue eased up on her, sniffing her out, and she stooped to rumple his ears and coo something soft and senseless that made him plop down on his back, belly up. That was no way to treat a cow dog. Cade's grip tightened on the fork handle. He forced his feet to stay put.

After a few more laughing words that lilted back to him like a song, Mae Ann went to the small room where he kept his tools. She soon left with a shovel, hoe, and rake. No gloves. No hat. Not even a bonnet, confounded woman. She'd be burned and blistered before noon.

He leaned the pitchfork against the wall and walked to the house. Betsy's room had been closed off since she left. He didn't like digging into old wounds, but a situation like this called for practicality. And if Cade was anything, he was practical.

At the upstairs landing, her door stood like a barrier to his past. With a hand to the cold knob and a rock in his throat, he entered to find everything exactly as Betsy had left it the day of their parents' funeral. He'd fought his head about going after her, but Deacon talked him out of it. Good thing. He didn't know if he would have let that no-account she ran off with live long enough to apologize.

He crossed to the small table in front of the window and ran his fingers through the thick dust. A drafty room with its north-facing wall, it took every storm head-on. He wiped his hand on his trousers and searched the chest of drawers for a split skirt and shirts. He fingered Betsy's butter-soft, doeskin riding gloves. They'd be ruined in a day.

In another drawer he found the heavy work gloves he wanted.

He took Betsy's hat from the bedpost and her boots from beneath the bed, then shut the door quietly behind him. He stopped at his room—Mae Ann's room—but didn't go in. She might not appreciate him trespassing on her private area. A growl worked up from his chest, and he headed downstairs and left everything but the hat on her chair by the hearth.

Just when had it become *her* chair? Distinctive and apart from his? With Betsy's hat in hand, he charged outside to prevent a disaster—and split wide open at a woman's high-pitched scream.

~

Mae Ann jumped back from the shovel handle, pushing off so hard that she stumbled and fell on her backside. She screamed again and scooted backward on all fours until she bumped into booted feet and two strong hands that lifted her up as if she weighed nothing. Mortified, she wrestled out of Cade's grasp and away from the temptation to throw her arms around his neck and weep in relief.

Her chest heaved beneath her hand, and she leaned over to catch her breath, all the while keeping her eyes pinned on the severed snake head at the opposite end of the garden.

Cade chuckled.

Chuckled? How dare he? If she had her wind, she'd give him what-for.

He picked a hat up off the ground and handed it to her with humor lacing his words. "This is for you. And remind me never to make you mad when you're holding a shovel."

He looked at her with something akin to admiration, and her anger leaked away.

"You scared the living daylights out of me, woman, with that Apache shriek of yours." He was laughing at her, so much so that his perfect white teeth showed.

She drew herself up and dusted her backside. "Well, you don't have to mock me."

He shook his head. "I'm not mocking you, I'm relieved. I thought you were being scalped."

The idea made her itch, and she pushed at the hair that had escaped her ribbon. She must look a sight—an image that tugged on her lips. She let go a small laugh and tension eased from her shoulders and arms.

Cade grabbed the shovel, chopped the rattles off, and tossed the body over the fence into the brush. Mae Ann clapped a hand over her mouth. Self-preservation had emboldened her to react defensively to the snake's chilling rattle, without hesitation or qualms. But in the absence of fear, her stomach rebelled.

He scooped up the head and carried it to the edge of the garden, where he dug a hole and dropped it in as if he expected it to grow.

"You're planting a snake in the garden?"

His lips twitched in that irritating way. She really must stop watching his mouth.

"Sure. Why not?"

"Cade Parker, I am not a d—"

"I know. You're not a dolt." His eyes glinted as he tamped the soil. Then he handed her the shovel and gentled

99

his voice. "We bury the head so the dog doesn't get snakebit. There's still venom in the jaws and if an animal—or you— nicked a fang, it could prove deadly." He sobered suddenly and concern crinkled his brow as if he cared about her safety.

She took the shovel and averted her gaze. "I see."

"Next time—"

Her eyes flew to his face. "Next time?"

"There's always a next time. So you want to keep an eye out. If there's one rattler, there's likely another nearby."

She felt the blood leave her face.

His features softened. "With the weeds and brush cleared away, they'll be less likely to come in here, but you always want to be prepared." Stepping back, he angled a look at her feet. "Hitch your skirt up."

Her breath jammed in her chest. "I beg your pardon?"

He jerked his chin up as if giving her skirt a tug. "Let me see the tops of your shoes."

She waited a beat and then did as he asked, inching the hem just above her ankles.

"That's what I thought. Those aren't tall enough."

Forgetting her modesty, she hiked her skirt and leaned over to judge the worth of the footwear she'd paid so dearly for. He chuckled again and turned away with a final command. "Wear the hat."

Her face burning, Mae Ann dropped her dress hem over her boots, painfully aware that she'd lifted it too high, revealing her stockings. Cade returned to the barn, his head wagging. If she had a tomato or an apple or just about anything besides a shovel, she'd throw it at him.

Instead, she shoved on the hat.

Judging by the heat of the sun on her back some time later, she stopped at midday and assessed her progress.

Precious little, for the way she felt. Tomorrow she'd surely pay, for already her limbs ached and her hands bore blisters. She leaned her tools against a corner post and went inside to fix dinner.

Refreshed by the hand pump's cold water, she dabbed some against her sweaty neck, retied her hair ribbon and donned her apron. Three place settings topped the table before she remembered that Deacon had taken a hearty meal with him when he left that morning.

That meant she and Cade would be eating alone. Together. Alone together.

She let out a huff. What a sissy she'd become. She returned one place setting to the cupboard and pulled the coffeepot over the front burner. The small roast, potatoes, and onions she'd started that morning simmered nicely, and when she lifted the lid to check their progress, the rich aroma filled the kitchen and her soul. Good food. Strong walls. The makings of a home.

"Could it be, Lord?"

"Could what be?"

Startled by Cade's voice, she dropped the heavy lid and it clattered against the kettle. "I didn't hear you come in."

He frowned and walked past her to the sink, where he washed without being asked. Why did he frown when she least expected it? Did she trouble him? Annoy him?

"Dinner smells good. Deacon won't know what he missed." Cade came up behind her. "Coffee hot?"

She sidestepped and skirted the table. "Not quite. I just set it on. I got so involved in the garden, I let time get away from me."

"Speaking of the garden, I have a few things for you." He left the kitchen, and she followed him around the end of the wall to see where he was going. When he stopped at one of the chairs by the hearth, he looked over his shoulder with one brow cocked. Mind-reading must be one of her expected chores. She joined him.

He handed her a pair of tall leather boots, then picked up several other items and sat in the opposite chair, motioning for her to be seated. "Try those on."

"Now?" She clutched them to her and stood stock-still.

He sighed heavily and leaned back. "If you wouldn't mind. I'd like to see if they fit you, though I can leave the room while you put them on."

"No. That won't be necessary." Heavens, she had never been so prudish. What had come over her? Besides, he was her husband. Why could she not remember that?

She took her seat and, keeping her eyes fixed on the floor, untied her now dusty shoes and set them aside. At least she didn't have holes in her stockings. Drawing a deep breath through her nose, she took the right boot and slid her foot into it. She wiggled her toes and grudgingly admitted it was truly comfortable, much more so than the unforgiving new shoes she'd brought from St. Louis.

She pulled on the mate, flounced her skirt over the tops of both, and stood.

Cade nodded, looking pleased with himself. "Walk across the room and see how they feel."

She did so, surprised that they didn't pinch her in all the wrong places. Were they from his boyhood? Or had they belonged to his mother or sister? "They're perfect."

"Good." He lifted a white shirt from the mound of clothing on his lap and held it to the side. "What do you think?"

She thought it small for him, so he must intend it for her. She examined the seams. "It's nicely made. Whose is it?"

A shadow licked his face as he held up a blue chambray. "These were my sister's. Not exactly women's high fashion, but she wore them riding. The boots too. I thought these might fit you as well."

She accepted the shirts. Not a lady's attire, but sensible for ranch life. When he held out a split skirt and leather belt, the picture clarified. "You don't think she'll mind?"

"Betsy left it all behind." Another frown knit his brow, and Mae Ann felt the oddest urge to relieve his discomfort.

"This is very generous. Does a horse come with them?"

Her words had the effect she'd intended, and he addressed her with a spark of humor. "You're a smart one, Mae Ann Rem—" He swallowed the remaining syllables, not taking his eyes from her. "Parker."

Her heart winced at his mistake. She hugged the garments to her. "I'll run these upstairs and then we'll eat."

She felt his eyes on her and did not breathe until she reached the safety of her room. Laying the clothes on the bed to put away later, she smoothed each item, as if smoothing the wrinkles from her soul. It was the not knowing that bothered her so. Not knowing what Cade really thought. At times—like this—he treated her with consideration and kindness. Then his mood abruptly changed. He was not a drinking man, so liquor was not to blame as she knew was so often the reason women had sought shelter at the boardinghouse.

Would he be like this forever—hot and cold, bitter and sweet?

. . . and give thee peace.

This time the words hit her from a different side. If she were *given* peace, then it was hers to accept or reject.

She'd signed up for this odd arrangement. In fact, it had been her idea. There was no room for fanciful thoughts of love or approval, simply survival—a role she'd learned from her mother before she took ill.

Standing before the dressing table mirror, she pulled the ribbon from her hair, brushed out the knots, and retied it. She would accept God's gift of peace, and do her best to wear it with gratitude. Along with the boots and clothes that had once belonged to Betsy Parker.

CHAPTER 10

The next morning, Mae Ann stepped into the split skirt and buttoned the white shirt, curious about the woman who had worn them yet chosen to leave them behind. If what Willa said was true, Betsy had run off with a man without the blessing of marriage, no doubt bringing shame to Cade in the wake of their parents' funeral. That alone would account for his frowning countenance yesterday.

She pulled the belt tighter and tucked the end under, refusing to judge Betsy. She did not have all the details. Perhaps heartbreak had made the girl flee. Mae Ann certainly understood the pain of losing one's mother, and the memory sent her hand to her throat only to stall at the cameo's absence.

The woman now facing her in the dressing table mirror looked like something from the cover of a dime novel—quite unlike her former self. She flattened the open shirt collar, pressing it against her collarbones, no brooch to close the gap. How long before she relinquished her habit of reaching for the touchstone of her mother's love?

After cleaning the breakfast dishes and planning what to prepare for dinner, she pulled the work gloves from her skirt pocket, donned the hat she'd left on a hook by the front door, and headed for the garden.

The gate stood straighter, obviously repaired since the day before. As she lifted a wire loop from the gatepost, she surveyed the buildings that flanked the wide yard on three sides. No one was about. Busy with their own chores, no doubt. Neither Cade nor Deacon had mentioned the gate at breakfast, though Deacon did lift a bushy eyebrow when Cade told of her snake-killing episode. If she didn't know better, she'd think the old cowboy was impressed.

With a steady, unhurried eye, Mae Ann surveyed every inch of the patch, looking closer at any discoloration that could be another serpent. *Humph.* Serpent in the garden. How droll. A prophetic sign or simply ranch life in the West?

She chose to believe the latter and began clearing the last corner where brush had piled thick against the fence. The hat, gloves, and comfortable boots made the work much easier, and gratitude came just as easy until her rake snagged on a dried cane cluster. She knelt to pull away the debris.

Her heart lifted at sight of a small green stem fighting up through the thorny clutter. She worked the soil around the determined shoot and pressed it into a bowl shape. Inspired by her discovery and relishing the fresh air and sunshine, she did not sense Cade's approach until she stood to stretch her limbs.

He was watching her, the hard planes of his face softening. "You've made progress."

She filled her lungs, eager to share. "I found a rose-bush."

He came inside the fence and squatted by the dried cane, running a finger along the brave little branch. "It's still alive." Wonder filled his words.

Kneeling beside him, she leaned closer to the bright new growth. "Do you know its color?" It didn't matter, but perhaps she could draw him out and learn more about who had planted the rose and when.

"Yellow." He thumbed his hat up. "My father told stories of how his mother brought it from Texas when she and Granddad homesteaded this place."

Mae Ann admired the struggling stem of family history, fighting for life right here, generations after its arrival. "Your mother must have cared for it too."

A shadow dashed across his face and as quickly disappeared. "Faithfully. She and Betsy trimmed it back every fall and nursed it to life each spring. I thought it must have died."

She stood and brushed dirt from her knees. "The pieplant is doing well, but it will be a while before I have enough for baking or canning."

Movement caught the corner of her eye, and she looked up to see Deacon leading two horses across the yard toward the hitching rail. She tugged at her gloves, wishing Cade didn't have to leave so soon to go and do whatever the two of them did all day with the cattle.

He walked out the gate. "How 'bout a change of scenery?"

She stared at him.

He chuckled and tipped his head toward the horses. "Take a break and come for a ride with me."

Her breath snagged in her throat. "But I . . ."

"Don't ride?" Laughter pulled at the corners of his eyes. "I know. Come on." He held the gate open and waited for her.

Well, she'd brought it on herself when she asked about a horse last night. She should have kept her mouth shut, though somehow she suspected he would have gotten around to getting her up on one at some point. Her ability to ride had been his only question when confronted with her *business proposition.*

Several excuses for why she should not be engaged in such a venture presented themselves, but they failed to reach her lips, and she stopped abruptly at the rail. The darker horse she recognized as Cade's mount from the day they met in town. The other, a bit shorter, glistened near red in the morning light, its soft brown eyes watching her calmly. She pressed her hands against her hips and took a deep breath, uncertain as to which was the bigger challenge—rattlesnakes or horses.

Cade approached the smaller of the two and took the reins, gathering them in his left hand atop the saddle—a heavy-looking thing quite unlike any livery she'd seen in St. Louis. Then he held out his right hand and motioned for her to come around the rail. "Ginger here is a good ol' girl. You've nothing to worry about with her."

But she might have plenty to worry about with me. Mae Ann moved in next to Cade, who laid his free hand against the hollow of her waist.

He patted the tall knoblike object where he'd draped the reins. "Grab the horn here."

She complied.

"Now put your left foot in the stirrup and pull yourself up. While you're doing that, swing your other leg over the back and put your right foot in the other stirrup."

And dance a jig while I'm at it. Mae Ann gritted her teeth. She didn't need to hike her split skirt, for it was already short enough, just below her boot tops. Now she knew why.

As soon as she pushed herself off the ground, Cade released the horn and grabbed her around the waist, easing her into the saddle. Every nerve in her body tensed, and the horse danced backward.

"Don't pull on the reins." He covered her hands with one of his and stilled them against the horn. "That makes her think you want to back up."

"I don't." Mae Ann's voice was sadly lacking in bravery and at least one octave higher than normal.

Cade chuckled and stroked the horse's neck. He squeezed Mae Ann's hands until she met his eyes.

"Ginger's reading you. She picks up on your fear or confidence or whatever you're feeling."

Mae Ann swallowed and shifted in the saddle.

His voice softened and he squeezed her hands again. "Don't be afraid. I wouldn't put you on a dangerous animal. Ginger will be good to you if you're good to her. Relax. Let her do the work."

The tenderness in his voice nearly undid her, but he'd think her a fool if she let on. She leaned forward to pat Ginger's neck. "I understand."

The horse stepped sideways, away from Cade. "Relax your legs. You're squeezing her."

How did he know that? Embarrassed by his mention of her limbs but willing to believe him, she forced her muscles to loosen. How was she to stay on?

Cade gathered his horse's reins and led it a few steps away before mounting in one graceful move. He turned and rode up next to her, his stirrup brushing against hers.

Tempted to tighten her grip even more, she gritted her teeth instead.

"Hold the reins in your left hand and do what I do."

He held the leather strips loosely.

Mae Ann looked down at her fist and turned it halfway over, relaxing her grip. Feeling returned to her fingers.

"Good. If it makes you more comfortable to hold on to the horn, use your right hand to do it."

She had that part down cold.

"Now don't do so until I say, but when you want to go forward, click your tongue and press your boot heels into her. Not hard. Easy, like this." He made a clicking sound and his spurs touched his horse's side, and it stepped forward. "Pull on the reins when you want to stop."

She wanted to go neither forward nor back, but to get off.

He turned his horse to face her and crossed his arms on the saddle horn. "Now you try it."

She drew in a deep breath and tapped her boot heels against Ginger. The horse turned an ear in her direction but didn't move. Mae Ann glanced at Cade, who looked as though he was trying not to laugh.

He'd just better not, or he'd have a heavy dose of salt in his corn bread tonight. She pushed her heels again. Nothing.

Cade coughed suspiciously and palmed his mouth. "You're giving her mixed signals."

"I am doing exactly what you told me to do." She didn't need to learn to ride a horse. What was wrong with the wagon? Or walking, for that matter?

"Yes, you are."

She glared at him.

"But you're also tugging on the reins and you didn't click your tongue. Push the reins forward and click your tongue."

"I don't know how to click my tongue." She was certain she could hear his eyes snap with hilarity.

"Sure you can. Like this." He made the noise again, but this time he drew one side of his mouth back. He looked as if he was having a fit.

She tried it.

"Good."

The only thing *good* was his effort to not laugh outright.

"Do it again, but push the reins and heel her all at the same time."

Mae Ann would do this or die. Again, she made the ridiculous sound, lifted her left hand, and kicked the horse. It leaped forward, jerking her backward until she nearly fell from the saddle.

Cade was at her side in a heartbeat, his teeth showing themselves in a full-fledged grin. He reached over and tugged on the reins until Ginger stopped. "Whoa there, girl."

The light in his eyes betrayed his enjoyment. "Good," he lied.

Mae Ann's face burned and she dipped her head to hide her embarrassment. Cade leaned over and looked under her hat brim. "You're doing fine."

"You, sir, are a horrible liar."

He laughed aloud.

After several more stops and starts, she relaxed somewhat, and when she got the hang of reining Ginger to the right or left, a shy confidence settled within her. Perhaps she really could be a rancher's wife.

An odd endearment rose in her breast toward the horse who so patiently endured her awkward attempts. Not once did it buck or run off with her. It shook its head, no doubt in exasperation, but its patience was exemplary. An apple was in order, right after dinner.

Cade rode up next to her again and assumed his relaxed arm-on-the-saddle-horn pose. "You up for an easy walk through the near pasture?"

How could she say no to his warm regard? "Certainly." Already she knew her legs would betray her once she dismounted, and she wanted to put off that humiliation for as long as possible.

Cade set his horse into a slow walk, and she signaled Ginger to do the same. Thankfully, the mare was content to walk beside him and not vie for the lead. A horse race she did not need. The easy gait relaxed her shoulders and back, and she took note of the land rolling around them like a green blanket. A clear, brief melody rang out from her right, answered a moment later from Cade's left. A third matching call broke ahead of them, and her delight escaped in a small laugh.

"They're meadowlarks. They sing like that all spring and summer, especially in the morning."

"It's lovely. But where are they? I don't see any birds."

He looked across the pasture beyond her and lifted his hand toward a scraggly bush. "There's one," he whispered. "On the highest point of that sagebrush."

The little gray bird tilted its head and let loose a flute-like call. Again another answered, and then a third. Such a strong, clear voice from a creature no bigger than Mae Ann's hand. And with no particular beauty other than its yellow breast and black collar.

But as she had already come to see, everything was beautiful here—from Ginger's shimmering coat to the blue sky behind the mountain's jagged peaks. What glory she'd not known existed. What life even her dreams had never imagined.

~

Cade hadn't ridden for pleasure since he and Betsy used to take off as kids, not a care in the world other than staying out of their pa's way when he was in one of his tempers. When Cade lost them both within a week—plus his ma, and soon after, Alexandra—life had gone sour.

The ranch had saved him, its demands flowing into all his open sores and making him forget the pain. It required daylight-to-dark work that ensured sleep, and with Deacon's help and a few extra hands each fall and spring, he'd made a go of it.

Until last week, the ranch had been enough.

Then that gunslick shot Henry Reiker and everything turned inside out.

Mae Anne made him realize he hadn't been living, that he'd left behind the simple pleasures of riding across the land and seeing it like the way she did right now. Teaching her to ride filled him with a sense of companionship that he didn't have with Deacon and had never shared with Alexandra.

Her simple delight in their surroundings was childlike. She drank in the high park like a soul dying of thirst, and it made him proud of what he and his family had worked so hard for. She hadn't looked down her nose at one thing he'd shown or offered her, not even his sister's clothes. Alexandra would never have ridden anything but a sidesaddle, nor worn any clothing other than her high-dollar habit and fancy hat.

113

Relaxed, with the breeze tossing her hair, Mae Ann had a beauty that surpassed that of any woman Cade had ever known, including Alexandra. Maybe he should be thanking God for San Francisco dandies.

He turned them toward the house, and as they neared the barn, a rider approached from the opposite direction. Todd Price. Cade figured Mae Ann was sore from riding, though he doubted she'd admit it. She'd done fair today. Hadn't quit or whined or run off. At the hitching post, he dismounted and dropped the reins on the rail, but she sat stone still, a wrinkle between her brows.

Stepping in close to Ginger, he thumbed his hat up. "Gettin' off is just like gettin' on, only in reverse."

She cut him a look that said she didn't quite trust him. He bit back a laugh, and let her make the first move. She did fine until her boots hit the ground, and then she buckled like a newborn foal. He caught her about the waist until she got her legs under her. Holding her like that, so close her hat brim crushed against his chest, he forgot all about their visitor.

"Mr. Parker!"

Todd Price had a very poor sense of timing.

The old plow horse clopped to a halt, and the rail-thin boy slid down. "Ma sent some dried apple fritters along with the milk."

Cade let go with one hand but slid an arm around Mae Ann's waist as he faced Todd. She pulled her hat off and picked at her hair.

Todd drew a jar of near-clabbered milk from his saddlebags and a cloth-wrapped bundle that Cade hoped hadn't squashed on the ride over. Travine Price's fritters were the next best thing to yesterday's chocolate cake.

"Mae Ann, this is Todd Price, the neighbor I told you about with the milk cow."

"Nice to meet you, Todd."

"Ma'am." The boy looked between the two of them a couple of times, fritters in one hand, jar in the other.

Cade leaned close to Mae Ann's ear. Her disarrayed hair tickled his nose and he lowered his voice. "You got enough to invite him to dinner?"

She nodded and answered his whisper with her own. "If I can make it to the house without falling."

Her lips pulled into a tight seam. He stepped back, and she grabbed his arm. "Not so fast. Just give me a minute. Have him help you do something out here while I get to the house." She scorched him with a frown. "You didn't tell me I wouldn't be able to walk afterwards."

His chuckle escaped of its own, but the way she held on to him knit him to her in a peculiar way. "Do you need my help getting inside?"

"I do not." She let go and reached for the rail. A couple more steps and she was on her own to the front door.

Cade turned to the boy. "Help me with these horses while Mrs. Parker gets dinner on the table." The proper title rolled out before he gave it any thought, and it felt odd on his tongue.

"Sure thing, Mr. Parker." Todd tethered his horse, set the milk jar on the stone pathway, and gathered Ginger's reins. "Don't mean to be rude or nothin', but when did you get hitched?"

Cade coughed and dragged a hand down his face as they led the horses away. "Recently."

"She sure is perty."

He smiled, a little proud. "Yes, she is."

"Shucks. I didn't know you were sweet on anyone." At the corral, Todd dropped Ginger's reins, hooked the stirrup on the horn, and loosened the cinch. "You weren't last time I was here, least not that I could tell."

The boy had a lot to learn about such things, sweet or not, and Cade wasn't about to be his teacher.

"She's not from around here, is she?"

He hefted Cricket's saddle and set it on the top rail. "Nope."

"Did you order her out of a catalogue?"

He stopped and glared at the boy.

Todd flushed girl-pink and hung his head. "Beg pardon, Mr. Parker. Heard my folks talking about the mail-order bride from Missouri that Henry Reiker was waitin' on."

St. Louis, Missouri. That was the only thing Cade knew about her background, and apparently, other folks knew near as much. Guilt snaked around his collar. "When was your family last in town?"

"About a month back. Ma and Sophie went in for some cloth goods."

Cade didn't want to discuss his marriage with a kid when he was just getting his balance on the whole matter himself. But news was important to folks who lived out from town. Neighbors depended on one another to keep them posted on important events.

"When you get home, tell your folks that Henry Reiker passed on. He was shot during a bank robbery Monday afternoon."

Todd stilled, and his blush faded at the news. "Yes, sir, Mr. Parker. I'll be sure to do that."

"Sheriff Wilson has word out about the two men, and they're probably a couple counties over by now. But just the same, you keep your eyes peeled on the way home."

The youngster puffed up like a skinny toad. "I can handle myself. Got my grandpa's pistol in my saddlebags. But thanks just the same."

Cade headed for the house, the boy on his heels. It didn't exactly brighten his day to know that Todd Price thought he could hold off cold-blooded killers with his grandfather's flintlock.

CHAPTER 11

"Please thank your mother for the milk." Mae Ann laid a healthy slice of chocolate cake on the boy's plate, keenly aware of Deacon's jealous glare.

Todd dug in and rolled his eyes. "This is even better than what Sophie makes."

Deacon huffed.

"More coffee?" Mae Ann held the pot above Deacon's cup and gave him her warmest smile. She also filled Cade's and caught his enjoyment of the foreman's cake-grudging discomfort.

"How far is it to your farm, Todd? I'd love to ride over for a visit."

"About three miles if you cut across the pasture." He washed down his last bite with coffee and laid his fork and napkin across his plate. Manners.

Mae Ann nodded approvingly.

"But don't tell Sophie what I said about your cake or she'll get her feathers all ruffled and quit baking."

Mae Ann laughed. "We can't have that, can we?" She reached for the plates. "Did Cade show you our new milk cow?"

Disappointment dropped the boy's head. "Guess I won't need to come anymore."

A bit remorseful, Mae Ann feared she'd taken something important from him. Independence, perhaps. Mornings away from chores, carrying milk to a bachelor neighbor. "I'm sure you're welcome anytime."

He scooted back from the table. "I best get a wiggle on. Ma'll be lookin' for me. Thanks for dinner and the cake."

Deacon mumbled in his mustache, and Mae Ann squelched a laugh. "You are most welcome, Todd. We'll enjoy your mother's fritters at supper tonight."

He paused and addressed Cade. "Do you have the other jar I brought last time?"

"Sure do." Cade went to the pantry and returned with a clean quart jar and lid. "Tell your ma I appreciate her keeping us supplied in milk for so long."

Mae Ann followed Todd to the door and watched as he stashed the jar in his saddlebag, then mounted his big-boned horse and rode away. Cade came up behind her, close enough to brush her skirt. For a moment she felt like a proper wife standing at the door with her husband, seeing a traveler on his way. A fanciful thought, and fleeting.

Deacon squeezed by. "Thank you kindly, ma'am."

"It's my pleasure, Deacon." And it was. Simple appreciation lifted her spirit more than almost anything. The old cowboy had cleaned up his mustache and his manners in the last few days, and Mae Ann liked to think it was on her account. His spurs jangled an odd cadence as he strode toward the barn, one of his steps longer than the other.

"About riding to the Price place."

Cade's throaty comment brought her around, and his brows snagged on a disagreeable thought she was certain she wouldn't like.

"You can't be goin' off alone in this country."

She tilted her chin and headed for the kitchen. "If a twelve-year-old can do it, I imagine I can as well."

Cade followed, boots *thud-clinking* his argument against the plank floor. "Not until you get better acquainted with Ginger."

Mae Ann cleared the remaining dishes. "I thought you said I did well today."

He stopped behind his chair and gripped the back of it. "I did. You did. But it's not as safe as you might think in these high parks. You know there are rattlers."

"And lions." She couldn't resist a sarcastic tone.

His brows drew farther down. "I'm serious. What if Ginger spooked and threw you? What if you came upon—"

Mae Ann lifted the kettle heating on the stove and stopped to face him. "Came upon what?"

His frown deepened. "Men could be out there. Men that Sheriff Wilson is still looking for."

Her chest seized. *The men who robbed the bank and killed Henry.* Shamed for mocking Cade's concern, she set the kettle down and smoothed her apron. No one but her mother had ever cared about her safety or warned her of possible danger.

His voice gentled. "I don't want anything to happen to you."

Unsure what to do or say, she picked up the kettle again. In spite of his valid worries, she'd not be kept a prisoner in this house. "That is very kind of you. But I am a grown woman and perfectly capable of taking care of myself. I cannot live shut up each and every day without the freedom of the outdoors."

He let go the chair and took a step toward her, his face awash with dark irritation. "I promised to take care of you and I intend to do so. But you sure make it all-fired hard."

She sagged inwardly. Of course, obligation. How addled could she be to forget their business arrangement? She carried the kettle to the sink.

Cade stomped from the room, and she held her breath until the front door slammed behind him.

Steam rose as she poured hot water into the dishpan, fogging the window. She wiped the glass with a towel and frowned out at the garden. Filling the role of dutiful wife was one thing, but living fenced in like a delicate rose was quite another. She had little to go on where men were concerned, other than the infirm or aged who had found shelter at the rooming house. Her father's abandonment was a faint memory, but it had driven desire deep into her breast. All she'd ever wanted was a real home, and the bridal advertisement in the *Chronicle* had seemed a chance in that direction.

She shaved soap into the hot water and sloshed it around, recalling Henry's straightforward letters. Her harbored hope that love would grow in time melted away like the thin shavings. How naive she had been.

Gripping the edge of the sink, she weighed her determination to be her own woman against her vows and recent prayer for graciousness. How these things would ever work together was indeed a miracle that only God could enact.

~

Cade clenched his hands as he walked to the barn. Every woman who'd ever meant anything to him had left him behind. He hadn't been able to hold onto any of them.

Alexandra. His sister. His mother—though she'd not left by her own choice.

Now Mae Ann insisted she could ride off whenever and wherever she wanted, in spite of his warnings.

She had a mind of her own—that was clear from the moment she'd asked if he needed a wife. A grim laugh rolled through his chest, and Ginger swung her head to look in his direction. He turned the mare out and resaddled Cricket. Blue trotted up as if sensing adventure, and Cade took off for the west end.

A ride would do him good, hard and fast, not pussy-footin' along as he had with Mae Ann. He ground his teeth against the way she made him feel, screwed his hat down, and kicked Cricket into a gallop.

Cresting a small rise, he came upon his band of saddle horses, startled by his wild approach. They watched him, heads high, tails swishing. Blue charged ahead, circling the band in expectation of bringing them home. Cade reined in and whistled the dog back, but not before he made a quick lunge toward the lead mare and drew flying hooves and a near miss. As Blue trotted to him, tongue hanging out and grinning like a kid, it hit him.

He'd get Mae Ann a dog.

Not a cow dog like Blue, but one to shadow her, defend her if need be. She would ride to the Price Farm, and Lord knew where else, whether he wanted her to or not. Of that he was more certain than the price of beef come fall.

Blue's ears perked toward the north, and Cade reined around. A rider headed his way at an easy lope. Deacon.

Cade rode that way and met his foreman at the draw behind Pine Hill.

"Something's been gnawing at me since I checked them late heifers up north the other day, so I swung up by Reiker's to have a look-see." Deacon tugged his hat brim lower and looked in the direction he mentioned. "I just come from there."

The back of Cade's neck prickled. "Find anything?"

"'Fraid so. Someone's been there, and recent. Fresh hoofprints in the corral say about a half dozen head been holed up there at least one night."

If MacGrath was moving one of his hands in to squat on Reiker's place, it'd mean another trip to town to see the sheriff.

Deacon turned cold blue eyes on Cade. "Weren't no one around, but I found tracks of two horses in the yard. Neither of 'em was MacGrath's black."

Cade's ire rose. Rustlers or squatters, with no clear link to MacGrath. Either way, Mae Ann had no business out by herself.

Deacon rode on to check a section of fence, and Cade turned for the house, taking the trail up to the hilltop and a clear view of Parker Land and Cattle.

Twin crosses stood in the ponderosa's shadow, and as he approached, the wind sighed through its branches, big-voiced and as heavy as a whole forest rather than a single tree. It had amazed him as a boy and it still did—the lone survivor his grandfather had left standing after harvesting other trees for building.

He stopped near the graves and stood in the stirrups, stretching his legs. There was no easing the ache in his heart.

His pa had known better. But knowing and being bullheaded were two different things. The colonel's determination to beat the storm home rather than spend the night in town had cost him his life as well as Cade's mother's. That one bad decision changed the course of everyone's future and taught Cade a hard lesson.

Pride could kill a man and destroy everything he held dear.

Was it pride chewing at him, making him distrust MacGrath? Or was it a common sense warning? Either way, he had to allow that there could be more players in these high parks than he first figured.

He turned Cricket downhill, mentally spurring his own hide instead of his horse's. If he hadn't been out courting Alexandra that wintery night, he might have convinced his stubborn father to wait out the storm.

He still didn't know which man he resented more. The colonel or himself.

~

Mae Ann woke to thin gray light teasing at the window, and it drew her to peek through the lace curtain and watch. Cade and Deacon slipped like shadows among the buildings. Blue trotted close behind.

"Thank you, Lord."

The words were her first each morning, and as the days had turned into weeks, she meant them more and more. God had used a horrible tragedy to redirect her life along a path that would have been otherwise undiscovered.

Life at the rooming house, narrow and constrained by lack and loneliness, held nothing of the anticipation that energized her as she dressed and tied back her hair. By the time she descended the stairs, dawn had turned up the wick and brightened the eastern sky with another fresh promise.

May had stretched deep into June, and Cade still kept a polite distance. But he took her riding in the long, lazy evenings, and truth be told, she looked forward to those rides all through the day. Whether cooking or baking or washing or cleaning, she projected herself into the solitude of those side-by-side encounters, scouting the countryside, enjoying the sunsets that often blazed silent and bold above the mountains. Cade rarely spoke, but he would sometimes rein in and cross his arms on his saddle horn and heave a sigh. Worried, she supposed. Or something else?

Still, she held those moments as sacred between the two of them, as if they really were man and wife. As if he *wanted* her beside him.

But they never rode to the farm.

Maybe she'd just go by herself. After today's expedition.

She tied on her apron and set the table with transferware plates and tin cups for the men's coffee. Hotcakes and eggs kept her hands busy while she mentally mapped her journey. Today she would visit Todd's mother, Travine. On one of their rides, Cade had pointed out the deer trail that skirted the ranch on the west. Follow it until it cut down to the creek, he'd said a bit grudgingly. She smiled at the memory. Turn left, watch for the windmill, then keep it in view. Within a mile and a half, she'd be at the farm.

The men rounded into the kitchen, and Deacon went to the sink. For some reason, Cade always let the old cowboy wash first. He poured himself a cup of coffee and stood as if taking in the room. Mae Ann's neck warmed, a sure sign that he was taking her in as well.

She offered him a cheery smile. "Good morning."

He peered at her over the edge of his mug. "You braided your hair."

Called out by his observation, she reached behind her neck and touched the plait that hung to her waist. Perhaps he suspected her plans. Now was as good a time as any to let him know. "As soon as breakfast is finished, I'm riding to the Prices'."

Showing no reaction at all, he took his turn at the sink, exchanging a look with Deacon as they passed each other.

She had no idea of the message, nor did she care to know. She was going to see Mrs. Price even if she had to walk. She brought the coffee from the stove and sat down. "Would one of you gentleman please saddle Ginger for me when you're finished eating? That way I can get an early start and be back in time for supper."

"Supper?" Cade hung the towel on the peg and joined them at the table.

"Yes. I have sliced roast and bread for dinner. And I made extra gravy, so you'll also have that while I'm gone. I'm sure you'll do fine without me for one meal." Secretly, she didn't want them to do fine without her. She wanted Cade to need her, but she had to admit he'd been without her for quite some time prior to her arrival.

He rumbled something deep in his throat and bowed his head for an abbreviated grace.

Deacon tucked in to his meal. "You're not taking all them gingersnap cookies to the Price place, are you?"

"What a wonderful idea." Mae Ann bit one side of her cheek to keep from laughing at Deacon's dismay. He was much too fun to tease, so transparent where his stomach was concerned. "Thank you for suggesting it. I made a double batch, so there will be plenty to tide you over."

The man's shoulders drooped, poor fellow. So protective of the sweets he enjoyed. Cade, on the other hand, scowled and said nothing other than, "I'd rather you didn't go."

Well, she'd rather she did. If he wanted to pout like a child, it was no concern of hers.

After breakfast, she cleared the table, washed the dishes, and wrapped a dozen gingersnaps in a napkin, wishing she had more to take to the neighbor who had been so generous. But this fall after harvest and canning, she'd have all sorts of preserves and pies and goodies. If she had excelled at anything growing up, it was cooking. Mama said she had a knack for it.

She squirmed inwardly. Mama also said she had a knack for being stubborn. Mae Ann preferred to use the word *determined*, and today she was determined to ride alone all the way to the Price farm and back.

She gathered the napkin and her hat from the door and found Ginger saddled and waiting at the rail in front of the house, a yellow slicker rolled and tied behind the cantle.

Whoever had saddled the mare had thought enough to prepare her for rain, but the men and Blue were out of sight. Just as well. She could do this by herself and would. She set her hat and strode to the horse, who watched her with those kind eyes.

Mae Ann pressed her cheek against Ginger's neck, earning a deep chesty rumble in reply. "You dear girl. We're going to do fine today, aren't we?"

"I expect you will."

Mae Ann spun to see Cade standing just beyond the railing. Where had he come from? "You startled me." Her fingers involuntarily fingered her collar and she jerked them down, irritated by the annoying habit.

"That's how easy it would be for someone to sneak up on you." He came around and took the bundle from her, then tucked it into the saddlebag. He loosed Ginger's tether, led the horse away from the railing, and waited for Mae Ann to mount.

She squared herself and reached for the reins dangling from his fingers. "Thank you." Gripping the saddle horn, she hiked her left foot to the stirrup, but before she could grab the cantle with her right hand, Cade encircled her waist and lifted her lightly to the saddle.

Tingling from the warmth of his hands, she pulled on Ginger's reins, and the mare backed several steps before Mae Ann regained her wits. He hadn't touched her once over the several weeks they'd ridden together. Why now, when she needed to concentrate on what she was doing and not the way he made her feel?

He thumbed his hat up, planted his fists on his hips, and captured her with a hard glare. "Take Blue. If something happens, send him home for help."

His tension was tangible.

Even Ginger sensed it and sidestepped.

"What could happen?" But she didn't want to know. She wanted to lose herself in the wildflowers and grassland and drink in the meadowlarks' songs. Cade was being protective again. Obligated. At least he hadn't insisted on riding along.

"If I send Blue back, will you call for the cavalry?"

His eyes narrowed. "Where you're concerned, I *am* the cavalry." His graveled voice backed up his words and thwarted any possibility of lighthearted conversation.

She gathered the reins in a tighter hold and turned Ginger away before she said something completely foolish.

CHAPTER 12

C ade snapped his fingers and gestured toward the departing horse. "Blue, go."

Obediently, the dog trotted away.

Cade shoved his hands in his pockets and watched Mae Ann ride across the yard, no longer awkward atop the trustworthy mare. Sending Blue was the best he could do for now, other than following her himself.

He snorted. She'd have a wild-horse fit. The idea was almost worth her ire—watching her eyes snap like firecrackers on the Fourth of July. He dismissed the idea and marched for the barn.

How was he supposed to concentrate on his chores with her gone?

The same way you did before you brought her here.

He dragged his hand down his face and reset his hat. Nothing would be the same as it was before he agreed to her infernal business proposition.

Deacon stood at the barn's open doorway, leaning on a pitchfork, watching him with his mustache cocked up on one side. If he said one thing about anything, Cade was liable to knock the grin right off his smirking face, friend or no.

By dinnertime, Cade had the barn stalls as clean as the kitchen floor. He'd replaced two worn poles in the round pen and restrung the barbed wire around the garden patch. Mae Ann was still gone—just as she said she would be.

At the water trough, he stuck his head beneath the pump's cold flow and plastered his hair back. Then he climbed up to the hayloft, skipping a broken rung that dangled from the barn wall, and scanned the long park that spread between two cedar-covered ridges. The Sangre de Cristo's snowcapped peaks cut above the horizon, surprising him as always with their snowy shroud so late in June.

His scrutiny returned to the grassland where the sun glinted off the Prices' windmill, a tiny flash from this distance. Still, it gave him a sense of bearing. Of knowing which way Mae Ann would be coming from. But there was no sign that she was headed home.

The word burned a hole through his sweating chest. This was her home now too. At least he wanted her to feel that way about it. He climbed down, hoping Deacon hadn't seen him up there. The old man would never let him hear the end of it.

He headed for the house, not because he was hungry but because he couldn't think of anything else to do.

Deacon already had the gravy bubbling and sliced bread on the table. Cade washed with soap—another change Mae Ann had brought. Through the window the garden lay like a quilt patch, the soil rich and dark where she had worked it and watered it every day. Smart rows of corn lined up like soldiers guarding hills of beans and squash. The rosebush and pieplant thrived from her care.

A chair scraped across the floor. "You eatin' or you gonna stand there all day mopin' like an orphaned calf?"

Cade joined him, took a slice of bread and beef, and smothered them with gravy. "Not unless you figure on eating it all yourself." He still wasn't hungry, but he could take only so much ribbing from the old codger.

Deacon guzzled his coffee and wiped his mouth on his sleeve. No napkins. "I figured you'd gone after her by now."

"Well, you figured wrong."

Deacon grumped. "Then that's my one for this month."

Cade shoved the gravy-swamped bread in his mouth to pack the words down. He didn't need to say what he was thinking.

"I'm takin' an iron up to the north section after dinner. All them mamas got a calf by 'em. Don't need some poke to slip a sticky rope on 'em and mother 'em up to one of their cows 'fore I get a Lazy-P burned on their hide."

Cade huffed. "You got that right." He sopped the rest of his gravy.

Deacon downed his coffee and took his plate to the sink. "A quick fire and hot iron'll do the trick. But I'll be wearin' my piece just in case."

Cade's blood chilled. Time was a man wore a sidearm in this country only for rattlers—and not the two-legged kind. "Drive them down this way when you're done. We'll keep 'em in the Pine Hill section."

When the wind kicked up late afternoon and a gray front tumbled over the mountains, Cade saddled Cricket and headed out, though not to help Deacon. He'd get those cow-calf pairs home just fine. But Mae Ann didn't know to come in before a storm.

He turned south at a fast trot. She should have been home by now. Plus, he'd not told her to keep an eye on the horizon. Summer storms had a way of rolling up in a matter of minutes, and her first brief hailstorm wasn't enough to warn her of the danger. He'd lost cattle to lightning strikes over the years, even a horse standing too close to the fence line. Images of the charred animal swamped his worry over Mae Ann, and he kicked Cricket into a lope.

He rode a mile along the deer path, relieved to find Ginger's trail and even Blue's tracks in the soft dirt alongside. At the creek, he veered left but rode closer to a line of scrub oak above the trail so he could keep an eye on the horizon. And then he saw her.

His chest cinched and his fingers tightened on the reins, pulling his horse to a shorter stride. He stopped to watch her, letting his breathing slow to normal. Thank God, she was all right. But she was in no hurry. Her braid must have come loose, for her hair flapped free below her hat brim like a horse's mane. She sat easy, as if she'd ridden all her life.

Blue's head shot up and he sniffed the wind. Cade reined Cricket around a thick sagebrush and trotted away from them. Upwind, if Blue got a whiff of him, it would tip off Mae Ann. He didn't want her to think he didn't trust her ability. But neither did he want her completely on her own.

Confounded woman had him so hobbled he didn't know what he wanted.

He loped home and into the yard against a strong headwind. Deacon's horse was in the corral. Cade unsaddled Cricket, gave him a quick brushing, and turned him out. Then he scuttled up to the hayloft.

He'd spent more time up there today than he had since he was a kid dreaming about running the ranch on his own with a wife and family to carry on the Parker name. He could just make out Mae Ann coming in from the creek, and he shuddered like the loft doors as a sudden gust blew a thought across his heart.

What if it wasn't his decision to bring Mae Ann home that had changed his life so drastically? What if it had been God's plan all along?

The revelation charged him like lightning as he shot down the ladder. A rung gave way beneath him, and if not for the grip he had on either side, he would have fallen. Sobered but still surging with the new perspective, he promised himself he'd come back later and reinforce the ladder that clung to the wall.

Blue's yap announced their arrival, and Cade ran from the barn. Mae Ann had dismounted but still held the reins.

Thunder cracked and lightning crashed into the pasture. Ginger danced on her back feet, head high and eyes wild.

"Let her go!" The wind caught his words before they reached Mae Ann.

Another clap sent the horse straight up, jerking the reins free. Mae Ann threw her arms over her head. Why didn't she run?

He grabbed her and whirled away. Ginger's hooves slammed down behind him. His heart slammed into his throat.

Mae Ann turned into his chest, fisting his shirt in her hands as the sky opened up. He wrapped his arms around her trembling body and pressed her close. Let Ginger settle herself. Mae Ann was worth more to him than his entire herd of horses.

The truth struck him square in the chest. As shocked by the realization as he was by the next lightning bolt, he scooped her into his arms and ran for the house.

~

They crashed through the front door, propelled by another explosion so loud that Mae Ann's ears rang. She pressed her face against Cade's neck, her hammering heartbeat answering his. Never had she heard such a storm. Her skin tingled and a metallic taste settled on her tongue.

He dropped into a chair, his arms still clutching her close, his head against hers. "Are you all right?" His voice rumbled from his chest into her shivering body.

"I am now." She touched her head. "I lost my hat."

His hold eased some, and he stroked loose hair from her face. "I'll look for it. Stay here."

She caught his hand. "Where are you going?" Surely not out in the storm.

"I won't be long, but I have to check on the barn, in case it was hit."

Fear squeezed her voice into a whisper. "What if *you're* hit?"

Her plea drew longing across his features, and again he fingered her hair back. "Stay here. Please—this time—do as I ask."

How could she not?

The door slammed shut behind him and a blinding blue flashed through the windows. *Oh, Lord, have mercy on him!* Eyes squeezed tight, she groped toward the sill and chanced a quick peek to see Cade at the rail, his shirt soaked through already, only steps from the door. Rivulets streaked the yard, and hail splashed here and there. He pulled his hat down farther and raced to the barn.

The garden!

Mae Ann ran to the kitchen window and found more than a rivulet rushing through her hard work. The hail would strip the rosebush, just beginning to bloom. She looked around for something to cover it, but her unspoken promise to Cade stilled her search. His urgent tone pressed her feet to the floor and her heart to her throat, so she watched from inside as the hail increased, growing in size, pelting her fledgling plants into the earth.

Defeated, she returned to the cold hearth and fell into her chair, helpless as a wind-tossed fledgling. Was this what it meant to be a rancher's wife? To pour all one's energy and strength into making a home and a life, only to have it blown away or drowned at nature's whim?

No.

The need to fight shot through her hands, and she gripped the cool leather arms. She would not sit and fret and feel sorry for her lost efforts. Both Cade and Deacon would be soaked and starving when they came in from battling the storm. Gathering her resolve, she went to the kitchen and stoked the fire, glad to see that someone had tended it in her absence.

Hot coffee and a fresh batch of biscuits would sit well with the men, especially with the strawberry preserves Travine Price had sent with her. She stopped. The jar still sat tucked in Ginger's saddlebags, as did a potato with a fresh cutting from one of Travine's lovely rosebushes. Mae Ann had wanted to plant it on Pine Hill between the crosses as a small gift for Cade.

Tying on her apron, she pulled a tight bow and considered how Travine might handle the storm. What a cheerful sort she was, and so welcoming. But her bright smile had not hidden the dry creases that etched her face. Life in the "high parks," as Cade called it, must be harsh on a woman. For the weathered skin that strengthened a man's countenance into rugged handsomeness left a woman looking old and worn.

Mae Ann touched her cheek, and loose hair brushed her hand. Another booming crash rattled her nerves, though it hit farther away. The storm was moving on, perhaps pouring down on the Price farm this very moment.

She'd completely forgotten her hair had come loose when the wind tore the ribbon from her braid. She pushed back the loose strands, then finished the biscuits and tucked them into the oven before taking a pail of warm water to her room to freshen up.

At her window, the breath left her. The hail had stopped, but a lake swamped the barnyard from building to building. Cade and Deacon splashed through it with Blue on their heels. She washed her face and quickly braided her hair, then dashed downstairs.

All three stood just inside the door, soaked and dripping. Without a word, she returned upstairs and crossed an invisible barrier into Cade's room. Some things were more important than propriety. Cade and Deacon were roughly the same size, Deacon more wiry, but both in desperate need of dry clothes. Cade's moccasins lay by the bedside table, and she picked them up as well.

Upon her return, a fire crackled on the hearth and Blue lay as close as possible. The men stood with their backs to the warmth, feet bare of even their socks. A strange sight on a June evening, but not so foreign that it didn't fit this surprising country with its heart-stopping beauty and sudden storms.

She handed each a change of clothes and set the moccasins by Cade's chair. "I'll be in the kitchen, and we'll eat as soon as you're ready." At that, she left them with a parting word. "Put your wet clothes on the back porch."

"Bossy thing, ain't she?"

A smile spread from Mae Ann's soul to her lips at Deacon's rough words. The crusty old cowboy had a core as soft as eiderdown.

~

Cade cut Deacon a look. "And considerate of your sorry hide, I'd say." As well as his own. He wasn't surprised that she'd braved his room and gone through his things to bring them dry clothes. But bringing his moccasins—the thoughtful act moved him more than he cared to admit.

Deacon let loose a laugh and tugged off his wet drawers. Cade turned away and did the same. A whiff of hot biscuits vied with the logs snapping on the fire, and Cade's insides warmed with the sounds and smells of home at his wife's hand.

No—not his wife. His bride. There was a difference, and that difference was starting to rub him raw.

He gathered his wet clothes, took them out back and hung them over the porch railing. The tang of rain and wet earth filled the evening, and the dying sun broke through a spent cloudbank skimming the western ridge. Contentment settled in his chest. Right next to deep longing.

He raked through his memory for the exact wording of Mae Ann's proposition:

If I do not appeal to you, we can live as man and wife in name only.

Appeal to him? Lord have mercy on his stubborn soul. No woman had ever appealed to him like Mae Ann. But he sure enough hadn't told her in so many words.

He looked down at his feet and wiggled his toes in the soft comfort, recalling other aspects of their agreement. Something about sending her away if he wasn't satisfied with her help. A groan rolled up from his chest and he let it out on the cool air.

He was a coward. That was all there was to it. He'd given his heart to Alexandra, and she'd tossed it aside as soon as a better option came along. Now he was afraid to make the same mistake again.

A second groan followed the first. Life had become more than just cows and grass and rustlers since Mae Ann came, but what if she wasn't willing to return his affection?

Confound it all, he'd rather face a rattler bare-handed than be rejected by another woman.

But she'd brought his moccasins.

He plowed through his hair, digging deep for a clear thought as the sun slipped behind the mountains. If he didn't tell her how he felt, he might lose his mind. And what good was a heart without a mind to follow it?

CHAPTER 13

The hail had beaten through a few old shingles on the barn, but they could wait until Cade knew all the stock was healthy. He rode out with his Winchester the next day to check on the horses, make sure none had spooked and broken a leg in a badger hole or been hit by lightning. He didn't care to put one down, but he wouldn't let an injured animal suffer either.

Deacon followed the fence lines out, starting with the north end. The storm had driven in from the northwest, but that wouldn't keep MacGrath from claiming the herd busted through the fence and onto his land while one of his boys with an extra cinch ring ran brands on a few calves.

If it was MacGrath.

Cade couldn't accuse him outright, not after what Deacon found at Reiker's. But he hadn't heard of any MacGrath cattle gone missing. Peculiar coincidence, since Cade had lost a dozen by his last count.

He topped a knoll and found the band of horses grazing in their meadow as if nothing had happened the night before. He leaned on his saddle horn and counted heads. Watched the herd's movements, his eyes sharp for a limp or stumble. Satisfied they'd fared well in the storm, he turned toward home and circled around to the ponderosa.

It called to him of late, as if reminding him he needed to get his footing when it came to being part of a family. He pulled up near the crosses, but Blue's low growl turned his attention to the ranch buildings below.

A horse and rider crossed the yard at a slow walk and pulled up by the garden where Mae Ann worked. She clearly didn't hear the approach, for she stayed low, facing away from the dark horse and its heavy rider.

Blue growled again. His ears pricked toward the scene, his scruff stiff as a porcupine's. Cade reacted in kind. His neck crawled and a growl rolled through his chest. The man who sat watching Mae Ann had no reason to ride onto Parker land. No peaceable reason.

Cade drew his rifle from the scabbard, turned Cricket down the hill, and skirted the barn. He'd not let the rider know he was coming. His kind needed no warning—only watching.

~

The softened earth let loose its hold, and Mae Ann pulled the weed with little effort. The chore was much easier after yesterday's storm, but her boots much worse off. The mud stuck like plaster and caked up on the heels until the weight of them sent her to find a stick to scrape off the excess.

She squatted unladylike in the garden, not willing to touch her knees to the wet earth. Cade was trying to sneak up on her, and she probably shouldn't let him catch her in this position. Her mother would have a fit to see her now, bless her soul. If only she could.

Cricket's steps were slow, plodding heavily as he approached from behind. Did Cade really think she wouldn't hear him? She clapped off her gloved hands and turned as she stood, pleased to see him so early in the day—

The black-booted man stared down at her from atop a thick-chested horse. The longer he stared, the wider he grinned until he laughed and slapped his leg with an oath.

Mae Ann took a step back.

"If this ain't my lucky day. We meet again, Widow Reiker. Or at least that's what you'd like everyone to believe."

She stiffened at the accusation.

Another bawdy laugh, and he pulled off his hat and swept it beside him in mock deference. "Surely you remember me from the mercantile. Sean MacGrath, at your service." His black horse sidestepped at the gesture, and he jerked it back with a heavy hand.

Her blood chilled.

He looked over his shoulder, then stepped from his horse and dropped the reins to the ground. She reached for the shovel she'd left by the gate, but MacGrath grabbed it and lifted it to his side of the fence. She held his look, refusing to cower.

"Need some help there?" One long stride brought him through the gate.

Mae Ann stood fast. "What do you want?"

He moved closer, animal-like in his focus. As he raised his arm, Mae Ann braced for him to drive the shovel into the earth, but he stopped, then slowly offered it to her.

"Land," he said in a slippery tone. "Land with water that shouldn't be *wasted*." His cold glare gripped her, and his voice dropped an octave. "Wasted on some sodbuster with a plow."

He smelled of sweat and tobacco and clothes gone too long unwashed.

She took hold of the shovel, but he yanked it toward him, pulling her off balance.

A metallic click made them both go still.

"You're not welcome here, MacGrath." Cade's deep-voiced threat rolled along the rifle barrel aimed squarely at the man's chest.

Mae Ann's knees quivered with relief. So focused on their rude visitor, she hadn't heard Cade ride up.

Dropping the shovel, MacGrath snarled up at him. "I've got business with your woman, not you."

"Get off my land." The cold threat in Cade's voice sent a shiver up her spine.

"That's what I was tellin' her." MacGrath jutted his chin at her. "She's got no right to the Reiker place. It ain't hers."

"It *is* mine." She stepped forward, refusing to stand in the background while two men argued about what rightfully belonged to her. "I have Henry's will to prove it."

MacGrath turned slowly, a sneer curling his lip as he took her in from foot to face. "I hear that will names his *widow* as heir. And you were never married to him. Isn't that right?"

A burning sensation swept through her middle, and her fingers curled into fists.

He pulled his head back and stuck out his chest. "But I'm a fair man, and I've come to offer you a fair price for that no-good piece o' dirt."

"If it's no good, then why do you want it?"

MacGrath's dark brows drew down at her challenge. "Take my offer, and I won't contest the will. If it goes to auction, I'll have it anyway, and at a lot less than I'm willing to give you now." His black eyes bored into her as if he could force his desire upon her.

Her fingernails threatened to pierce the palms of her hands. "My farm is not for sale."

"Leave." Cade's tone said much more than his words. "Now."

MacGrath's dark glare raked her one more time before he strode through the gate and swung into the saddle. The horse danced beneath him, ears pinned, head tucked, and he whirled it around with a cruel grip.

"We ain't finished, Parker. Not by a far piece."

Blue ran hard after MacGrath's galloping black.

Cade sheathed his Winchester, jumped down, and charged through the gate. Grabbing Mae Ann by her arms, he looked into her quivering soul, his eyes deep and alarmed and full of something she didn't recognize.

"Did he hurt you?"

The pain in his voice nearly broke her with its urgency. She shook her head. "No. He just frightened me."

Cade crushed her against him, his strong arms binding her tighter than any vow they'd spoken. She welcomed his embrace and looped her arms about his waist. His heart beat wildly against her chest, and she tucked her forehead into his neck.

Pounding hooves broke them apart, but Cade kept one arm around her shoulders as Deacon dismounted before his horse came to a full stop. "You all right? I just seen MacGrath slappin' leather outta here like the devil hisself was after him."

Cade drew her closer, and she had no desire to put distance between them in spite of Deacon's presence. "He'll have more trouble than that if he comes back here with his threats." The heat of his anger burned through his shirt and into Mae Ann's hand braced against his side.

Deacon let out a breath, pulled off his hat, and dragged his sleeve across his forehead. "Threats, you say?" The old cowboy's blue squint iced over.

"Reiker's farm." Cade tightened his hold, and the act warmed long-cold places in Mae Ann's heart. "Turn Cricket out for me and then meet us in the kitchen. We need to talk."

Reluctantly, Mae Ann stepped away from her husband. "I'll make coffee. And I have a fresh batch of cookies."

Cade gave her a look that said she'd not ride anywhere again on her own.

Mae Anne held her tongue and gathered her garden tools. MacGrath or no, she'd not kowtow to fear, but that was a conversation for another time. At the moment she relished the unfamiliar taste of being protected and held securely.

Maybe even wanted.

~

Mae Ann needed more than a good horse and a dog.

A few yards ahead of Cade, she marched into the house, no worse for wear or the tension he'd felt leave her body when he pulled her close. But he was worse. Much worse. He knew how well her soft warmth melded her against him as if she belonged in his arms.

He jerked his hat off and slapped his leg as if he could slap sense into his muddled brain. Yanking the back door open, he stopped short at the smell of coffee cutting through his fog, and hooked his hat on a peg.

144

Deacon came in the front, stashed the rifle on the rack, and pegged his hat. "Wish I'd gotten here sooner. It'd pleasure me some to pepper that thievin' scoundrel's hide."

Cade shoved both hands through his hair and cut his foreman a look. "It's worse than that."

Mae Ann had three tin cups on the table and a plate of cookies in the center. She stood by the stove, her apron wadded around the coffeepot handle.

Cade stopped in front of her expecting to find tears tracing her cheeks but found none. He touched her jaw, tight and determined beneath his fingers. Her head tipped slightly toward his hand, and it was all he could do not to kiss her right there in front of Deacon and God and whoever else barged in.

A chair scraped louder than usual, and Cade reluctantly stepped away and took his seat at the head of the table. Mae Ann sat in her usual place to his left, and Deacon helped himself to a couple of cookies before passing them on.

Cade sipped his coffee and bit into a gingersnap. Under different circumstances, the combination would have tasted a whole lot better. He waited for Mae Ann to finish dabbing her mouth and look at him. When she did, her dark eyes were clear and confident. As glad as he was to have her with him, he wanted her out of harm's way. If that meant sending her back to Missouri, then he'd do it, in spite of the hole it'd leave in his gut.

He'd not pried into her business over the will. Hadn't asked to see it or even discussed it with her since she read it on his wagon seat the day they buried Henry. He'd just taken her word that Reiker left her the land.

His blood heated at the thought of who had seen it. His guess was Ward, before he'd given it to her. How else could MacGrath make such a claim?

The envelope had been sealed, but that didn't mean the barber couldn't reseal it. The one with the money was too thick to seal. Maybe he'd helped himself to some of that as well.

Cade slid his hand toward Mae Ann, palm up, and folded his fingers around hers as she accepted his offer without hesitation. She met his look straight-on.

"Is what MacGrath said true?"

She blinked. But just once.

"About the wording of the will?"

She slowly pulled her hand away and left the table, returning in a moment with the stained envelope. Flattening it against the table, she gave it a little push toward Cade as she sat down. "You may read it."

It was important that he let her know he didn't want to horn in on her private affairs. But if he was to help her, he needed to know what he was up against. He picked up the envelope, pulled out the paper, and handed it to her. "You read the pertinent part to us."

She glanced at Deacon.

He scooted back. "I'll just step outside, ma'am. This is between the two of you."

"No." Her left hand rose above the table as if to stop him. "Stay, please. I've no secrets where Henry is concerned."

Which could mean she had secrets, just not about Henry. Suddenly, Cade wanted to know everything. Everything that had happened before they met in the bank that day. Everything that had driven her to answer a mail-order bride advertisement.

She unfolded the thin paper, the center discolored with Henry's blood and one side filled with dark, blurred writing. Her lips moved as she read to herself, and then she stopped. She pulled a tight breath through her nose, and her chest rose. "To my beloved wife, Mae Ann Remington Reiker, I leave all my worldly goods, including the farm and buildings and livestock, to do with as she wishes."

Her eyelids fluttered and she folded the letter and held it to the table as if it would fly away. When she looked up, tears shimmered. She loved Henry Reiker. Cade was a fool to think otherwise. His heart slammed to the floor.

"What did MacGrath say?" Deacon hid behind his coffee cup, his eyes flicking between the two of them.

Cade swallowed hard, shoving down all the things he wanted to say and forcing himself to focus on their neighbor to the north. "He said she's not the legal heir. Since she never married Reiker, she doesn't qualify as his widow and therefore shouldn't get the land."

Deacon drowned a curse in his coffee cup and shoved a whole cookie in his mouth.

"If she doesn't sell it to MacGrath, he'll contest the will."

Mae Ann returned the paper to the envelope and slid it into her skirt pocket. "Which means he has seen it or spoken with someone who has."

She looked at Cade. "Do you think Henry filed a copy somewhere? The bank maybe, or the courthouse?"

"The courthouse is twenty miles away in the county seat, but it's possible." Cade gripped his cup with both hands to keep from touching her. "I think Ward read it and got loose-tongued at the saloon."

Her brows dipped. "Ward?"

"The undertaker."

Her lips parted in a way that tugged at his gut, and he chugged the rest of his coffee. He'd be having words with Bartholomew Ward.

~

The next morning, those words pinned Ward to the barber chair where Cade found him feet up, asleep. "Early for a nap, wouldn't you say? Or you been here all night?"

Ward startled and his eyes flew open, wide and frightened behind his spectacles. He strained against Cade's hands that pinned both wrists to the arms of his brand-new leather-cushioned chair. "Wha-what brings you to town so early, Cade?" His Adam's apple bobbed from collar to chin.

Cade spun the chair to face the fancy wall glass. Then he leaned close enough to smell tonic on the barber's skin and met his panicked stare in the mirror. "You read Henry Reiker's will before you gave it to Mae Ann?"

Ward's head slowly bobbed down and up, his eyes never leaving Cade's reflection.

"Why?"

"Curious?" He squeaked like a trapped mouse.

Cade spun the chair again and stopped it with a vicious grip on the padded arms rather than Ward's skinny throat. "You been drinkin' lately? Flappin' your gums?"

Sweat broke out on the man's forehead. "Well . . . I . . . did step into the saloon night before last. Just a friendly drink or two. Pays to keep up relations with folks in town, you know. Business, and all."

"And how much did it pay you to tell Sean MacGrath what Henry Reiker's will said?"

Ward blanched as white as his apron. "N-n-nothing. I swear!" He raised his palms chest high. "I never took a cent from MacGrath."

Cade leaned in. "You'll never take another one from me either." He spun the chair again and marched out the front door without closing it. Even if his beard and mustache grew to rival Deacon's, he'd not darken the door of Bartholomew Ward's establishment again.

The boardwalk echoed beneath his boots, warring against the pounding in his head. He crossed the street and stopped outside the jail to let his blood cool, but Sheriff Wilson came out to greet him.

"Parker." He offered a hand. "What brings you to town? More rustler trouble?"

Cade shook his friend's hand and looked off down the street, hoping to keep the fire in his chest from flaring in his eyes. "In a manner of speaking."

Wilson stuck his thumbs in his belt, and Cade took note of the ever-present Colt strapped to his right hip. The holster was tied down. Not a common practice among ranchers and farmers. But Wilson had been in his share of shootouts and didn't balk at being prepared for the worst.

Cade told him what Deacon had found at the Reiker place. "But I'm in town to wire Judge Murphy. MacGrath is contesting Henry Reiker's will that leaves the farm to Mae Ann."

Wilson crossed his arms and spread his stance. "How does he know what the will says?"

Cade darted a glance at the barbershop. "Ward digs up more than dirt."

"And MacGrath's complaint?"

"She was never married to Reiker."

The sheriff nodded and looked up the street. "That could be a problem."

More than he knew. Cade fisted his hands, and Wilson caught the reflex. He didn't miss much. "If the judge rules in Mae Ann's favor, the land's hers. If he doesn't, and the farm goes to auction, I'll bid on it. But I can't be certain MacGrath or someone else won't outbid me."

"He's wanted that land for a long time. He'd be a fool not to with that water."

Cade glared. "You takin' his side?"

The sheriff remained calm and steady. "Maybe you don't need the headache. Let somebody else worry over the place. Can you talk her into selling it?"

Cade looked away, rubbed the back of his neck. "You ever tried to hold oil in your hand?"

Wilson huffed and shook his head. "Just be sure you know what you're up against."

"Afraid I do. MacGrath was out to the ranch yesterday, trying to intimidate Mae Ann."

The lawman's right hand dropped to his holster and he absently fingered the butt of his gun. "What can I do to help?"

Cade emptied his lungs, let his frustration drain away, and drew in a clean breath. "That yellow dog of yours got any pups?"

Wilson snorted. "When does she not?" He slapped Cade on the shoulder. "Come around back. There's two half-grown, and you're welcome to both if you want 'em. Pick 'em up on your way back from the telegraph office."

CHAPTER 14

M ae Ann served Deacon eggs and steak for breakfast and set a plate in the oven for Cade, about whose absence Deacon had nothing to say. He merely raised or lowered a bushy brow at her questions, feigning a mouthful of coffee or meat. His timing was impeccable in that matter, but he did not fail to offer his gratitude for the meal, as always.

She was happy to give him the peppermint stick from another Arbuckle's bag. Old enough to be the father she'd never had, the man was childlike when it came to grinding coffee beans for candy. Imagining him in a paternal role was a bit of fancy that couldn't hurt. She knew his crusty shell hid a kindhearted soul that thought the world of Cade.

And evidently, Henry had thought the world of her. Why hadn't the word *beloved* registered with her six weeks ago when she read Henry's will the first time?

The endearment had been written before they were even married—which they never were, as Sean MacGrath had charged so cruelly. As if it were a crime. The memory of his cold stare made her shudder. But he was right. She'd never been Mrs. Henry Reiker, in spite of Henry's kind words. What if a judge ruled against her and she lost the farm? Though she'd never felt it was really hers, she bristled against a stranger trying to claim it, particularly MacGrath, whom Henry had withstood for so long.

She pulled her apron off and folded it over a chair back. Why hadn't Cade told her he would not be at breakfast? His absence contradicted his feverish embrace after MacGrath's visit. She would never forget it, regardless of what happened next. Henry had called her his beloved before he met her. But Cade had rescued her and drawn her into his arms as if she really were.

With her kitchen chores out of the way and sweet beans baking for dinner, she went upstairs to gather the laundry. Frankly, she did not care to know what Cade had done for clean clothes before her arrival, but she appreciated the tubs and wringer set up on the back porch.

Sparrows chittered from the trees as she worked, lessening her chore with their merry song, and cottontails hopped and chased among the junipers in clear abandon.

She filled her apron pocket with clothespins from a kitchen drawer, and pinned the wash to a wire strung between two poles behind the house. As she spread the shoulders of Cade's chambray shirt, the sound of an approaching rider sent her heart to her throat. Quickly, she pinned the shirt and hurried to the corner of the house to see who approached. When Cade and Cricket came into view, relief left her nearly light-headed.

Relief, or the sight of such a kind and handsome man. She must get hold of herself. Swooning over one's husband while hanging his shirts to dry was simply not done. She smoothed her hair away from her face and returned to pinning the wash. If he wanted to see her, he would seek her out.

At a soft whimper, she turned to find him standing a few feet away with a squirming yellow bundle in his arms, all leg and tail and floppy ears. Her insides melted.

"Like him?" From his expression, Cade desperately wanted her to.

Mae Ann dropped to her knees and patted her lap. "Come here, little fellow. Come here."

He set the gangly thing on the ground and it galloped into her, knocking her over in its exuberance. She couldn't stop laughing as Cade rushed in to pull off the dog and help her to her feet. By the time she righted herself, he was laughing too and ruffling the dog's ears.

"Where did he come from?" She stooped again to hold the pup's head between her hands and look into his amber eyes while the rest of his body wagged. How dearly she missed her beloved Percy. But he'd been a morsel compared to this beast. "Look at the size of his feet. He'll be a giant."

Cade's features flushed with good humor, something Mae Ann hadn't seen much of lately. How handsome he was when he smiled. No worry creases. No frown.

"I got him from the sheriff."

Straightening, she brushed paw prints from her apron at his admission. "You were in town."

His smile dimmed, and he avoided her eyes. "Wired Judge Murphy about the will."

"I see." So much for a pleasant moment between them.

Blue bounded up to welcome the new playmate, and the two of them romped around the porch, yapping and scampering as only canine comrades could. She returned to the clothesline, arguing against her irritation that Cade was only trying to do the honorable thing.

She snapped out his sister's shirt, the one he'd given her for riding. "The dog is wonderful. Did you think Blue needed a companion?"

Cade thumbed his hat up and stood just inside her field of vision, his hands on his hips. "He's for you. I wanted *you* to have a companion."

A companion? Disappointment vied with gratitude. Did he think she did not enjoy *his* companionship? Then again, he was busy most of the day with chores, or gone for hours with Deacon, checking the herd. And theirs was a business arrangement, after all.

She chose gratitude. "How thoughtful of you."

The turn of his lips said she'd chosen well. "What will you call him?"

She pinned the shirt to the line, then tapped her chin with a finger, watching Blue nip at the big pup's heels. "I'll have to give it some thought. He's going to be as big as a bear, but bears aren't the color of dark honey."

Cade rolled his eyes. "You're not going to call him *Honey*, are you?"

Though dampened earlier at mention of Henry's will, good humor thrummed through her and, with little effort, spilled out. "Of course not, silly. He's much too masculine for a name like that."

"Good."

She slid him a glance. "I could follow your lead and call him a color."

"My lead?"

"Yes. You have Blue and Ginger. I could call the dog Goldenrod. Or Mustard. Buttercup . . . Peaches."

Cade's jaw dropped.

"That's it—he's such a lovely peach color."

"No!"

Fully committed to egging him on, she picked up the empty basket and propped it on her hip. "You wanted to know what I intend to call him."

He stared at her, speechless.

Empowered by triumph, she hurried inside before she burst out laughing.

~

Cade moaned and dragged a hand over his face. Blue and—God forbid—*Peaches* splashed through the mud where Mae Ann had dumped the wash water. Some guard dog.

Surely she wouldn't give it that sissy name, but who knew the mind of a woman?

He watched the dogs romp, grateful all over again that he'd arrived when he did yesterday. Twice now MacGrath had trailed Mae Ann, and it made Cade's blood boil. He might not be around the next time, and he reloaded an idea that had struck him at the sheriff's.

Mae Ann excelled at what she did, but she needed to know more than how to ride a horse. Washing and cooking and cleaning were fine for a city gal, but out here in the high parks, God-knew-what could show up without notice. Like MacGrath or some stray no-account.

She needed to know how to handle a gun. They carried easier than a shovel.

He stomped off his boots and walked through the back door into a mouthwatering aroma. Mae Ann reached into the oven with a length of toweling in her hands, then set a covered pot on the stove and closed the oven door with her foot. His ma used to do that.

Her dress sleeves were rolled up to her elbows, and loose curls fell around her face. She was the prettiest thing he'd ever seen.

"Hungry?"

He swallowed.

She brought him a cup of cold water and waited while he downed it. With the back of one hand, she pushed her hair off her forehead and braced the other on her hip, watching him as if he were an invalid. "You all right?"

No, he was not. "Right as rain." *In Noah's flood.*

He handed her the cup. "Thanks."

At the sink he splashed cold water on his face and neck and ran his fingers through his hair before drying his hands.

Deacon came in the front and around to the kitchen. "Smells mighty fine, ma'am. I swear I've put on weight since you come."

"You are too kind, Deacon."

He took his seat and cut Cade a look. "I see ya brung home another critter."

If Mae Ann called the dog *Peaches*, he'd never hear the end of it.

"Got a name for it?"

Mae Ann rolled her lips, but her cheeks puffed out with pent-up laughter. After she sat down, Cade said grace and reached for the serving spoon. He dished up her plate, hoping to catch her eye.

"I've given it some thought." She took a bite and set her spoon down without looking at him. "He's such an unusual color, and I think he'll grow to be huge by the size of his feet."

Cade grabbed a thick hunk of cornbread and buttered it, waiting. If she said *Peaches* while his mouth was full, he'd spew cornbread all over the table and his foreman.

He slid her a glance only to find her watching him. Doubt crawled up and perched on his shoulder. Was she foolin' with him?

"I think I'll call him Cougar."

He choked, but not for the reason he'd expected. *Cougar?* Where'd that come from?

Deacon shoveled in his beans as he always did, though he took care not to dribble in his beard. "You're givin' the dog a cat name?"

She flicked her dark eyes at Cade, and he knew for certain she was toying with him. Made his chest warm, and he shoved the buttery bread in his mouth.

"It was something Cade mentioned that day at the farm when you tried to catch the chickens." She took a dainty bite of beans and set her spoon down again.

Deacon took the bait. "I'll get 'em. I told ya I would."

She dabbed her mouth and gave him a warm smile. "I'm sure you will. As soon as we have a full moon."

Deacon squirmed.

Cade swigged his coffee, fully determined to take her with him when he drove his yearlings to the stockyards come fall. She'd run a hard bargain with the buyer, and be sure to get top dollar.

"Cougar's a fine name," he offered. "Suits him." After only one bowl of beans, he shoved himself back and took his dishes to the sink. "We'll ride earlier today. Meet me at the barn when you're ready." He left before she had a chance to reply.

On his way out he grabbed his .45 and a box of shells and stuck the colonel's old long-barreled Army issue in his belt.

~

Cade led them around Pine Hill to a spot where he and Betsy used to target-shoot when they were kids. He tethered the horses to a cedar twenty yards from an old, bleached cottonwood that had fallen the year he turned twelve. Riddled tins still littered the ground behind its white mass, rusted evidence that he and his sister had been pretty good shots.

He stepped off twenty yards in the opposite direction. Mae Ann knelt in the grass, talking to her dog and Blue. Confounded mongrels looked as if they understood every word she said. He turned away, before his anger at MacGrath and the rustlers—whoever they were—spilled over on her. It wasn't her fault Reiker died before he said *I do*.

But that wasn't all that ate Cade. A new worry gnawed, and he set the shells on a stump and loaded the Colt. Last night when she'd read the will, he'd seen it in her eyes. She still had feelings for Henry.

How was he supposed to compete with a dead man who'd won her heart?

"Are you going to shoot?"

He flinched at the nearness of her voice and fumbled a shell. She'd come through the grass like an Apache. Either that or he was losing his hearing along with his mind.

She stooped to retrieve the bullet and dropped it in his hand with so much trust in her expression it was sure to be his undoing. "Yes, and so are you."

She blinked. Twice.

"I know. You've never fired a gun." Her nervous *tell* hitched his heart. "I'll make a gunslinger out of you yet."

At her shock, laughter escaped from where he'd thought he had none. He narrowed his eyes. "Unless you're not up to it."

She stiffened like a barn board, exactly as he'd bargained.

Her hands cocked at her waist. "Show me what to do."

That's my girl. The words swirled through his head, soft and warm, and he coughed and cleared his throat, hoping to clear his wits.

"Stand right here and face the tree." He pointed to the ground in front of him. When she stepped into place, he reached around her with both arms, holding the Colt in his right hand and overlapping it with his left. "Both hands on the gun. Just like this."

She nodded and her hair brushed against his face.

"It's going to be loud."

"I know."

So she did. His chest squeezed at his oversight, but he pressed on. "Ready?"

She nodded again.

He cocked the hammer and fired. A peach tin kicked off the cottonwood, and Mae Ann flinched so hard she fell against him. He lowered the gun and laid his left hand on her shoulder. "You all right?"

Gathering herself, she pushed loose hair from her face. "Of course I'm all right. You weren't shooting at me." She looked at the dogs. "But I'm not so sure about Cougar."

Cade followed her gaze. The yellow dog was runnin' tale-tucked for the house. Blue watched him go. Cade chuckled.

"It's not funny, poor thing. I should have warned him."

"You can't warn him. Besides, he'll get used to it."

"I can too." The steel in her tone made him almost believe she could.

"Face the tree." He reached around her again. "One more. Then it's your turn."

"I don't need one more. Let me try it." She held up her hand.

Fitting the gun in her fingers, he covered her right hand with his. "Don't pull the trigger. Just get comfortable with the way the gun feels. Now wrap your left hand around your right."

He looked easily over her shoulder, grateful that gunpowder masked the smell of her hair. "See the sight at the end of the barrel? Line that up just below the next tin."

"Shouldn't I aim right at it?"

"No, because you'll probably shoot high."

She turned her head.

"Don't look at me. Look where the gun's pointing."

She let out an exasperated puff.

"Now cock the hammer with your right thumb. When you've got the sight lined up just below the tin, squeeze the trigger with your finger. Don't pull it or jerk it. Just squeeze nice and—"

The gun fired and she fell against him again but quickly recovered. "I did it!"

She looked up at him, head tilted back, her smiling lips inches away. He swallowed hard and reached around her to cover her hands with his. "Keep your eyes out here. On your target."

"Oh, all right."

"Try it again." He lowered his hands but stayed close against her.

She sighted, cocked the hammer, and fired. A tin sailed into the air.

"I hit it, I hit it!" She whirled around and hugged his neck before he could grip her wrists.

"Be careful where you point that thing. You don't want to shoot the horses."

With her laughter washing over him like a torrent, she handed him the gun, tipped up on her toes, and kissed his cheek. "Thank you."

The warmth of her lips shot him clean through the heart. Knocked off balance as sure as the old peach tin, he slid the gun in his holster and realigned his sights.

CHAPTER 15

Mae Ann stepped back, her cheeks aflame. She'd been so excited—only two shots and she'd hit the target! And ridden a horse. And been given a dog. Her heart was overflowing, and the flood had swamped her good sense as surely as the storm had swamped the garden.

But that one careless act had changed everything. The tension between them stretched like barbed wire. She hugged her middle. "I'm sorry. I don't know what came over me."

Cade quickly reclaimed the distance she'd made and cupped his rough hand against her face, sending the heat in her cheeks even higher. A passion in his eyes held her rooted to the ground, and his voice dropped to the deep tone she'd first heard at the bank. "Don't you?"

Surely he felt her pulse beneath his fingers. She drew air in through her nose, determined not to faint from the lack of it.

"Mae Ann—"

The last tin flew off the cottonwood and a shot cracked the stillness. Cade threw her to the ground and covered her with his body, his breath hot and sharp in her ear. He lay atop her as rigid and unyielding as the dead tree, every muscle in his body a rock. Slipping his hat off, he raised his head to scan the horizon.

His heartbeat hammered against her own and she pushed at his chest. "I can't breathe."

He covered her mouth with his left hand, but bent one knee to ease his weight from her. "Don't make a sound." His graveled voice held no desire as before, merely a warning that chilled her as thoroughly as a sudden hailstorm.

Did he think someone had deliberately shot at them? Who would do such a thing?

She craned her neck toward the horses. They'd pulled free but hadn't run off. Blue stood half the distance to them, his ears pointed toward a small rise, the same direction Cade looked.

"Blue." His harshly whispered command flattened the dog's ears, and it trotted to him and dropped to the grass.

Something like a growl rumbled in Cade's chest and he rolled off Mae Ann. She pulled in a precious breath but missed his warmth against her. Uncertain what to think or feel, she also rolled to her belly and looked toward the rise. Grass, juniper, rocks.

"Crawl over to that bush, but stay low. I'll cover you."

Afraid to push any higher than the grass, she dragged herself to the nearest bush. Cade scuttled right beside her, shielding her from the rise. He gave her the gun and crept back to the stump for the box of shells. When he returned, he pulled another gun from his belt, holstered it, and tied thin leather thongs from the holster's tip around his leg. Then he took the first gun and reloaded it.

His features remained hard and cold as he pressed the weapon into her hand. "Don't be afraid to use it. Follow your instincts. If MacGrath or someone you don't know shows up and threatens you, wait until they're closer than the cottonwood is, aim low, and squeeze the trigger. Don't forget to cock the hammer first."

"Where are you going?"

His fingers skimmed the hair at her temple as his eyes darkened. "If I'm not back in a half hour, get to Ginger or Cricket—either one—and ride to the house. Deacon may already be headed this way if he heard the rifle shot."

She gripped his fingers that lay against her head. "Don't go."

His eyes grazed her mouth before he touched her lips with his own. "Do as I say. Please."

Then he reached for his hat, rose to a crouch, and scuttled off to the nearest scrub oak.

Mae Ann held her breath until he reappeared, running hunched over to the next cluster—*heading toward the shooter!*

Blue trotted after him, dropping when Cade dropped in the long grass, staying close by his side. With shaking fingers, she skimmed her lips, tracing his kiss.

How long was a half hour? The sun hung hot in the afternoon sky, not yet to its journey toward evening, and she marked the shadow clinging to a nearby bush. Could she shoot a man in self-defense? What if Cade was hurt in the meantime, or worse?

Banishing the pointless questions, she propped herself up on her elbows and squinted at the hill for any movement there or in the wide expanse of grass and scattered juniper between. She felt completely and utterly alone, yet she knew she wasn't. Cade was out there somewhere with Blue.

A horse stamped a foot. Its tail swished as it grazed. No meadowlark sang. No quail alerted its fellows. All was still but the buzzing flies and her thumping heart.

She waited.

Perhaps five minutes.

Sweat trailed into her eyes. She'd left her hat on Ginger's saddle horn, and now it lay in the grass. A scuffle behind her jerked her head around to a yellow patch shifting in the blanket of green.

Mae Ann checked the rise one more time, then grabbed the box of shells and rolled to her left, closer to where the horses grazed.

"Cougar, come." Her urgent whisper raised the pup's ears, and his amber eyes seemed to smile at her call. He crawled toward her on his belly. Was he really that smart, or did he think this was a game?

She hugged his body to her, welcoming his wet kisses. "Shush now, Cougar. You must be brave. No crying." He licked his jowls and looked toward the rise as if he understood. If that were truly the case, she'd send him for Deacon.

Oh, Lord. Please protect Cade.

Another noise broke behind her, but this time she rolled to a sitting position and raised the pistol. Cougar's ears flattened and his soulful eyes looked away. He didn't like the gun. Neither did she, for that matter. But if it came down to herself or someone like the man who shot Henry . . . Well, she'd make that call when she had no other choice.

She thumbed the hammer back and bent her knees as a rest for her quivering arms.

A light whistle shot through the brush. Cougar's ears rose and he thumped his tail but didn't make a sound.

"Stay," she commanded.

Another whistle, closer.

What if the shooter had crawled around behind her as Cade made his way to the hill? But if Deacon had heard the rifle shot, he'd come in under cover rather than riding in, making himself a target. She had a fifty-fifty chance of shooting Cade's foreman and a man dear to her heart.

Then again, there could be two shooters, like the two bank robbers. The not knowing made her head hurt.

Cougar raised his ears toward a sharp hiss. Mae Ann quickly aimed toward the sound.

"Cougar!" The whisper came from the brush. Only two people knew what she'd named the dog, and Cade had headed for the rise. It had to be Deacon.

She pointed the gun skyward and took a chance. "Deacon?"

A hat poked out of the brush on one side and wiggled. It looked like the old cowboy's, sweat stain and all. Cougar thumped his tail again.

Mae Ann leveled the gun. One chance was enough. If this was a distraction, then she'd at least take down one of the shooters. Or frighten him. Or deafen him. She reached down deep in her chest for a heavier voice. "Show yourself."

The hat wiggled again and Deacon stuck his gray head out on the other side of the bush.

Mae Ann's breath jammed against her rib cage and she lowered the gun.

Deacon hurried to her, crouched as Cade had been. "That Cade boy picked hisself a winner in you, he did." His mustache spread the width of his face.

Boy? Mae Ann filed that tidbit away for later. If there *was* a later. And she had done the picking, thank you very much. Maybe Deacon didn't know. It didn't matter. She pointed north. "He thinks the shot came from that small rise."

Deacon narrowed his eyes and grumbled something unintelligible.

"What?" She crawled closer.

"MacGrath. I'd lay money on it."

Mae Ann swallowed hard. "You really think he'd try to shoot us?"

"Try to scare you is more like it. Fool varmint could have hit one of you or either of the horses."

"From the expression on Cade's face when he left, he was not the least bit frightened."

Deacon grumped. "If you're the prayin' sort, then you need to pray MacGrath or whoever it was skedaddles 'fore Cade gets there."

~

Enough dust hung in the air to prove that whoever had been there had just ridden off in a hurry.

Cade skirted a cedar patch and came up on the other side of a rock outcropping near the crest. A quick search of the ground netted the rifle casing, still warm. He clutched it in his fist and scanned the horizon north of Parker land. It had to be MacGrath.

Cade pocketed the cartridge and headed back to Mae Ann, his head so full of conflicting desires he could hardly think.

She'd kissed him.

And then he'd kissed her because by that point there was a chance it'd be his last opportunity.

He kicked into a trot, Blue at his heels. By the time he got to her, it'd be more than a half hour.

A hundred yards out from the cottonwood, he saw both horses still grazing. She hadn't done what he'd told her.

Confounded woman. How could he keep her safe if she didn't listen to him?

As he neared, he moved out into the open so she wouldn't shoot him. "Mae Ann."

She and Deacon came from behind the scrub oak. Cade's irritation lifted at the sight of his friend, then landed again. He couldn't take Mae Ann in his arms the way he wanted.

Nor could he keep her. Today's near miss changed everything.

He'd put her on the next train. After the dust settled over the will, maybe she'd come back to him, not as a last-chance grasp at security, but because she wanted to.

He wiped his face with his neckerchief and tossed the cartridge to his foreman.

"MacGrath?"

"Gone just before I got there, so I can't be sure."

"No-good outlaw." Deacon returned the shell. "Too bad he didn't carve his initials in the casing so we could nail his sorry hide."

The relief on Mae Ann's face made Cade's chest hurt. She held out the gun. He took it from her and eased the hammer down.

She blanched and raised both hands to her face with a gasp. "I didn't think to do that."

"I didn't tell you. Or show you." Deacon or no, Cade pulled Mae Ann to him and held her close. "Thank God you're all right."

She looped her arms around his waist and let loose a shuddering sigh.

Another time, another place, he promised himself.

He set her at arm's length, drinking in her tousled beauty and nerve. She was more woman than he'd bargained on. More woman than he deserved. "You can ride double with me. Deacon'll take Ginger back."

Deacon handed him Cricket's reins and gave Mae Ann her hat. Cade stowed the gun and shells in his saddlebag and mounted. He pulled his left foot from the stirrup and reached for her. "Wrap your hand around my wrist."

She set her foot and grabbed hold, and he easily lifted her up behind him. "Hold on."

Both her arms encircled him, and he turned Cricket and his heart away from the fallen cottonwood and toward the house.

Cougar fell in step with Blue and they scouted ahead—the yellow dog nose to the ground and Blue sniffing the air. Quite a team. Complete opposites. Like him and Mae Ann.

He covered her clasped hands with one of his, and her warmth against his back fired the longing inside him. He needed to get her to town as soon as possible. Before he lost his nerve.

~

Mae Ann anticipated a rough and hurried ride back to the house, but at Cricket's easy pace, she laid her head against Cade's broad shoulders. His rib cage expanded and contracted with a deep sigh that seemed to match her own surprising sense of well-being—in spite of their close call.

Contentment was a rare treat, but lately she'd tasted it more and more. Especially when she and Cade spent time together, as they had today until someone fired over their heads.

When he'd covered her hands with his, she closed her eyes in gratitude, but not just for their safety.

At the barn, she slid off Cricket and waited as Cade dismounted. Deacon took the horses, and Cade took her elbow and led her toward the bench. Her arms still held the warmth of his body, and it spread all the way to her toes as she seated herself and he joined her.

The same rough hand that so easily held a gun and reins gently turned hers over and stroked her palm, sending rivulets of longing through her arms.

"About our business agreement."

The rivulets swelled. She searched his rugged face for signs of affection, but inwardly froze at the pain she found there instead.

He pressed her hand between both of his, capturing her breath with his worried eyes. "I made a vow before God and man that I would protect you."

Dread nearly strangled her, and she fought for her voice. "But you did. We made it home, didn't we? And you taught me to shoot. What is that, if not protection?"

The muscle in his jaw flexed. He slowly shook his head and turned her hand palm down, closing his strong fingers around it. "I think you should go back to Missouri."

Hope shattered, falling in fine glass shards at her feet. Go back to what? The boardinghouse?

A quail beckoned its mate, and she slowly withdrew her hand. How poorly she had read his intentions.

He leaned on his knees and stared at his empty hands as if hunting something. "It's not that you haven't kept your end of the deal."

She gripped the bench and dug in her nails until they threatened to break. She would not shed tears in front of him. Not at his rejection.

What of the shooting lesson? The riding lessons? Cougar? She dare not ask these questions, for her voice would betray her. To open her mouth would open the way for all her dreams to gush out onto the ground. All the graciousness she'd been harboring. All the peace for which she had prayed.

She drew her feet together and tucked them beneath the bench.

He turned to face her, determination displacing pain. "Whoever shot at us today could have killed you. I won't let that happen. I'll put you up at the hotel in town until the first train east. After the will is settled, then . . ."

His voice trailed off, and she squeezed the board until splinters pushed beneath her nails. *Then* she'd be right back where she started. No home and no prospects.

Unbidden, Cougar angled toward her, uncertain, hesitant, but finally sitting beside her knee, where he laid his golden head. At least *someone* appreciated her.

"I see."

"Do you?" Frustration edged his voice, and it raised her hackles.

Cougar whined and she patted his soft head.

"Do you see that I am right?"

She stared at the dog, losing herself in his adoration and blinking back tears.

"Mae Ann, look at me."

She could not. If she did, she would lose every stitch of starch and self-respect. His words squeezed a welling into her throat that she refused to reveal in her eyes. And their

171

message contradicted what she'd believed was growing between them. Clearly, she couldn't trust him.

She pulled at her collar, in need of air. And to think, she'd believed he'd grown accustomed to her, possibly cared for her. He'd *kissed* her.

"Mae Ann."

What must he think of her, making herself so comfortable in the clothes he'd given her, in his mother's kitchen? In his home. His *bedroom.*

"It's not safe for you here. You saw that today." He tipped her chin with a rough finger and turned her face to him.

She stared at his shirt buttons. If she looked any higher, she would melt into his arms and beg him not to send her away.

She squeezed her eyes shut, refusing to beg.

He let out a heavy sigh. "Mae Ann, it's for the best. For your safety."

Anger shot her to her feet, and Cougar darted away with a yelp. "For your convenience, you mean. What I *see* is that I am more trouble than you bargained for." She raised her chin. "I shall be ready first thing tomorrow morning."

She spun to walk away, but his hard hand caught her arm. "Let me finish—"

She pulled free and spoke over her shoulder, avoiding his stormy eyes that had power to weaken her knees. "You've more than finished."

CHAPTER 16

O nce the ranch house door closed behind her, Mae Ann fell against it, a dart piercing her soul with each ragged breath. The cold hearth and chairs mocked her, proving she was no better off than when she had arrived, empty of all but hope. Now bereft of even that small grace, she must leave. Had God not heard her prayers, or had she misread circumstances as His leading?

And give you peace . . .

A small huff escaped her lips and she pressed a hand against her aching chest where the once-comforting words now sliced her to the quick. She swiped at her stinging eyes and marched to the kitchen. At least she had a meal to prepare. Idleness was bread she could not afford to ingest.

Nor would she be ingesting cornbread, for the men had eaten every last crumb for dinner. She was weary of beans, but with Cade insisting they leave so early today, she'd had no time to fix anything else. Even a vinegar pie would take too long now. They'd have to be content with syrup on fresh biscuits if they wanted something sweet.

In no time, she had the meal ready, but when the front door opened, she jumped like a frightened child. Self-reproach tightened her grip on the coffeepot, and she filled the three cups that waited on the table.

Deacon clomped into the kitchen and stopped. "Thought Cade would already be here."

Mae Ann shrugged, feeling all of twelve. "I wouldn't know."

The old cowboy looked at her sideways as he passed to the sink, and she was certain he knew what had happened. How could he not, with her stomping away from Cade like an ingrate? Deacon, she was certain, missed very little, though he might not know the extent of the marriage arrangement.

At the table she sat with her hands in her lap while he sipped his coffee in obvious pleasure. She'd done one thing right, one of many, she'd thought, after Cade's praise of her riding and resurrection of the garden. She linked her fingers and squeezed until the joints ached more than her heart.

"Should we wait for his sorry hide or go ahead?" Deacon's eyes twinkled in his leathery face, forcing a grudging murmur from her.

"Go ahead. We don't know how long he'll be, and I can heat a plate for him when he comes." *Or let him eat his supper cold and alone, which would serve him right.*

Deacon picked up his fork. "Thank you, Lord." Apparently satisfied that his brief thanks sufficed as a blessing, he dug in.

Mae Ann supposed it did, considering the mood.

Darkness inched from the corners of the kitchen, and she rose to light the lamps, uneasiness pushing words onto her lips. "Maybe you should check on him. He's never been this late." At least not since she'd been at the ranch. Perhaps he had fallen into his former ways before her arrival. Or he was avoiding her.

Deacon grumped and shoved the remainder of his biscuit in his mouth, then *thud-clinked* his way out the front door. The familiar sound that she'd first noticed in her groom threatened to spur her wound anew.

She pulled the beans to the front of the stove, wiped the counter, and washed her cup and clean plate for something to do. Food held no appeal, whether Cade showed up for dinner or not. Her mind was a mess of knots and loose ends with no hope of sorting it all out.

The door crashed open and heavy steps pounded into the front room. She hurried around the wall to find Deacon ashen-faced above his bushy mustache, his arms holding a limp, unconscious man. Cade.

~

Mae Ann ran to him and pressed her hands against his temple, his chest, searching for the strong beat of his heart. His arm hung at an odd angle, tightening her voice to an unfamiliar pitch. "What happened?"

"I found him in the barn, out cold. My guess is he fell off the rungs that climb the back wall to the hayloft. A couple of them were busted through."

"He may have broken his arm. Let's get him upstairs."

Pausing at her bedroom door, she pushed it farther open and stood aside as Deacon laid Cade on the wide feather tick. She lit the lamp on the dresser and another that she moved to the small bedside table.

"He's got a gash on the back of head." Deacon's voice was thicker than she'd ever heard it. "And you may be right about that arm. But I don't know if anything's busted up inside." He stepped back. "I'll go for Doc Weaver."

Alarm lit the old cowboy's eyes, and Mae Ann resisted the temptation to allow it into her own soul. "Do you think he'll come now, at night? It's so late."

Deacon's voice dropped to a low rasp as he turned through the door. "He'll come."

She followed him down the stairs to fetch rags and warm water from the kitchen. Returning to the bedroom, she dragged the washstand from the corner to the footboard and filled the bowl with warm water. Then she pulled off Cade's boots, set them by the armoire, and concentrated on cleaning him up as best she could.

No frown or sign of pain marred his handsome face as she held the warm cloth against his brow. Gently, she cleaned the scrapes and cuts, but her touch brought no reaction. He lay as if dead, and fear knifed beneath her ribs. She dunked the cloth again and refolded it into a clean square to wipe bits of hay and dirt from his jawline. A strong jaw. Something she'd noticed in the bank that day, along with his dark, penetrating eyes that she longed to look into again.

Pressing the cloth against his cheek, she recalled the kiss she had placed there earlier. Those brief moments of excitement and pleasure seemed now like the clouded past, a distant time shared between two different people. She smoothed his hair and gently slipped her hand beneath his head, where a sticky warmth met her tentative touch. Dark red stained her fingers as she drew them into the light. She dipped a fresh cloth and squeezed it out, then carefully slipped it like a hammock between his head and the feather pillow.

His broad chest rose and fell with nearly imperceptible change, but he breathed, and she leaned close to feel the assurance on her cheek. She washed his hands, stroking his calloused palms and knuckles. His sleeve was ripped, and she checked the rest of his clothing for seeping bloodstains but found none.

No fever touched his brow, but oh, he was deathly still. How angry she'd been with him a mere hour before. How he had broken her heart! She lowered herself to sit on the edge of the bed, and it tipped him so that she quickly stood. Retrieving the chair from his room across the hall, she pushed it against the tick and lifted his left hand to her lap.

His strong fingers lay uncharacteristically idle but cool against her own, hardened by the demands of ranch life yet with such capacity for gentleness that it broke her heart anew.

"Lord." Her whisper seemed a shout in the quiet. "Please touch Cade and bring him back to us. To me."

Grief weighed upon her, and she rose against it to trim the lamps and check outside. The barnyard remained darkened and empty of life. Even the dogs had taken refuge in some hidden spot. Deacon would be gone for hours, but still she squinted into the shadows, hoping to see him ride into the yard ahead of the doctor. Resigned to waiting, she settled in the chair and again leaned close over Cade, allowing his slight puff to caress her cheek. She gathered his hand once more and closed her eyes.

"I'll go," she whispered over his still form. "If that's really what he wants, Lord, I'll leave in peace if You'll just spare him."

~

"Doc Weaver's here." Deacon's hushed voice drew her from fitful dreams and a slumped position, the muscles in her back punishing as she dragged the chair away.

The doctor set down his bag. "Mrs. Parker."

Not really. She tucked her ringless hand behind her. "Thank you for coming at such a late hour."

He removed his coat and pulled the cloth from beneath Cade's head. It was soaked with blood. "I'll need to stitch that up, but you did right to let him lie still."

Another lesson from the rooming house when a tenant had been beaten and robbed on his way from work. Mae Ann, still a child, and her mother cared for the man who lay unconscious for days. *Please, not Cade.*

Clutching her apron, she moved to the footboard.

"First we need to get his shirt and trousers off so I can check him thoroughly."

We? She swallowed.

At her pleading look, Deacon backed away. "I'll leave you to it." The door clicked shut behind him.

She stared at the solid, dark wood. He didn't know.

"Mrs. Parker?"

She hiccupped.

"Mrs. Parker, are you all right?" The doctor studied her face as if reading her from the inside out.

"Yes," she lied. "Quite."

He waited a moment—for her confession, she supposed—but she gathered herself and stepped to the opposite side of the bed. Cade was her husband, legally and in the sight of God. She could not afford to be prudish. Nor could she afford to let the whole town know they were not— well—If Doc Weaver figured it out, he might let the truth slip. *Oh, Lord, send grace.*

She forced her thoughts to the battered man she'd helped her mother care for, but doing so did little to diminish her reaction at the sight of her husband's masculine form. Without his shirt, his pale, muscled chest contrasted sharply with his face and hands, bronzed by years in the Colorado sun. His right shoulder, however, was near black.

Focusing on the doctor's methodical inspection, she pinned her eyes to his balding head, but they wandered to caress Cade's corded arms, his broad shoulders where she had laid her head.

"It's dislocated," the doctor said, pressing into the bruise and making Mae Ann cringe. "I'll need your help to set it. Trade sides with me."

He motioned her toward the headboard. "Wrap your arms around him, high up under his arms, and throw your weight into pulling him toward you."

Urgency helped her disregard the intimacy of embracing Cade so, and she forced her right arm beneath his back and laid the other across his chest, locking her hands. "Ready."

"All right, pull."

As she tugged, the doctor wrenched Cade's arm and the joint snapped into place with an audible pop. Mae Ann released her hold and studied her husband's expressionless features. He'd felt nothing.

Dr. Weaver continued with deft fingers, poking Cade's flat stomach. Mae Ann's clenched, anticipating pain, but Cade made no response, which worried her even more.

"He appears to be in good condition, considering." The doctor rolled up his sleeves. "If you'll get me some hot water, we'll turn him over and have a look at the gash on his head."

Moments later she returned with the kettle and stacked clean rags on the washstand. She emptied the basin's bloody tepid water into the pitcher and replaced it with hot.

"All right, Mrs. Parker, take your position across from me and catch him as I roll him toward you." The doctor bunched the edge of the coverlet into his hands, scrunching it until he reached Cade's arm. "Now."

He turned Cade as easily as she turned bread dough out of a bowl and rolled him facedown on the bed.

"Push out a hollow beneath his nose and mouth so he doesn't smother while I sew him up."

The doctor cut away Cade's dark, matted hair, revealing a jagged gash that angled across the back of his skull. With a tailor's skill he closed the wound, and as they turned Cade to his back, they pulled free the quilt and sheet and covered him. Relieved that the deed was done but also that she'd no longer be tempted by what was not hers, she let out a tight breath, drawing the doctor's scrutiny once again.

"It's difficult to see our loved ones in pain. Speaking of which . . ." He dug through his bag and pulled out a small corked bottle of laudanum. "He's not suffering at the moment, but I imagine when he comes to, he'll appreciate a spoonful of this."

Dr. Weaver pressed the small bottle into her hand and held on to catch her eye. "While you're taking care of him, don't forget to take care of yourself." He patted her hand. "Rest is the best medicine for both of you."

"How long before he wakes?"

As methodically as he had stitched Cade's gash, the doctor unrolled his sleeves, drew on his coat, and gathered his bag before answering. "Only the Lord knows the answer to that question. But with his wife's prayers and attention to his needs, I'm sure he'll soon be fine. I'll return in three days to check on him."

His wife. She felt like an imposter.

Dr. Weaver opened the door and looked over his shoulder. "If he rouses before then, don't let him get up. We wouldn't want him tumbling down the stairs, now, would we?" His chuckle cushioned the warning, but the seriousness of the situation was not lost upon her. Evidently, the good doctor knew Cade's determined nature.

"Thank you again for coming." Forgotten manners pushed her forward. "We have an extra room if you'd care to stay until morning." She knotted her apron in her hands. "And your fee. I—"

Raising a palm in refusal, he looked beyond her and she followed his gaze to the window that was brightening by degree. "I'd say morning's just about here, Mrs. Parker, but thank you just the same." He gave her a slight smile, compassion warming his eyes. "Next time you're in town, stop by my office and we'll take care of the bill."

He left the door ajar, and silence settled in the room. Mae Ann returned to Cade's side to check his breathing, as light as goose down against her skin, but reassuring just the same. Dare she take a moment's rest before starting her day? She knelt on the braided rug beside the bed and lightly cupped his dear face with one hand. How drastically one incident had changed everything—every emotion, every need.

The irony swirled through her. Death lurked at all times, even in unexpected places, but by God's grace it had failed to steal Cade. Her conditional promise churned in her breast, and she would keep it once he recovered—if he still insisted on her departure. Until then, she'd not leave him

181

unattended. Weariness escaped on a sigh, and she laid her head on the tick, pressing her arm against the warmth of him seeping through the coverlet. She moved closer, drawing comfort even as she sought to give it.

It might be as close as she'd ever come to loving him.

~

"Ma'am?"

A strong hand squeezed her shoulder, and she sat up, keenly aware that she'd fallen asleep ill-positioned. Two booted feet appeared on the rug, and she looked up at Deacon's worried face.

"I come to spell you." He helped her to her feet and kept a hand on her elbow until she stood steady.

Pain shot through her legs and feet as the blood flowed freely again, and she shifted her weight from one foot to the other. "The doctor said to make sure he doesn't get up." She rubbed her face and studied their patient. "He hasn't stirred or even moaned. Nothing."

Deacon doffed his hat and folded his long self into the chair. "I'll let you know if he does. But I'm sure there's plenty o' time for you to catch a few winks yourself."

How tempting his suggestion, but he was no doubt hungry. "Hot coffee seems a better idea."

His mustache twitched and he cast a look at Cade. "Jerked beef and a cold biscuit'll do me fine. The chores are done, so I'll just set here and keep this boy from leapin' out o' bed and down the stairs."

Against all propriety, Mae Ann leaned over and kissed the top of Deacon's snowy head. "Thank you. You are a kind man."

He grumped and blustered as she left the room, and it did her good to hear the old cowboy short on words. She would miss him and his seasoned speech, so unlike Cade's slightly more refined manner. But now was not the time to go all maudlin. She had work to do.

A bucket of milk sat on the counter—bless Deacon's softhearted soul—and she strained it and poured it into clean jars. Then she set the coffee on, rolled out a pan of biscuits, and sliced salt pork into the cold skillet.

She hurried outside to pick eggs but stopped short at the yellow ribbons lacing the eastern horizon, marveling at the beauty unseen by so many. No view of dawn's waking had met her in the rooming house, and she'd felt blessed beyond belief to see it spread before her every morning at the ranch.

Quail scrabbled outside the chicken pen, and sparrows and finches fussed in the slender trees—a symphony, were she to describe it to anyone.

Cougar bounded up with his youthful glee, and Blue trotted along more sedately, as if demonstrating good manners for the youngster. "You boys—such good dogs you are." She stooped between them and gave each a hearty hug, then entered the chicken pen. The setting hen pecked her way into the yard, imitated by four hovering hatchlings, and Mae Ann's spirit lifted at the promise of a future generation.

Bunching her apron, she filled it with warm eggs from the nesting boxes, sadly recalling Henry's hens. She couldn't very well ask Deacon for such a trivial favor when Cade's recovery and all the regular chores would take their every waking moment. She'd ride to the farm herself and check on things once Cade was up and about.

A bitter taste set her teeth on edge. The farm seemed more trouble than it was worth. If she sold it to MacGrath, then he wouldn't be a threat and Cade wouldn't send her away—at least not for that reason. Doubt wagged a worrisome finger. Maybe he just wanted out of their arrangement, and the farm was as good an excuse as any.

Then why his fierce protectiveness, his kiss?

CHAPTER 17

Mae Ann turned the bacon strips and cracked three eggs into the hot grease, praying Cade would rouse at the smell of breakfast frying. She started a bone broth on the back of the stove, admitting that as much as she wanted to draw him to consciousness with the aroma of solid food, he would need nourishment when he woke, and broth was the better choice.

When the biscuits were done, she made a plate for Deacon, filled two tin mugs with hot coffee, and carried them upstairs on a tray.

The old cowboy sat with his legs stretched out, arms folded, and head down, mustache fluttering with each snore. She nearly laughed, but instead backed from the doorway and loudly cleared her throat, entering as he shuffled and sputtered.

"That smells mighty good, ma'am." His standard comment at every meal.

She set the tray on the bureau and handed Deacon his plate and cup.

"Ain't you eatin'?"

"Coffee is what I need right now."

He narrowed his eyes at her, about to give her a cowboy comeuppance, but she cut him off. "I'd really prefer you called me Mae Ann. Every time you say 'ma'am,' I feel like you're talking to my mother."

He chortled and lifted the coffee to his mouth for a quick sip. "Just seems proper, you bein' the missus and all."

Proper? If he only knew how improper the whole situation was. She walked around to the other side of the bed, grateful that he *didn't* know. "Thank you for milking the cow."

He nodded, his mouth full of biscuit and bacon.

"If we plan a schedule for chores, one of us can always be with him." She risked sitting on the edge of the tick and succeeded in not tipping Cade to the floor. "I'll not leave him unattended."

Deacon snorted and washed his mouthful down with more coffee. "Ain't it a fact? He'd roll hisself down them stairs if he thought he could get away with it."

She shuddered. "My thoughts exactly."

Deacon sopped his egg yolk with a biscuit and finished off his coffee. "Let me take the first day watch since the herd's faring well and most of the calves have dropped. You take the second. We'll switch off until night, when I'm sure Cade'd rather have his wife with him than the likes of me."

Heat prickled from her chest into her neck, and she prayed Deacon wouldn't notice her unbecoming blush. "That's a wonderful idea. I'll put on a stew so we can serve ourselves between watches, as you call them."

As soon as Deacon finished, she stood to gather his dishes, a bit light-headed. She hadn't eaten since yesterday's dinner, and the image of herself tumbling down the stairs convinced her that at least a biscuit was in order.

Deacon leaned over Cade and held a finger beneath his nose, frowning. "You got a hand glass?"

"I did, but . . ." It had gone the way of her money and reticule. Another thing she'd not get into now, but she knew why Deacon asked. Looking about the room, she settled on the chest of drawers. "I'll see if I can find one."

Like an interloper, she opened the top drawer and removed a beautifully carved wooden box. She lifted the lid to find a cluttered collection of things a woman would value, topped by a lovely gold ring, Cade's mother's wedding band, no doubt. She slid it onto a finger and pushed other items aside in her search for a small mirror. Finding none, she returned the ring, set the lid, and placed the box in the drawer.

The second drawer contained a woman's undergarments, an old sachet—its fragrance long spent—and at the back, a matching porcelain-backed brush and mirror set with hand-painted violets in lavender hues. Her fingers brushed across the lovely artwork, so delicate and intricately detailed. Cade's mother must have been a fine lady to have had such accessories. Or dearly loved by her husband. Perhaps he'd given it to her as a wedding gift.

Whisking away the idle fantasy, she returned the brush and gave Deacon the mirror, which he held beneath Cade's nose until the glass fogged. Deacon huffed out his satisfaction and laid the mirror on the side table. Mae Ann preferred her method of checking Cade's breathing.

By late afternoon, there had been no change. No fever, thank the Lord, but no response either. The aroma of a savory stew meandered up the stairs and into the room, teasing Mae Ann's empty stomach. The morning's hastily eaten biscuit was a mere memory. She dashed to the kitchen for a bowl and on her way back grabbed the padded footstool from her chair by the hearth—a much more comfortable way to spend the night against the tick rather than growing stiff on the floor or in that unforgiving chair.

When daylight followed the sun over the western range, she trimmed the nearest lamp, wrapped herself in a quilt from the bed across the hall, and settled onto the footstool. Cade's scent lingered on the quilt, and she pressed it against her face to catch her welling grief. If only he wanted her to stay. Readjusting herself, she laid her arm alongside his to cushion her head. If he stirred, she would feel his movement and waken.

And if he woke out of his mind and frantic like the man from the rooming house, she was prepared to physically restrain him.

As if she could.

~

Cade's head pounded. The whole herd stampeded through it, and his right shoulder throbbed. Frowning, he opened his eyes and grimaced against the pain. His left arm lay pinned against something soft and unfamiliar, and he pulled it free to rub the back of his head. The stampede rounded anew, striking hard where his fingers pressed. Where was he?

A pale rectangle hung to his right like the window in his bedroom, but he didn't go in there anymore because . . . he wasn't sure.

He blinked several times, trying to focus. The warm weight he'd felt earlier meant he wasn't lying next to a fallen tree for protection from the cattle. The ground beneath him was also soft. He felt for his neckerchief to cover his mouth and nose and found it gone—as well as his shirt.

The shock drove him upright, and swirling pain shoved him back down.

"Cade," a woman's urgent tone whispered at his ear. "Cade, can you hear me?"

The herd split in two, circled around his head on both sides, and joined up again in the middle. He pressed a hand against his forehead, but it did no good. He couldn't catch the leader to turn them.

An arm slipped under his neck, and a cold spoon touched his lips, tipping liquid between them. He coughed, spooked the cattle, and sent them crashing back the way they had come. Another spoon against his lips and he knocked it away, hearing it clatter. Where was he that the ground was first soft, then hard?

The woman's gentle tone resumed. "This will help the pain, Cade. Please take it. The doctor left it."

Again the arm, the spoon, the liquor-like substance. *Doctor?* Too weak to resist, he swallowed the gall and slumped against the pillow. That was it. A pillow. He cut a glance at the gray light and found it brighter. It *was* a window. His window.

Fingers combed through his hair, and he caught the wrist in a fierce grip. Welling dark eyes looked down at him above a quivering smile, and loose hair fell against a familiar cheek. He loosened his hold. "Mae Ann?"

Her full smile pushed a tear over her lashes and she swiped at it. "Yes," she whispered. "Yes!"

She leaned in and kissed his temple, and the sweetness of her lips against his skin cooled the throbbing. He caught her against him with his good arm and held her close until the sound of spurs on hardwood pulled her from him.

"Well, that's just about the pertiest sight I ever did see." Deacon clomped to the bed, sending maverick steers running through Cade's skull with every stomp of his boots.

Mae Ann blushed and backed away. He'd rather look at her than Deacon's bushy mug.

The man hooked his thumbs in his belt and gave Cade a smooth once-over as if figuring his price for market. "Fair to middlin', I'd say. How do you feel with that knot on your noggin?"

"Don't make me laugh, old man. It hurts."

"Guess that tells me what I need to know." He reached for a small bottle next to the bed and held it at arm's length to read the label. "You had any of this yet?"

"Two spoons," Mae Ann said. "Most of two spoons."

Deacon cocked a bristly brow. "Most?"

A smile stole across her lovely face. "He wasn't exactly cooperative about his medicine."

Deacon snorted. "I can ear him down for you if you want."

She laughed outright and the music washed through Cade's soul like a summer stream, clear and fresh, but he met his foreman's threat with a dare of his own. "I'd like to see you try it."

Mae Ann stepped between them, her skirt brushing the tick. "Another time. No roughhousing until Dr. Weaver says it's safe, which means bed-rest all today and tomorrow until he returns."

"How long have I been here?" The cattle slowed and milled in a circle, and Cade's eyelids grew heavy. "What happened?"

"You recollect climbin' to the loft?"

Cade pulled at his memories, but they churned with the herd, spinning just out of his reach. He closed his eyes and rubbed his forehead. "The loft? Yeah, I think so. Went up there to think. I think."

Deacon huffed. "That'll teach ya to overtax your brain box."

Spurs sang out the door and down the stairs, and all Cade wanted was to cradle Mae Ann against his chest again and sleep.

~

Thank you, Lord—thank you. Mae Ann's silent offering winged from her heart on two levels—that Cade lived, and that the laudanum sent him back to sleep. At least she wouldn't have to worry about him trying to get out of bed for a few short hours.

Deacon returned after milking the cow, smelling of animal hide and the manure that edged his boots. She'd not chide him, so grateful she was for his help and Cade's waking. Instead, she fried him a steak and took it upstairs with a cup of broth in case Cade woke on his watch.

She hadn't washed or changed clothes in two days, so while Deacon was busy with breakfast, she gathered what she needed and carried warm water to Cade's room. It would now be her room, as it should have been from the beginning. A long soak in the tub downstairs was what she craved, but such luxury could wait. Revived by her morning ablutions and fresh clothing, she braided her hair and hurried downstairs to do as much as possible in what little time she had.

Strong coffee braced her as she paused at the window, and it set her racing mind into a more reasonable pattern of thought. Cade's accident gave her a brief reprieve from his intent to ship her off. It also got him off his feet and out of the thick of things, and she intended to make the most of it. His arm would no doubt be in a sling for some time, and he could use her help more than ever.

After adding to the stew pot, she headed for the hen house. Cricket and Ginger were in the near corral, and the sight of them stopped her in her tracks. *The rose clipping.* She'd forgotten all about it, and it had been how long since Travine Price slid the shoot into a raw potato and wrapped it in a wet napkin?

She ran to the tack room, uncertain which saddlebag she'd carried that day, so she went through each one until she found the bundle. The napkin had dried, but the little stem remained firm and green—not wilted or dry—just as Travine promised. Mae Ann held it against her heart, awash with more thanksgiving. This was the perfect opportunity to plant it.

And she'd not tell Cade. If it rooted and thrived, as she prayed it would, he'd find it someday and perhaps count it a blessing. Perhaps guess that she had planted it and think well of her.

She left the egg basket in the kitchen and hurried out the back door with a small pail of water and a trowel. As if sensing her intentions, Cougar ran ahead of her across the open field toward the small rise. She marveled at her strength of limb and lung, for she would not have been able to hike so hurriedly when she first arrived. Colorado had been good for her, with its clean air and food for the soul. She had flourished, and she believed the rose would do so as well.

Billowy clouds hung against the sky like freshly washed petticoats, adding to a sense of new beginnings. A small picket framed the matching plots, and she easily stepped over onto revered ground and knelt between the crosses. The bottom of the tree had been limbed, and morning sun slanted in, warming the earth.

She loosened the soil, planted the cutting—potato and all as Travine had directed—and patted the dirt around it. A small thorn snagged her finger, and she jerked her hand away as a red bead formed at the first knuckle. She sucked it between her teeth and with her other hand, pushed the soil into a shallow bowl. She pressed her fingers in as if investing herself in a family she'd almost become a part of. Then she emptied the pail around the cutting and watched the dirt drink it in.

Sitting back on her heels, she drew a deep breath. A breeze soughed through the big pine, and she looked up into its spreading arms, a protective canopy from the ravages of summer's heat and winter's blasts. No wonder Cade had picked this spot.

I made a vow before God and man that I would protect you.

The words snagged her heart and drew blood as quickly as the thorn had from her finger.

It was in Cade's very nature to be protective, and everything he had done on her behalf stood as proof. From giving her his sister's hat and gloves and boots, to teaching her to ride and begrudging her solitary visit to the Price farm. Why couldn't he see that he had indeed kept his vow?

She stood and brushed off her skirt, taking in the ranch buildings below and the vast grasslands that spread in every direction like the sea around an island. A cloud passed before the sun, casting the hill in shadow, and a cool wind licked the back of her neck. With a sudden sense of premonition, she looked north toward poor Henry's even poorer farm, and movement drew her eye to a distant rise. She squinted, trying to make out the object, whether man or beast or both. The fine hairs on her neck rose as she watched the silhouette drop from view behind the crest of the knoll.

Cougar whined and she turned to find him ears alert, eyes asking. She gathered the pail and trowel and stepped over the picket to pat his head. "Let's go, boy. It's time we got back to the house."

She'd tend the rose until the day Cade sent her away, but she'd not tell him she planted it. Nor would she tell him that someone watched them like a hawk observing its unwitting prey.

~

Mae Ann held the cup of warm broth against Cade's resistive lips. He'd slept until noon, then woken disgruntled and in pain and insistent that she sit with him and not Deacon. Had he forgotten he wanted her gone?

She convinced him that broth would speed his recovery and managed to lace it with laudanum, tsking against his complaint that her broth was the most bitter he had ever tasted. As he settled against the pillows she'd gathered from every bedroom and bunched behind him, his brow soon relaxed and he drifted again to that place of healing sleep.

Quickly, she set the cup aside and emptied the armoire of her clothing, took it to the room across the hall, and exchanged it for everything she could find there of Cade's. She filled the armoire shelves, for the chest of drawers contained his parents' things, it appeared, most of it his mother's. Then she lifted one end of her trunk, toed a small braided rug beneath it, and used it like a sled to drag her trunk across the hall. The task was easier than she'd anticipated, but again, she was stronger than before.

After re-placing the rug, she returned to the footstool, content to remain there until Deacon would come to "spell her" at suppertime. Not one moment did she begrudge at Cade's side, and she spent most of the time memorizing his features as she had done with Henry's letters.

If only she could capture him in a sketch as some of the women in the rooming house did, drawing images of their loved ones or flowers from happier days. She would draw his strong chin, broad shoulders, and capable hands. The way his hair insistently fell across his brow when he was without a hat. His handsome face and straight mouth—lips that had grazed hers near the fallen cottonwood and set hope fluttering anew for a marriage of love.

But it was not to be, and nothing would be gained by pining over what she could not have. Thankfully, she was not staring at him when Deacon filled the doorway. He had removed his boots and spurs and she'd not heard him climb the stairs, so lost she'd been in her own thoughts. So much for belling the cat.

"How's our boy today?"

Did the man know how such inclusive endearments tormented her? "He grumped at the broth and said it was the most bitter he'd ever tasted." She picked up the corked bottle and held it aloft with one hand, a single finger to her lips with the other.

Deacon's eyes twinkled and his shoulders bounced with silent laughter as he grabbed the chair and rested his feet upon the cushioned stool Mae Ann had vacated.

"I'll bring supper shortly, and a mug of broth in case he wakes as a bear once more." With a final look around the room, satisfied she'd removed all that was hers, she went downstairs.

While a pan of cornbread baked, she sat at the table with pencil and paper, making a list for Deacon to take to the mercantile tomorrow. The doctor would be out to check on Cade, so she'd not be left alone while Deacon was in town—a small comfort against the sense of having been watched. She could not be absolutely certain it was their dark-hearted neighbor to the north, but who else would it be? Her crawling flesh said it was MacGrath on his black horse, biding his time.

That night as she settled on the footstool and stretched her arm along Cade's side, he lifted his left hand and laid it over her arm. His eyes remained closed and no sound came from his lips. No telling twitch that so often betrayed his hidden humor, yet she wondered if his hold was an involuntary gesture welcoming her nearness. Weary in heart and body, she rested her head upon the tick, relishing the warmth of his hand and not caring that her grief and gratitude blended and bled onto the coverlet, soaking it with her tears.

CHAPTER 18

D eacon left in the buckboard right after breakfast. From Mae Ann's position at the bedroom window, he looked ill-suited to a wagon seat and envious of the good doctor, who passed him on horseback in the yard. Dr. Weaver tied his mount to the rail, seeming better fit to a carriage. Two men out of their element if ever there were.

Unwilling to leave Cade long enough to greet the doctor at the door, she watched as he untethered his bag from the saddle, certain he would come right in. He disappeared beneath the porch roof, and soon the heavy door hinges creaked his entry.

She stepped out to the landing that overlooked the great room. "Thank you for coming so early, Dr. Weaver. You do keep the most difficult hours, riding out to ranches in the middle of the night or near after sunrise."

"All part of the job, Mrs. Parker." He smiled as he reached the landing, but the creases at his eyes spoke of his total disregard of his most highly recommended medicine—rest. He crossed to the chair and sat heavily upon it to study Cade's sleeping form. "How is he doing?"

Mae Ann pulled the footstool out of the way and stood back. "He wakes twice a day and grumbles at my gruel, but so far we've managed to keep him in bed."

"Nightmares? Fits or frights?"

She clenched her hands behind her, grateful again, yet uneasy at the doctor's questioning. "None that I know of. Deacon has not mentioned any such thing, and only he or I attend Cade."

"Have you tried to wake him?" The doctor took off his coat and let it fall over the back of the chair.

"No, I let him wake on his own."

Dr. Weaver leaned forward to feel Cade's brow, and after a moment he shook him gently by the left shoulder. "Mr. Parker."

Cade turned his head toward the doctor and frowned.

Another shake, less gentle. "Mr. Parker. You awake?"

Cade drew his left hand across his face and squinted. "I am now."

"Good." The doctor leaned over, slipping an arm behind his patient's back and taking Cade's left hand. "Sit up."

Cade grimaced as he pulled himself upright and swung his bare feet to the floor. Mae Ann moved closer in case he toppled forward out of Dr. Weaver's capable hands. She would catch him, support him, right? Cade rubbed his immobile arm, and sweat broke out on his forehead. She gripped her apron with both hands and glanced at the corked bottle on the end table.

"I'll stabilize that shoulder for you. See to it that you don't use your right arm for six weeks."

Cade grumbled under his breath and looked up at Mae Ann. She blushed at his undressed state but held her ground, reminding herself that she was his wife. Keeping him from using his arm would be more of a challenge than anything she had yet faced, but she and Deacon were managing just fine with the chores and could continue to do so for as long as it took.

Cade grumped again. "Six weeks puts me almost into the roundup. I can't be laid up that long."

Dr. Weaver ignored the remark as he riffled through his bag and withdrew a rolled black cloth. He shook it out square, folded it into a triangle, and fashioned a sling to support Cade's right arm, knotting it behind his neck. "If you don't let this shoulder heal all the way, you'll pay for it the rest of your life. Now stand up."

Tempted to add an emphatic *amen*, Mae Ann instead rolled her lips at the scolding. With a hand beneath Cade's left elbow, Dr. Weaver steadied him as he unfolded to his full, glorious height. Her heart raced to see him once again where he needed to be—upright. But he looked lean and tired and pained. How she longed to comfort him. Instead, she turned to fetch a clean shirt from the wardrobe.

At first Cade seemed unsure of himself, but within a few steps, he managed a more solid stance and walked to the window unattended. Bracing his left arm against the frame, he stood looking down on the yard and corrals and barn.

"Now come back this way." Not one drop of sympathy colored the doctor's order.

"I have a chore to take care of while you are here, Doctor, but I'll return shortly." She laid the shirt across the foot of the bed and went out, glancing over her shoulder to find Cade frowning after her.

In the kitchen she filled two small pails with water and hurried out the back door and up the hill, grateful that Cade's bedroom window did not give him a view to the north. And thankful that the fledgling rose had not failed.

She brushed pine needles from the bowl-shaped depression and emptied both pails.

The wind sighed through the great pine's boughs, surprising her again with its full and rushing voice, as if from a chorus of trees instead of just one. No horseman watched from the distant rise, at least not that she could see, but she hurried back to the house just the same, gooseflesh rising on her arms. Voices in the great room warned that Cade had ventured downstairs.

"You're weak, but that's to be expected." Dr. Weaver's tone had not softened. He evidently knew how to handle his more stubborn patients. "You are to spend the rest of the day resting and none of it on a horse."

Cade fell heavily into his chair at the hearth, grumbling again about ranch work that needed to be done. Mae Ann stoked the fire in the stove, brought the broth to the front, then hurried out the back door and around to the corral, where she loosed the horses and shooed them out of the near pasture, waving her apron and calling Blue and Cougar to her aid, a task in which they delighted. Winded from all her running, she slipped through the kitchen door in time to hear Dr. Weaver's final orders.

"I'll be back next week to look you over unless your wife drives you into town in the buckboard." He tugged his coat on and picked up his bag. "But that may even be too much for that hard head of yours. Best take it easy and let others do your chores for a while."

He turned to locate Mae Ann. "Do you need any more of that remedy I left with you last time?"

"No, she does not." Cade shoved his free hand through his hair and glowered at the doctor, who humphed at him and ambled over to Mae Ann. "You let me know if he gives you any trouble."

"I will. Thank you again." It was all she could do to keep a sober face with Cade's disgruntled frown in her line of vision.

"Good day, then." The doctor jerked a nod at Cade as he passed and let himself out the door.

She smoothed her apron. At least Cade was dressed, his shirt buttoned awkwardly over his right arm, pinning it and the sling inside. Possibly the doctor's way of making movement inconvenient. "Would you like some coffee?"

"If you swear you won't put gall in it."

For all his bravado, fatigue tinged his voice and he sounded like a petulant child.

She joined him at the hearth and perched on the edge of her chair. "You don't want it 'horned and barefoot'?"

A faint spark lit his weary eyes, and his mouth ticked in that familiar way.

Thank you, Lord.

"Speaking of that old badger, where is he?"

"I sent him to town for supplies." She rose against the urge to throw her arms around Cade's neck and kiss the frown from his brow.

"I'll take some food too. But no more broth."

Gasping, she pressed a hand to her chest. "You don't like it?"

He nearly smiled. "Give me what you give that foreman of mine. Biscuits. Gravy. Eggs."

Her heart danced with relief, and she moved past him, stopping abruptly when he grabbed her wrist.

Looking up at her, he probed her countenance with that same deep appraisal from the day they were married, and his voice sank to the dark, gritty mine. "You were always there. Caring for me."

She swallowed against her tight throat and covered his hand with hers. Would he let her stay? Did he *want* her to stay? "I was happy to." *I love you.*

The admission, even to herself, made her tremble, and she freed herself from his grasp lest he discover her secret.

In the kitchen, she stopped behind a chair, gripping its sturdy back to brace herself against her storming emotions.

~

Cade closed his eyes and turned his head against the cool leather. He sure hadn't figured on falling—off the ladder or for a woman. And not just any woman, but this bride of his. Both acts complicated his life and required more concentration than he felt capable of at the moment. He reached for the stool with a bare foot, then sat up to look for it, wrenching his shoulder in the process.

Then he remembered. It was in his room. Her room. She'd probably spent every night on that stool beside him.

He tracked her movements by the sounds she made in the kitchen. Opening the oven door, shifting the skillet on the stove. The aroma of coffee and cornbread threaded from his nose to his stomach and tightened it into a knot. He couldn't lose her.

He couldn't let her stay.

She brought his coffee in a tin cup, not china, and he took a whiff. No laudanum, but he wouldn't put it past her. As he tested the brew, she went upstairs and quickly returned with the footstool and something tucked under her arm.

"While I dish up your food, you can make yourself comfortable." She set his moccasins atop the stool and left a pair of clean socks on the table next to his chair.

Actions rarely lie. His ma's words twisted around his knotted gut as he slipped his feet into the soft sheepskin.

He dozed off and on in his chair for the rest of the day, not as comfortable as he'd been in his bed, but not as quarantined either. He looked to the door for his boots, but they weren't there, which meant they were upstairs. Feeling stronger than he had that morning, and counting on Mae Ann being busy elsewhere, he took his time climbing the stairs, his left hand skimming the banister. He didn't need her finding him in a heap at the bottom.

As he suspected, his boots were tucked under the footboard. Even as he reached for them, he wondered if he could pull them on by himself, a question that graveled him more than anything. He didn't take kindly to dependency on other people, especially when it came to getting dressed. But he wanted to walk outside, check on the horses, breathe fresh air. Even if he had to do it barefoot.

And horned. His pulse kicked. He checked the wardrobe, and just as he'd figured, Mae Ann had moved all her things out and his clothes in. A quick glance into his old room across the hall confirmed that she'd moved her trunk too. Confounded woman. At the landing he dropped his boots over the edge with a *thunk*, then made his way down.

Sitting on the stone hearth, he worked his socks on with one hand, stuck his left foot in his boot top, and pulled. Pain shot through his right shoulder anyway, as surely as nails through the ladder rungs on the barn wall. If he'd taken care of repairs when he should have, he wouldn't be here tugging his boots on with one hand. The front door opened and

Deacon stomped inside, a flour sack over one shoulder and a crate under his arm.

He slid Cade a glance on his way to the kitchen. "You just gettin' up?"

Arrogant old man. Cade managed to shove on his right boot and, a bit woozy but under his own power, made it to the kitchen. Deacon was dumping flour in the baker's cabinet, and a fine white cloud rose from the possum-bellied drawer to dust his clothes and face. He puffed a breath to clear his mustache, and set about stashing sugar, coffee, and other stores in the pantry. Cade poured them each a hot cup that had cooked down to thick black brew and eased into a chair at the table.

"Got somethin' for you." Deacon turned his chair around and straddled it, then pulled a paper from his vest and slid it across. "Saw the sheriff and he said it's been waitin' at the telegraph office nigh on a week."

Cade leaned his good elbow on the table and gripped his cup. He felt weaker than a kitten.

"Your missus got any of them ginger cookies left?"

He shrugged—a painful mistake.

Deacon checked the covered crock on the counter, grabbed a handful, and deposited them on the table.

Cade dunked one in his coffee and shoved the whole thing in his mouth before unfolding the yellow paper.

Where was she anyway? He hadn't looked outside. She could be milking the cow this late in the day. Or at work in the garden. He didn't hear her washing out back, and he didn't expect she'd ride to the Price place while he was laid up. At least she'd better not.

"Were the horses still corralled when you drove in?"

Deacon shook his head, a cookie swelling one cheek. "Nope."

Cade's heartbeat jumped, and he attempted to follow it to a standing position. The sudden act shot needles through his shoulder and a small herd through his forehead. He dropped to the chair and considered swearing.

"I'll check on 'em." Deacon grabbed the rest of the cookies and left.

Cade looked again at the telegram. Judge Murphy wanted to see the will. Mae Ann was to deliver it to the courthouse at the county seat Monday morning. Decision to follow that afternoon. That meant a long wagon ride to Cedar City the day before and a night in the hotel. Maybe two.

He leaned back and dragged his hands down his face, finding close to a week's worth of whiskers in the process. He'd never shaved with his left hand, but he wasn't about to let Deacon at him with a straight razor. Nor that no-good, mealymouthed Bartholomew Ward. That left his choices slim to none, and he imagined Mae Ann taking a turn at him with his razor. His chest grew tight. He left his coffee on the table and walked out to the back porch.

Evening slipped across the high park with a cooling sigh, and he filled his lungs, hoping to cool his emotions as well. A distant cow bawled, a hawk screed. A dog barked and he looked up toward the ponderosa where a flash of yellow on summer's green grass charged downhill, rolled to a stop, and ran back up again. At the top, Mae Ann stood at the edge of the evergreen's branches, her faint laughter rippling down and through his soul. She bent over Cougar, then threw something the pup chased like a hound on a rabbit. Her unbound hair draped her shoulders in a dark cloud.

Why was she up there? He watched her make her way down with Cougar, who ran back and forth to fetch what she threw. Her laughter wafted to him again, as pretty as the meadowlarks she was so fond of. She carried a pail over her arm like an egg basket, but nothing grew atop that hill. No berries or currants. Only crosses.

She saw him leaning against the porch post, for her gait faltered and then picked up again more slowly. As she neared the house, she disappeared from view behind the cedars, then came around the side into the yard, past the clothesline. She stopped at the bottom of the steps to look up at him standing like a guard at his back door. A weak guard who wanted only to take her in his arms and declare his love.

Mighty strong word for a man who still bore scars from another woman's loose handling of his heart. But he might as well face it head-on. Mae Ann had tangled his spurs with her stubborn, gentle ways and convinced him that he couldn't live without her. So how was he supposed to put her on the train and send her away?

He steeled himself with visions of what could become a bloody battle over a dead man's farm. "I heard from the judge."

Expectancy drained from her face, leaving it pale in the fading light.

"Deacon picked up the telegram when he was in town."

Cougar dropped to his haunches at her side and leaned against her leg, his tongue lolling. The pail slid from her arm to her fingers, and with the other hand, she scratched the dog's head. "What did it say?"

"He wants to see the will. On Monday, at the county seat."

"I see." She hitched her skirt and climbed the steps to stand next to him, but kept her eyes on the door. "And your decision about me leaving. Is it the same?"

Anxiety cinched his chest, and he felt he'd snap in two. His first obligation was to keep her safe, in spite of what he really wanted. He swallowed past the stone in his throat and reached for her hand, but she stepped away and looked up with a challenge.

He had no choice but to tell her the truth. He owed her that much. "Yes."

Her head remained high as always, the little fighter who had lassoed him into this arrangement in the first place. She didn't even blink.

"But I—"

"Supper will be ready shortly." Without letting him finish, she swept into the house and shut the door, closing him out of her presence.

Exactly what he didn't want.

CHAPTER 19

M ae Ann set the pail in the sink and leaned against the
edge, pressing her fingers to her temples where her
heartbeat pounded. *Gracious. Be gracious.* Nowhere in the
preacher's blessing had it said graciousness was deserved.

She drew a ribbon from her pocket, then coiled her hair
at the base of her neck and tied the ribbon around it, praying
it and her heart would hold and not fray into a thousand
strands.

If she were not such a coward, she would have waited to
hear what else Cade had to say.

But she hadn't waited because she could not bear to
hear his argument again, not after his tender kiss that day at
the range and the fire in his eyes that said he would fight for
her. Not after she'd kept vigil at his bedside three nights,
praying that he would change his mind. She squeezed her
eyes shut and swiped away the pain leaking through her
lashes.

At supper Deacon mentioned he'd found the horses out
beyond the near pasture, and shot her a glance from beneath
his bushy brows. He knew what she'd done, and surely he
knew why. Other than that, the meal was a quiet affair, and
Cade soon retired upstairs. Deacon left for his cabin, and she
washed the dishes and started a batch of bread to rise

overnight. She added the remaining bone broth to the stew, plus an onion and turnips that Deacon had brought from town.

Come fall they'd have their own garden vegetables. But she'd not be here to see they were set in straw in the root cellar for winter. Nor would she preserve berries or dry apples or do any of the things she'd planned.

Climbing the stairs with a heavy heart, she forced herself to consider where she would go, for she'd not return to St. Louis. Nothing awaited her there, and she refused to scratch out a living in another rooming house in a stifling city. Or answer another bridal advertisement.

She sat on the edge of the rope bed, not much more than a cot, and strained to hear across the hall behind Cade's closed door. He more than likely slept, weary from the first day in four on his feet.

Three more days, and they would be on their way to Cedar City. If the judge ruled in her favor, and Henry's farm was truly hers, she would put it up for sale, withdraw her money from the bank, and rent a room in Olin Springs until someone bought the land.

But that someone would not be Sean MacGrath.

The man's name set her teeth on edge. The thought of him walking into the run-down house that was to have been her home turned her stomach, and she imagined him gloating if he did so, rubbing it in like salt on a raw and tender wound.

Cade wanted the land and its valuable water source. He'd said as much right from the start. Perhaps he would buy it.

She loosed her hair and pulled it over her shoulder to brush, the repetitive act soothing her frantic thoughts. All she had to do was survive until Monday morning. She'd leave baked goods for Deacon. A pot of beans. A ham from the smokehouse to feed him until their return. Then she'd prepare as much as she could for the two of them before she left, though she could not ensure that the garden would not be abandoned once more to the weeds and snakes.

And the rose on the hill?

It would die like all her dreams, for she had no intention of telling Cade, or even Deacon, that it was there.

~

"We leave tomorrow morning after church."

Cade's announcement on Saturday evening shredded Mae Ann's tenuous preparations and left her one day short on time. The trip was a good half-day's ride from Olin Springs by wagon, he said. They'd take rooms at the hotel in Cedar City so they'd be rested to meet Judge Murphy on Monday morning.

Cade might rest, as well he needed it, but she would not sleep soundly until the ordeal was over.

Whether he had told Deacon his plans to put her on the train, she did not know, but the old cowboy seemed to sense that more than a reading of the will was at hand. She felt his sky-blue eyes following her Sunday morning as she checked and rechecked the food she'd prepared for him. Cade had given her his mother's carpetbag, and after she'd packed her few necessities, Deacon took it to the buckboard.

He did not say good-bye, but strode to the barn in his uneven gait, where he stopped just inside the door. As they drove out of the yard, Mae Ann turned and raised her hand. He nodded and tipped the brim of his battered hat with a finger, nearly tipping her tears over the edge.

Cade insisted upon driving, also claiming that the mare was a one-handed horse that posed no threat. Mae Ann could not argue, so sore she was from wrestling with her emotions. She needed what little strength she had left for enduring the church service, the ride to Cedar City, and an appearance before Judge Murphy. She had nothing to spare for contending with Cade over his bullheaded refusal of her help.

In fact, she had nothing to spare at all, and the blue satin reticule hung empty from her wrist save for Henry's will and a few coins.

Perhaps this was all for the best. Life with a stubborn rancher might prove to be one argument after another, though up to this point she had enjoyed their banter and his ill-disguised humor. She darted a glance at his stoic form beside her, dark and mysterious with his shadowed face. The beard changed his appearance, deepened his eyes, and hid his sturdy jaw. Did he grow one against Colorado's winter storms?

A small sigh slipped away. She would never know. Nor would she see the first snowfall, watch Blue and Cougar romp and play through the drifts, or serve hot meals to two hardworking cowboys after hard days in the cold. She'd miss the roundup, spring calving, her new friend, Travine Price, and riding in the evenings with Cade. Shooting old tins off the dead cottonwood, and his arms around her even if just for a moment.

How full her life had become in little more than two months, and how empty it seemed now as she jostled on the wagon bench like a doll bereft of its stuffing. She smoothed her brown velvet skirt, the same one she'd worn the day she arrived, much too warm now beneath a July sun, even in the morning. But it was the best she had for traveling and for church.

The irony stung. Church and Pastor Bittman figured as prominently in her departure as they had in her arrival, but Millie Bittman's beaming face over the bundle clutched to her breast that morning assuaged the nettle somewhat.

After the service, folks lingered around the church door, visiting with the parson and one another, and Mae Ann sought out Millie. She touched a gloved finger to the babe's plump and bonneted cheek as a fine barb hooked her heart. "She is precious."

"Would you like to hold her?" Millie pressed the infant into her arms before Mae Ann could refuse the blanket-wrapped miracle.

Always a miracle, a baby. She shushed the longing that shifted in her middle at the rosebud lips and delicate lashes. The transfer woke the tiny girl, and gray eyes blinked up into her own with wonder. Mae Ann thought her heart would break.

"She's perfect, Millie. You must be so proud." Carefully, she returned the babe to its mother.

"I daresay, not as proud as her father." Millie blushed becomingly and rocked the babe in her arms, making little cooing sounds.

A hand at Mae Ann's elbow drew her from her yearning. "We need to be on our way if we want to make Cedar City before dark."

Cade's declaration raised Millie's brows with a question just as the parson stepped up to join their small group.

"Surely you'll stay for dinner. What takes you to Cedar City on such a glorious summer day that can't wait until after a solid meal?" The parson's openly honest expression made Mae Ann want to pour out all her heart's pain and passion, but she pressed her lips together to wait for Cade's explanation.

His deep voice seeped into her skin, increasing her sorrow. "We've business there with the judge over Reiker's farm. Should be back tomorrow. Or the next day." He shook the parson's hand and tipped his hat to Millie, both of them accepting his vague explanation. "A good afternoon to you."

He handed Mae Ann up to the seat, and while he circled around to the other side, she lifted a handled basket from the wagon bed and set it on the floor at her feet. They didn't have time to eat at the café, Cade had said. Perhaps it was so. Or maybe he did not want to be seen with a wife he had no intention of keeping.

When they passed the east edge of town—the edge she'd seen only from the train's smudged window two months before, she handed him a sandwich of ham and bread. Pickles would improve the fare, but she had none.

He took it with a somber look that caused her stomach to do all sorts of things it shouldn't. Instead of fixing her own stacked bread and meat, she drew out two Mason jars of lemonade, removed the lids and set one beside Cade against the bench back. Looking out over the grasslands and dwindling houses, she sipped the tart mixture, hardly noticing the sugar she had added.

Nothing could sweeten this journey for her. For she would not ask Cade Parker a second time if he wanted a wife.

~

If the gray didn't spook or misstep, Cade could manage. He'd draped the ribbons loosely over the fingers of his right hand, accepted the sandwich Mae Ann offered, and finished it in three bites. It lay in his stomach like a stone.

She hadn't said a word since they left the church house, just handed him his food and set a jar of lemonade against the bench back. A bullwhip wouldn't crack the tension between them, and the twenty miles to Cedar City might as well be two hundred.

Straight she sat, that ramrod spine of hers in proper place and her pretty face taking the brunt of the midday sun. Her hat was as handy as a leash on a bobcat. He knew she hadn't brought the one he gave her, for he'd grabbed it off the hook on his way out the door.

"Take the reins."

She looked at him as if he'd told her to jump out.

He laid them in her hand and reached under the seat. "You'll be as crisp as fried bacon by the time we reach Cedar City if you don't wear a real hat."

She hesitated, then took his offering and pulled the pin from the thing on her head. "Thank you."

The gray plodded ahead, her ears flicking back at their voices.

"You have the will?" His question garnered an offended scowl.

Her chin rose. "Isn't that the purpose of this trip?"

He swallowed a snort. Her clipped words could roach the mare's mane and shave his whiskers all at once. Draping the reins again over his right hand, he scratched his cheek. Too hot for a beard. Even a short one. And too hot for a sharp tongue. She should thank him for taking her all the way to Cedar City to see Judge Murphy. He picked up the jar of lemonade and downed half of it.

On second thought, he should thank her for packing them a meal. And making the ranch house feel like home again, and all the other things she'd done since her business proposal. Hang fire, if it weren't for MacGrath, he'd get down on one knee and offer her his mother's wedding band. Do it right, take her someplace fancy to celebrate and—

He coughed the idea from his head and shot iron pickets through his shoulder. Blasted bad time to be half laid up and out of commission.

She glanced at him, concern stitching her brow.

"I'm fine," he said to her silent question.

She huffed. No wonder Deacon tolerated her. More than tolerated her, the old coot. She didn't cut either one of them any slack, and that was exactly what they needed, whether he cared to admit it or not.

By the time they dropped down into the valley where Cedar City draped itself across the river, the sun's heavy heat had let up some as it slid toward the mountains. Shirt stuck to his back and smelling like a goat, he pulled up at the Stratford House Hotel and looped the reins around the brake handle. Before he could get around to Mae Ann, she'd shed her hat, climbed down, and took the carpet bag from the bed. He grabbed his valise. At least she accepted his arm as they walked into the hotel lobby.

"Two rooms, please," he told the desk clerk, who eyed them with open condescension.

Mae Ann coughed politely. Cade repeated the request.

"I take it you're here for the Founders' Day festivities." The clerk pushed his spectacles higher on his nose.

"No, we are not." Cade set down his valise and reached into his vest pocket, dislodging Mae Ann's fingers from his arm, which left an unpleasant emptiness in their absence. He laid two coins on the counter. "We'll need the rooms tonight and possibly tomorrow night. I'll know for certain tomorrow, but I'll leave this on deposit."

The clerk slid the guest registry across the counter with a fancy fountain pen, then turned to his honeycombed key boxes. Cade picked up the pen with his left hand and looked at Mae Ann. She took it from him and signed their names.

The clerk swiveled the book around, then glanced up. "Mr. and Mrs. Cade Parker." He closed the registry with a smug arch of his brows. "I am glad to see you are matrimoniously joined, for we have only one room available." He offered the key.

Cade was pretty sure *matrimoniously* was not a word. He took the key. "You're certain."

The clerk smiled, but it wasn't a friendly look. "I am absolutely certain. You are fortunate to find a room at all with the Founders' Day celebration in full swing. Marital spats aside, your room is the last on the third floor, to the left. Opposite end from the bathing room."

Cade leaned toward the man.

Mae Ann's fingers linked his elbow like a chain and tugged as she addressed the clerk. "Thank you so much. A bath sounds lovely after a long day's journey."

It was only the idea of a bath that kept Cade from wiping the smirk off the man's face and landing both himself and Mae Ann on the street.

"You'll find the lift on your right at the base of the stairs."

Lift? He'd like to lift that snooty gent out of his knickers and leave him hanging on a coat peg.

Mae Ann pressed close and whispered, "I'd prefer the stairs, if you don't mind."

He sliced the clerk a warning glare and headed for the broad staircase with polished banister and finials. Mae Ann lifted her skirt and ascended ahead of him. He pinned his eyes to the carpet-covered steps. He had other matters to deal with, and considering their predicament, watching the gentle sway of her hips would only make those matters worse. On him.

At the end of the third-floor hallway, he inserted the key, pushed the door open, and stepped aside for Mae Ann to enter.

She let out a gentle, "Oh."

A four-poster bed dominated the room, and a window with lace curtains allowed the faded day a final glance inside. Mae Ann moved from dressing table to chest of drawers to curtains, running her fingers across each item as if testing its reality.

Cade locked on the settee, half his length and covered in gold brocade, where he'd spend a painful night. Mae Ann turned, and he caught her reflection in the dressing table mirror. Her eyes held his, and color filled her cheeks.

He cleared his throat and hung his hat on a coat tree near the settee. "I'll sleep here, if you don't mind."

"I most certainly do mind." She set her bag on a padded bench at the end of the bed and crossed her arms.

He turned away and growled out his frustration. A chair in that fancy parlor they passed downstairs would serve his needs. *After* the clerk retired.

"You will take the bed."

She could not have said anything that surprised him more. He dropped his valise and matched her stance, brace for brace.

"I know this arrangement is against your wishes, but we are *legally* man and wife." Her hands began to flutter dismissively in the general direction of the gold brocade. "I will not have you, in your condition, folding yourself like a paper fan onto that—that ridiculous settee."

In his condition? He'd been in worse straits, and his good hand fisted in preparation for telling her just what he thought of her appraisal. But her high color and mother-hen demeanor conjured a chuckle and he bit it back. "Just what do you propose, madam? That *you* curl up on that spindly legged, oversized chair? No woman under my protection will spend the night rolled up like a slicker on a saddle."

She blinked, and he knew he had her. Then she glanced at the bed and blushed even deeper, a most becoming color that matched the spread. He suddenly feared she had him.

"It is only one night. Perhaps two. I believe we could rest civilly with cushions and such between us. Perhaps our bags as well."

Her proposal sucked the wind from his chest and, for a moment, robbed him of his ability to speak. She was right, but he would not have suggested such an arrangement. He cleared his throat and tugged on his sling. "Very well. I will take this side, closer to the door. Should I need to . . ."

Her brow arched. "Defend my honor?"

She tilted her head in an irritatingly appealing way and pushed at the hair once piled on top. Most of it hung loose after changing hats. "I would like to freshen up before supper."

"I'll take the horse and wagon to the livery and meet you in the dining room in an hour." Leaving his valise behind, he marched out the door, weighing the benefits of sleeping in a stall.

CHAPTER 20

M ae Ann leaned against the closed door of the bathing room, her fingers pressed beneath her jaw where her pulse hammered. Cold water—that was what she needed. A great deal of cold water.

She undressed down to her chemise and drawers, grateful to be rid of her corset after the long drive. She rolled her stockings off, delighting in the cold wooden planks beneath her bare feet. A glorious copper tub sat against the wall with spigots for both hot and cold water. Such luxury she'd seen only once in St. Louis when running an errand for her mother. The rolled edge was firm and cool beneath her hand.

She placed the stopper in the tub and turned the matching copper spigots. As the tub filled, she shook out her nicest dress, creased from the day's journey but cooler than her suit and much cleaner. With a clothes brush she'd tucked into the bag at the last minute, she brushed her heavy skirt and jacket, ridding them of the colorless road dust that clung to the fabric like frost on an iron handrail.

Satisfied that the tepid water was not warm enough to put her to sleep, she shed her remaining garments and slid into its cool embrace, stopping at the nape of her neck. It would not do to attend supper in public with wet hair.

Cade was determined to send her away, in spite of her care of him. In spite of everything. Clearly, he wanted out of their business arrangement, and claiming he was worried about her safety was his excuse. So be it. At least he'd invited her to dinner. They had never dined openly together other than at their own table. His table, rather.

Determined not to be late, she released the water and quickly dressed, refreshed with the soaking.

An elegant cheval mirror in one corner allowed her to do up her hair, and she clustered a few curling strands at one side. She pinched her cheeks and bit her lower lip, pleased with the overall effect, plain blue twill and all. Not that Cade would care. But she cared, and wanted to look her very best on what could possibly be their last—and only—outing together.

She knocked lightly at their room and, hearing no answer, slowly opened the door to peek inside. Cade's hat hung on the coat tree, but he was gone, not fallen exhausted across the bed as she'd half expected. A hint of tonic lingered in the room, and she checked the washbasin to find it filled and a used towel draped over the attached dowel. The room key lay on the dressing table, and she locked the door on her way out and dropped the key into her reticule.

He sat with his back to the far wall, watching the dining room's entrance. When she paused at the threshold, he rose and made his way to her, reminding her how handsome he was in spite of his shadowed jawline. Her heart raced up to perch in her throat as he greeted her pleasantly and offered his left arm.

"You look lovely." Though harnessed in his sling, the fingers of his right hand covered hers the way they had on their wedding day. Such memories and his current considerations chafed her already tender emotions.

"Thank you." Accepting his gentlemanly offer to assist her with her chair, she detected the woodsy tonic as he leaned close to scoot her nearer the table. He wore a clean shirt, and a string tie supplanted the ever-present silk neckerchief. Refusing to feel dowdy in her simple cotton frock, she straightened her posture and sipped the water that awaited her.

"They are serving roast beef tonight. Nothing special, I'm afraid, after living on a cattle ranch." His near smile melted against the edge of his water glass as the waiter stopped at their table, a linen cloth draped over one arm.

"Would you care for wine this evening, sir?"

"No, thank you. Water will do. Coffee with dessert." Evidently, Cade was familiar with the formalities of dining out—more acquainted than she—another surprise to his character that she would not have equated with the spurs and chaps he'd left at the ranch.

"As you wish, sir." The man bowed slightly at the waist. "Ma'am." Then he left them to an uneasy silence.

Mae Ann moved her reticle drawstring to her left wrist and positioned the bag in her lap. She glanced at other couples seated in the lavishly furnished room, envious not of the women's fine gowns, but of their gaiety and subtle touches of fingers across tables.

She forced a pleasant tone. "You have been here before?"

Candlelight from their table reflected in his dark eyes, and his mouth twitched, tightening the cord that held her to him. "My parents came here often when Betsy and I were young. It was our mother's desire that we learn the 'finer graces,' as she put it." He tasted his water again, and his deeply tanned hand rested starkly against the white linen tablecloth.

Indeed, he had slipped into a finer-grace mode, and she longed for his rougher cowboy ways. She felt a bit out of place in the elegant room, in his mannered company. The ranch house kitchen and their chairs by the fire appealed to her much more.

The meal was as delicious as Cade's attentions, and she found herself relaxing at last, warming to this side of her husband that she had never known. A fine custard followed the beef, vegetables, and gravy, with coffee served from a silver decanter, but in spite of her desire to enjoy the evening as long as possible, her eyelids warred against her.

"You're tired."

The gentleness of his voice pricked her conscience and stiffened her back as if he'd caught her doing something brazen. *Like falling helplessly in love.* She tucked her linen napkin beneath her plate. "The ride here, I suppose."

"And anticipation of what awaits you tomorrow." He slid his hand across the table and folded it around her own. "Are you ready to go upstairs?"

Her mouth opened, but her throat closed. She withdrew her fingers, clutched her reticule, and nodded before finding the weakest of all replies. "Thank you for the lovely meal."

He stood and assisted her with her chair, then again offered his arm. "Heavy for supper, but it will help us sleep well."

She glanced quickly at his face to find he meant just that and nothing untoward. The man was a gentleman to a fault. She sighed, relieved yet somehow disappointed.

At the door to their room, she handed him the key.

His mouth ticked on one side. "I knew you'd find it."

He stood aside for her to enter but did not follow. She faced him.

"I need to check on the mare." His eyes swept her from head to foot, his brows drawing down with the progression. "Lock the door."

It clicked softly closed at his hand, and she waited, pressing her ear against the polished wood. Did he stand on the other side awaiting her compliance? Feeling all of twelve, she stooped to peek through the keyhole and met his trousers there. She covered her mouth and turned the lock, and his footfall faded away.

Unlike the lit hallway, the room was nearly black, for she'd not trimmed the lamp before she left. Flicking on the gas wall bracket, she squinted against the suddenly harsh light, but used it to locate the oil lamp she'd seen earlier. Yes, there on the dressing table, where Cade had earlier left the room key. He'd thought of everything.

Except their unconventional sleeping arrangement. That blatant proposition fell completely on her own shoulders. She lit the lamp and lowered the flame, then turned off the gaslight before plopping onto the cushioned seat at the dressing table. The pins pulled easily from her hair and it fell unfettered. Freedom from restraint felt good, even if for only a moment. She brushed its length and dug the bristles into her scalp, loosening the road dust lingering there, then plaited it into a long queue.

Retrieving her nightgown from the carpetbag, she fingered the blue ribbon trim at the neck and hesitated, uncertain if she could lie beneath the coverlet on this warm night in such a state of undress.

Cade was her husband, but not really. He had made no advances toward her, other than his brief kiss at the old cottonwood. And it was she who had determined the conditions of their so-called marriage—*If I do not appeal to you, we can live as man and wife in name only.*

Clearly, she did not appeal to him or he would not send her away.

She returned her nightclothes to the bag, unbuttoned her shoes and discarded her stockings, then took two smaller cushions from the settee and laid them down the middle of the delightfully soft feather tick, her carpetbag at the foot. The whole idea was preposterous, but she didn't know what else to do.

Giving in to the lush lure of bed and pillow, she lay down on her half with not even an inch of space remaining because of the cushions. How would Cade manage in such a cramped arrangement, his arm in a sling?

She rolled to her right side, her back against the cushions, one arm beneath her pillow. It would have to do. At least he'd not be folded onto the settee or stretched out on the hard floor, though the idea of stretching out proved a tempting one even in her state of weariness.

~

The mare did not need checking, but Cade needed the walk to the livery to clear his thoughts, untangle his emotions, and convince himself that he couldn't accompany Mae Ann to court tomorrow smelling as if he'd slept in a barn.

On his way back, he inquired at the other hotel about a room. They had none.

His boots echoed his pulse as he stomped through the ornate Stratford House entry and into the lobby. The clerk was gone. Given his current agitated state, the man's absence was probably the Lord's doing.

He snorted. The second time that impression had crowded him.

He took the stairs a mite slower to let the idea simmer. If God really was behind this whole *business proposition* of Mae Ann's, then it was a whole lot more than Cade just showing up at the wrong place at the right time.

But how was he supposed to keep her *and* keep her safe?

At the third-floor landing, he dropped down on the stair and pulled the sling off his neck. The knot had worked him raw, and immobility made him stiffer by the day. It'd been more than a week since the ladder rungs had busted through, dropping him on his head. And it was his stewing over Mae Ann and MacGrath that sent him up there in the first place.

The loft had been a favorite hideaway when he was a boy shirking chores. The old barn's shady, hay-scented quiet cleared his mind. He could see better, get a different perspective, and rein in his thoughts. The top of the third-floor staircase didn't have the same effect.

He rubbed his neck and bent his head from side to side. Mae Ann had been the most beautiful woman in the dining room with her simple blue dress, softly curling hair, and gentle demeanor. And she was the most frustratingly stubborn and perfect embodiment of everything he'd imagined a wife should be.

But her suggestion for sharing the bed scared him to death. He wasn't as confident in his personal restraint as she was—a revelation that shamed and honored him all at the same time. A more trustworthy woman, aside from his mother, he'd never met. Nor one more trusting.

Slowly, he extended his right arm, welcoming the movement. He bent it a couple of times and, convinced he was in good shape, reached up to grip the rail. A dagger pierced the joint, and sweat broke out on his forehead. Bad call.

Rising carefully, he headed for their room. At the door, he drew the key from his vest pocket and turned it end over end. What kept a man from saying the things he wanted to, or pushed him to go against his heart in a matter?

Sean MacGrath, that's what.

As much as he didn't want to send her away, he had to keep Mae Ann out of harm's way. He'd vowed to keep her safe and he was a man of his word.

Slipping the key in the lock, he listened for the metallic click, then eased the door open to a welcoming glow from the table lamp. He was glad she hadn't left on the gaslight, but she had left on her blue dress and lay on the far side of the bed, shored up by gold brocade cushions and her carpetbag. He quietly closed the door and crossed to open the window for fresh air. Then he turned down the lamp, toed off his boots, and shed his vest and tie.

Standing by the bed in his stockinged feet, he stared at the narrow shelf she'd left for him. She made not a sound—he couldn't even hear her breathing. But if he felt the warmth of her through the tick, it would increase the ache in his chest far beyond the one in his shoulder.

He turned away, picked up his boots, and went downstairs.

~

The next morning, Cade's neck screamed louder than his shoulder as he unfolded from the parlor chair and opened his eyes. He alone remained, the other patrons absent and in their comfortable beds. He plowed his hair back and headed for the stairs and his room.

Mae Ann was gone.

Disappointment chaffed him, and he crossed to the washbasin. Warm water filled the pitcher, and a fresh towel waited on the rack.

Actions rarely lie.

Without the need to shave, his morning ritual took much less time, and he hurried downstairs hoping to find her in the dining room. Their appointment with Judge Murphy was set for ten, and by the slant of sun through the lobby windows, it was still early. His pocket watch and the floor clock near the stairs confirmed his observation.

She sat at the same table as the previous night, in the same chair, her profile facing him as she gazed out the window. Few patrons occupied the other tables this morning, and the distinct aroma of strong coffee stirred his appetite.

He caught the waiter's eye and indicated Mae Ann's table. Adept at reading the guests' wishes, the man filled the cup at the empty seat across from her. She turned to look over her shoulder.

At first glance, her eyes lit with pleasure, but she masked them and turned to her coffee.

"Good morning." Cade took the chair facing her, amazed that she looked so fresh. Her brown suit looked fresh as well, and the matching excuse for a hat perched defiantly atop her upswept hair.

"And to you." A brow arched. "How is your shoulder?"

Of course she knew. She wasn't blind. "Not bad, considering."

She sipped her coffee and pinned him with a darted look. "Did you not sleep well?"

Blast it all, he'd not be airing his personal battles over breakfast. "It was the forgetful raising of my arm that did the deed." He adjusted the annoying knot. "The sooner I'm out of this rigging, the better I'll like it."

Soundlessly, she set her cup in its matching saucer. "That seems a contradiction if the sling reminds you not to raise your arm."

He bit back a snort. As contradicting as his warring emotions—wanting her within reach but out of harm at the same time. He could not have it both ways. "Contradiction makes up a good deal of my life lately."

She dropped her gaze to the table, her hands to her lap. Her shoulders leveled and she pulled in a breath before raising her chin.

"If the judge does not rule in my favor, and Henry's farm goes to auction, will you make a bid?"

His chest seized. "Would you like that?"

Her chin rose another notch. "That is not what I asked."

"It is what *I* am asking. Do you want me to buy the farm if the judge puts it up for sale?"

She blinked. Twice.

He leaned slightly forward and lowered his voice. "Mae Ann, I want to know what you want."

Her beautiful eyes locked on his and drew him under, squeezing the air from his lungs.

"I don't want MacGrath to have it."

He fell against his chair back, stinging from her subtle dodge. "Neither do I, so I'll do my best to get the farm. But I can't promise anything. He is an unscrupulous man and may already have Judge Murphy in his pocket."

She blanched.

He mentally kicked himself. "On the other hand, the judge may declare the will valid. In that case, the land is yours to do with as you see fit."

The waiter arrived with poached eggs on toast—the same fare he'd eaten with his parents a dozen years before. It appealed to him even less now than it had then.

Mae Ann bowed her head, but before he could offer his hand for a unified prayer, she laid her napkin in her lap and cut into her egg. The yoke spread across her buttered toast like the uneasy dread that stained his heart.

CHAPTER 21

C ourt was held on the second floor of a Main Street
saloon, and Mae Ann feared her rights and interests
might flow away as easily as the liquor downstairs. It was a
short walk to the establishment from their hotel, but the
clerk, ever his smug self, assured them that the new
courthouse would be constructed and open for business by
this time next year.

As if that would do her any good.

The boardwalk was surprisingly crowded so early in the
morning, which was due, no doubt, to the Founders' Day
celebration, and she clung tightly to Cade's left arm lest they
be separated in the crush. Bright bunting festooned every
store window and door, inviting people to enter and browse
collections of hardware, pastries, millinery, and cigars. An
Oriental tea shop beckoned customers inside with spicy
aromas pouring from its open door.

At the saloon, an outside stairway ascended to the
second floor, and Cade stopped at its base for her to precede
him. Such as it was, the staircase was little more than a
railing and slats fastened precariously against the brick
building, and in no way mirrored the fine oak construction
they enjoyed at the Stratford House. She glanced back,
praying he did not crash through the rickety construction

and fall again. His hat brim hid his features so she could not see if he was as nervous as she. Perhaps it was best she didn't know.

She paused on the brief landing for Cade to open the door—not that she was incapable, but she felt the gesture somehow honored him as her husband. *In name only.* Oh, for the peace Pastor Bittman had prayed upon them at their vows. *Please, Lord. Shine Your face upon us.*

Her silent prayer had not risen past the door frame when her eyes landed upon a familiar figure standing against the back wall. Cade, too, caught sight of him, for his arm turned to stone beneath her fingers. Fear heightened her pulse at Sean MacGrath's presence in the courtroom, though he'd told them he was contesting the will. Perhaps Cade was right, and the cattleman *did* have the judge in his pocket. She schooled her expression, determined not to linger on MacGrath or show alarm.

Cade ignored their neighbor and led her to the front row of chairs arranged in an orderly fashion as if church were about to begin. An excessively large table served as the judge's bench, she assumed, for it sat atop a small riser with a leather-padded chair behind it and a gavel and block on its polished surface. Another chair, not cushioned, sat on the floor to the right, and twelve smaller chairs made two rows against the outside wall.

A door opposite opened and a bearded man in a long black coat entered, followed by another gentleman. Cade stood and she did as well. With a sharp knock of the gavel, the bearded man took the leather chair. "You may be seated."

She sat, clutching her reticule as if her life depended upon it, for it might.

The judge looked through several papers he had brought with him, then peered down at Cade. "Would you be Mr. Parker?"

Cade stood. "Yes, Your Honor. And this is my wife, Mae Ann Remington Parker."

Oh, Cade. This is futile! There is no Reiker in my name.

"Do you have the will in question?"

Mae Ann drew it from her reticule and handed it to Cade.

"Ma'am."

She went still. The judge extended his hand. "You may approach the bench and bring the will. This proceeding involves your interests, not your husband's."

Oh, Lord, a forward-thinking man. She glanced at Cade to find his regard warm and encouraging. A brief nod, and he sat down.

The distance to the judge's waiting hand proved a series of blows that struck her nerves with each step. As she handed him the paper, his scrutiny probed her very soul, leaving an unusual peace there. She thought immediately of Deacon and the way his old blue eyes missed nothing.

She held herself squarely, refusing to tremble, and stood silently before the judge's table. After reading for a moment, he glanced up and flicked his hand at her, brushing her away and back to her chair. Heat flooded her neck and face as she returned, humiliated that she did not know the proper protocol. Cade took her hand, enfolded it in his hard fingers, and held it possessively on his lap. The gesture threatened to charge a teary flood, and she blinked rapidly, staring at the fine needlework on her blue reticule.

Judge Murphy read Henry's stained and bullet-torn will three times, measured by the lift of his eyes from the bottom of the page to the top. She had never been so nervous in all her life. Usually she prided herself in her composure. A sin that goes before a fall? She knew the warning well, and though no such pride accompanied her today, she still feared she approached the edge of a precipice over which she soon might tumble.

"Mrs. Parker."

The title drew her head up to meet the judge's regard. "Yes, Your Honor."

"I will not readjourn this matter to this afternoon, but will announce my decision momentarily. However, I'd like to know if there is anything you care to add."

Her mouth dried to road dust. He wanted to hear her opinion—practically what Cade had asked the night before. She certainly had one, but dare she voice it in such a public place?

"Mrs. Parker?"

Cade squeezed her hand and whispered, "Go ahead, Mae Ann. You can do this."

Anchored by his apparent faith in her, she stood, gripping her reticule to her waist. "Your Honor, I believe Henry's true wish was for the farm to be mine in the event of . . . his death."

"Your Honor."

She flinched at the harsh voice behind her and followed the judge's glare to find MacGrath standing two rows back.

"She's not Henry Reiker's widow."

Judge Murphy scowled and banged his gavel. "Nor are you, sir. You are out of order, and will wait until I call for additional information or objections."

A chair barked against the plank floor as MacGrath dropped his heavy frame to the seat.

Mae Ann drew in as much air as possible, for most of it had been sucked from the room by MacGrath's venomous accusation—which was completely true.

Pastor Bittman's words chose this moment to meander through her mind, calming her senses as they played across her worrisome thoughts. *The Lord bless thee, and keep thee.* Had He not done just that and more? Kept her from being shot, or worse, during the robbery, and blessed her with Cade and Deacon and Cougar and the ranch, even if only for a short while?

"Your Honor?"

He nodded and turned one hand palm up, indicating she continue.

"Henry Reiker and I began a correspondence last fall when I answered his notice in the *St. Louis Chronicle* for a bride. We agreed upon a May wedding, and he met me at the train depot in Olin Springs. On our way to the church, Henry wanted to stop at the bank." The words stuck in her throat, jammed against a fierce pain resurrected in speaking them aloud.

"Go on." The judge folded his hands on the table.

"While we were there, the bank was robbed. Henry was shot and killed." Tears pushed disloyally against the backs of her eyes, and she scorned her feminine sensibilities for betraying her at such a moment. Clearing her throat, she looked down at her fingers, white knuckled in her attempt at self-control.

The judge leaned forward. "So you never actually married Henry Reiker."

Cloaking herself with the mantle of truth, she met his scrutiny. "My intentions were to do so, but we were not afforded the opportunity."

He raised the paper. "Is this hole the result of the fatal bullet?"

Her chest seized. She nodded.

"Have the thieves—and murderer—been caught?"

Her voice joined hovering tears in betrayal and squeezed itself into a weak whisper. "Not that I am aware."

"But you are now Mrs. Cade Parker, is that correct?"

Another nod and she reached for mettle that had once served her well. "I am. Mr. Parker came to my aid at the bank and agreed to uphold Henry's end of the agreement regarding the marriage."

"I see." One thick brow arched over his somber countenance, and he looked at Cade. "Mr. Parker, did you marry your wife for her property?"

~

Sean MacGrath snorted, and it took every ounce of Cade's self-discipline not to leap over the chairs and smash his face into the floor. His hands fisted, the right one shooting daggers into his shoulder.

He stood. "No, Your Honor, I did not. I married her for, for . . ." He felt Mae Ann wilt beside him though her body stood firm. How could he hurt her this way? But he hadn't married her for love or even companionship. He hadn't known her at the time, wasn't aware that he would fall—

"Did you know of Mr. Reiker's property?"

"Yes, Your Honor. A corner of the farm borders Parker Land and Cattle west of Olin Springs."

Scuffling feet behind him caught the judge's attention. "You, sir, what is your name and why are you here?"

MacGrath stood, shoving his chair back as he did so. "Name's Sean MacGrath, Your Honor, and the Reiker place borders my land also. It has good water on it, and I offered to buy it from the farmer. So did Parker here, but Reiker wouldn't sell."

From the hard set of Judge Murphy's mouth, Cade guessed he didn't take kindly to MacGrath.

"And?"

"And the land should be put to auction, judge. Your Honor, sir." He pointed a thick finger. "That will says Reiker left the land to his widow, Mae Ann Remington Reiker, but he never married her, so she can't be his legal widow."

Murphy read over the will again and raised a hard glare to MacGrath. "Are you related to Mr. Reiker?"

MacGrath grumbled under his breath before answering. "No."

"Are you his attorney?"

"No, Your Honor."

"Then exactly how do you know what the will says? Did Mr. Reiker or Mrs. Parker allow you to read it?"

Cade heard the wind leave MacGrath's chest, and he looked over his shoulder to see the big man go white in the face. His beefy hands gripped the back of the chair in front of him, and Cade anticipated the snap of breaking wood.

"I heard tell is all."

Murphy looked again at Mae Ann, laid the will flat, and ran a hand over it. "Did your husband-to-be have any living relatives that you know of, Mrs. Parker?"

"He mentioned in one of his letters that he had none living, Your Honor." Mae Ann was nearly stretched to her limits, based on the fiddle-string tension Cade heard in her voice.

"Can you produce this correspondence?"

She hesitated. "Henry's letters were in my reticule. The bank robbers took it and every other woman's bag."

Cade did not expect compassion from the judge, but he expected fairness and sent up a silent prayer to that effect.

"Very well. Based upon what I read here, it is my ruling, Mrs. Parker, that Henry Reiker, in all good faith, left his farm to you upon his death. I daresay he did not know said death would take place so prematurely, but I hereby declare the land to be legally yours to do with as you see fit."

The clap of gavel on wood rang out like a gunshot and Mae Ann flinched. Cade laid his hand against her back and moved closer. She'd fainted on him once before, and he intended to catch her if it happened again.

Judge Murphy gave the will to the man standing to his right, who in turn brought it to Mae Ann. Then he gathered his papers and left the room. The door closed behind him with crisp finality.

Mae Ann fell into her chair, her hands trembling like autumn leaves as she folded the will and tucked it in her bag.

"It ain't right." MacGrath rumbled an oath.

Cade faced him.

"It's right and declared so by the circuit judge. Unless you want to deal with me—and you don't—you'll leave well enough alone and keep your rope on your saddle and not drifting toward my herd."

MacGrath's black glare flicked to Cade's sling and back again and his lip curled in a snarl. "It's not my doing that's costing you cows." He lumbered out the side door without another word, the flimsy stairs to the street creaking beneath his weight.

Cade pulled his chair closer to Mae Ann and covered her gripped hands with his good one. Her eyes brimmed like a spring flood pool, and he longed to pull her to him and tell her he wanted her to stay at the ranch. To stay for love. "Mae Ann."

She drew a shaky breath and swiped at her face. "I'm putting the farm up for sale. Perhaps a nice family from Olin Springs will want it. With the money in my account, I can pay my own traveling expenses."

His gut twisted at her spoken intentions, but instead of airing his mind, he cupped her shoulder and drew her against him. "If that's what you want, then that's what we'll do."

She pulled away from him, avoiding his eyes. "I do."

The words shot deep until they joined up with a matching pair whispered in May. "It's early enough that we can head back now, if you're willing, and take a cutoff to Olin Springs and the land office on our way to the ranch. But I want to talk to you about something and this isn't the proper place."

She stood. "I'm willing."

"To talk?"

"To take the cutoff to Olin Springs. The sooner I sell the farm, the sooner I can leave and your life can return to the way it was."

He deserved that.

CHAPTER 22

Weak-kneed with relief as well as heartache, Mae Ann held so tightly to the rickety railing that she drove splinters into her hand. She needed a moment alone to sort through her emotions, but where? The crowds had doubled in the hour she and Cade were in the courtroom, and the heat and noise and smells wove into a suffocating web that threatened to send her running. She turned sharply at the bottom of the stairs and hurried for the alleyway behind the saloon, Cade close behind.

He grasped her hand and led her toward an open park at the intersection ahead. How did he always know what she needed?

As soon as they stepped from between the close stone buildings, the air freshened and her panic dissipated. Cade took her to a park bench beneath a spreading elm, where he joined her, but with distance between them.

"You may feel better if you remove your jacket." His mouth worked in that curious way, though hidden in part by his beard and mustache.

She took his suggestion to heart, and he helped her pull the snug sleeves from her arms. Immediately, she felt better. "Thank you."

"Wait here. I'll be right back."

She watched him stride away, the crown of his hat skimming above most of the other people milling about in the scattered shade. If only things had worked out differently, perhaps she could have grown old in the circle of his strong arms, made the ranch house a home, and filled it with children. She folded the fitted jacket across her lap and fingered lines against the nap of the dark velvet, considering her next step—what to ask for Henry's farm.

He'd had such good intentions, at least she assumed so by the wording of his will. Tears pricked her eyes anew, but not for loss of Henry. She'd been willing to marry him and work beside him, but she'd never known him. Now she was responsible for his land, and rightfully so, according to Judge Murphy. Was it wrong to sell it?

A light breeze fluttered through the park on ribbons of popcorn and caramel. Music played in the distance, and children's laughter erupted nearby where a family shared a picnic on a blanket. Cade approached her with a bottle in each hand and a smile forming on his handsome face. Another changing mood. Had he changed his mind as well?

His hat was cocked to one side, clearly revealing merry eyes. "Soda water," he said, standing before her and offering an opened bottle. "Chilled in ice."

She could not have been more pleased had he offered her a new set of unchipped china. "Thank you." His slinged arm hung at eye level, and she leaned toward it, sniffing. "Not to be rude, but you smell a bit like popcorn and . . . honey?"

His face bloomed into a true smile, like that of a young boy producing his best work for a parent. He reached into the sling and withdrew a brimming paper sack. "They called it kettle corn, and it smelled so good I couldn't resist."

Laughing, she accepted the bag, delighted in his relaxed enthusiasm as he settled beside her on the bench. She longed to know what he wanted to discuss, but refused to disrupt this hard-earned reprieve from their ordeal in court. Contenting herself with his presence, the breeze, and the delicious sweetened popcorn, she tucked her curiosity away. He would tell her when he was ready, and she prayed she'd have the fortitude to hear what he had to say.

In too brief a time, he drew a gold watch from his vest pocket, gave it a quick glance, and slipped it back, ending their pleasant respite. He downed the last of his soda water and set his hat to its normal position. "We best leave if we're going to stop in Olin Springs before the land office closes."

Her lightheartedness fizzled in the face of rough reality, but he was right. It would be hot enough traveling beneath the midday sun—again. Her suit might be beyond salvation by the time they made it home. The word pinged against her heart, leaving a small wound.

They returned their bottles to the soda stand, and she waited in the shade as he retrieved their bags from the hotel and brought around the wagon. After handing her up, he reached behind the seat for her broad-brimmed hat and gave it to her with his characteristically wry quirk. Then he joined her on the seat, flicked the gray mare on the rump, and they left Cedar City and its Founders' Day festivities behind.

~

If he'd not told Mae Ann she had to leave, Cade wouldn't be racking his brain for a way to unsay it. If he'd spoken up sooner and declared himself, they'd be spending another day in Cedar City. Strolling down Main Street, dining at the hotel. He'd buy her a fancy-made dress, try his hand at courting, and dadgum it, he wouldn't be spending another night in a chair.

Smoke clopped along as if this were just another drive from town and not a crossroads for the rest of Cade's life.

He huffed. With her sitting right next to him, he couldn't even think out loud. As it was, she'd made her wishes clear, and he had twenty miles to figure out how to tell her he wanted to buy her farm.

"I want to buy your farm."

So much for working around to a conversation.

The gray swiveled its ears at his voice, but Mae Ann sat stone-still.

He darted a look her way and found her stick straight as usual, the hat hiding her expression. Exasperating woman. Light as a spring flower one moment and brick heavy the next.

"Why?"

He swallowed. "Why?"

"Yes, why?"

He might as well jump in all the way. "I've changed my mind about you leaving."

The gray plodded on. Mae Ann remained her stalwart self.

"Seeing as how Judge Murphy ruled in your favor, and you're set on selling the farm, you might as well sell it to me."

He gave her a sidelong glance. "I figure if I buy the farm and join it to Parker Land and Cattle, you might feel you have an interest in the place and decide to stay on."

He drew in a bucket of air, unaccustomed to stringing so many words together in one breath.

"So this is about business."

Not a question, but he heard one just the same. What was he supposed to say? That in spite of what she thought, he didn't want the life he'd had before she came to the ranch—lonely, cold, and one-sided. The words stuck in his throat and he couldn't pry them loose.

"I see." She fiddled with the blue bag on her lap, but he hadn't missed the disappointment in her voice.

He plowed on. "If we do it that way, MacGrath'll back off and a third party won't be involved up in our country."

She looked at him, something like hope staining her voice. "We?"

The knot at the back of his neck rubbed, and his shoulder ached from flexing his right arm over and over. "Well, *you*, I guess."

Her shoulders slumped a bit, and Cade felt as if he were holding a losing hand in a high-stakes poker game. Only this was no game. "Mae Ann, what do you want me to say?"

He dipped his head to see beneath her hat brim and found her lips rolled tight, her eyes blinking furiously, but she wouldn't look at him. Just shook her head.

Confounded woman, she made him crazy. He clucked Smoke to a faster pace. The sooner they got to Olin Springs, the sooner he could breathe again.

The gray ate up the dry miles, and Cade stopped in front of a watering trough two doors down from the land office. While he let the mare drink, Mae Ann climbed down and brushed the dust from her suit. It was near the same time of day as when he'd taken her to the church in May. The sun inched closer to the mountaintops, and a distant rumble warned of a coming storm. He tied off the reins and slapped his hat against his trousers. Mae Ann looked past him to the land office, its shingle clearly marking the entry. Best get it over with.

He offered his left arm and she took it, much to his relief. But at the entrance she reined him in.

"I accept your offer."

He freed his arm, gripped her shoulder, and turned her to face him. "Look at me, Mae Ann."

Her jaw tightened, but her eyes—oh, those eyes. They brimmed once more, and for the life of him he didn't know how it was he hurt her so easily. "It's not about the land. It's not what the judge said, that I just wanted the farm. It's about keeping you safe and keeping MacGrath out of our life."

A tear slipped away before she could stop it. She lowered her gaze and pushed the back of each hand to her eyes, then locked on him again. "Tell me what you mean by *our life.*"

His heartbeat pounded in his skull, and he had no doubt she could hear it.

"Excuse me."

He spun around to a fella trying to get in the door that he and Mae Ann blocked.

Cade nodded. "Beg pardon." Gently, he pulled Mae Ann to the side, grateful for a minute to herd his thoughts. Her cheeks were damp, her lashes wet, and her fingers knotted in the string of her blue bag.

"I mean you and me. Together on the ranch." Fine courting words, but this was no stroll down Main Street.

She looked clear through him. Broke down the door to the cold room where he'd kept his heart chained. Her hand brushed his bearded cheek, and the chains snapped like the old ladder rungs in the barn.

"Let's go inside and see what the land is worth, and then I can transfer the papers to you at the bank."

The door opened and two people exited. They could have been walking, talking buffalo for all the notice he paid them. Mae Ann preceded him through the door, and they caught the land agent as he was closing up shop.

He greeted them without surprise. "I thought I might see you today, Mrs. Parker. Cade." He gave them a toothy grin. "Mr. MacGrath came in earlier and left this envelope for you, ma'am. He said to be sure and tell you that if this wasn't enough to buy your farm, there was more where that came from."

~

Mae Ann stared at the envelope the man offered, refusing to touch it. Of all the arrogant, presumptuous, and overbearing people she had ever met, Sean MacGrath took the prize. But that prize would not be her farm.

With a hike of her skirts, she bolted out the door and down the boardwalk toward the bank, Cade hollering behind her. He wanted her. She saw it in his eyes, even though he hadn't said the words she longed to hear. But he'd defined *us* as the two of them, and that was a start. The start to the home she wasn't about to let Sean MacGrath or anyone else get in the way of, no matter how much money they offered. Henry's farm was not for sale.

She was *giving* it to Cade.

The bank's door was locked, the shade pulled, the interior dark. She fell against it to catch her breath, then pounded her fists on the wood, rattling the window glass. "Open this door! I know . . . you're in there!"

A hard hand pulled her back and an arm clamped her against an even harder chest. "Mae Ann." Cade's deep voice rolled through her, settling into her very core, and she slumped against his restraint, her tears spotting his sleeve. She covered her face and turned into his chest.

His lips grazed her ear, his voice gentle. "We'll come back. I promise."

~

The wind cut into Mae Ann's unguarded side, and she longed for Cade's arm around her again. But he had only one he could use, and he needed it to get them home ahead of the coming storm.

"Tell me about your family."

His question startled her. In all the time she'd been at the ranch, he'd asked nothing about her background. That he wanted to know somehow warmed her against the sharp wind.

"Just my mother and myself before she died at the rooming house where we worked." Mae Ann sensed him looking at her, though with only intermittent flashes of distant lightning, she couldn't be sure.

"No father?"

The pointed query turned her face away. She peered into the cloaking dark, tamped down the shame, and chose to believe concern drove his interest rather than judgmental curiosity. "I remember very little about him. He left when I was a child, a decision that completely changed our lives."

Cade huffed disagreeably. "I understand how that can happen. The change, I mean."

Did he? He'd had a father growing up. Had his life changed all that much after his parents' accident?

Rain dappled her arm, and she thought of the garden she'd salvaged after the hailstorm, barren for so long but now full of promise.

"And your mother's death—is that why you answered Henry's advertisement?"

At least he cut right to the issue and didn't beat around the bush.

Swollen raindrops plopped against her lap and shoulders. Perhaps the pressing storm pressed his candor. "Yes. Henry offered a home and security, something I had long wanted."

She recalled telling Cade something very similar when he'd questioned her motives in May, but now she felt exposed by sharing it again.

The rain fell harder, and she hunched her shoulders beneath her hat brim, dreading the likelihood of hail.

"I'll give you that and more if—"

Light exploded ahead of them, and the horse reared. Cade tore off his sling and fought to keep the mare in hand. Again lightning speared the road and thunder slammed through the wagon seat and into Mae Ann's bones. She caught a glimpse of Cade's corded neck, his clenched jaw, and linked an arm around the bench back to keep her seat.

Lightning ripped across the cloud canopy, illuminating the scene and opening heaven's stores. The mare bolted.

Cade stood with one boot braced against the buckboard, leaning back, the reins wrapped around both hands and every rock-hard muscle in his arms and legs bulging against his drenched clothes.

Mae Ann had learned what a summer storm could do. Rain-gorged creeks became raging rivers, and if Cade didn't stop the wagon before they reached the upper crossing of

Olin Creek, they might not make it across without being swept away.

"Oh, Lord, we need your help." The slashing rain and wind tore the words from her lips. She thought of Jesus stilling the tempest, and pleaded for Him to calm their storm and give Cade the strength he needed.

Water ran off the brim of her hat and down her back. She tried to drape her jacket over her shoulders, but the wind caught it and ripped it from her hands. Soaked to her bones, she clung to the bench and prayed—for Cade, for Deacon. For the ranch, Cougar and Blue, the cattle and horses. The Price family.

Bless them that curse you.

Lightning broke like blue fire around them. The mare turned violently away and charged through the brush and trees until the wagon snagged and slammed Mae Ann from her seat. She caught herself against the buckboard before she could tumble beneath the mare's hooves.

Cade leaped out and cut the reins as well as the traces, and the horse charged into the night. He came back to lift Mae Ann to the ground, and together they crawled beneath the wagon. Though muddy and slick, the small knoll sent water running away from their makeshift shelter, and Cade drew her into his arms, arching his broad shoulders around her as they lay on the wet earth.

Without the rain slashing her face and back, her tension eased in his embrace, and she felt safe and protected from the storm. *Thank you, Lord, for saving us. Please, please protect Smoke and Deacon and Cougar and Blue.* She rolled her lips, struggling against resentment before acknowledging God's great love and provision for her. *And keep Sean MacGrath safe as well.*

As the words left her heart, the rain lessened. The moments between lightning and thunder lengthened, and soon the only sound was the dripping of water from the end of the tilted wagon and the thunder of Cade's heart against her ear.

CHAPTER 23

C ade's shoulder screamed for relief, but he refused to let go of Mae Ann. The soft warmth of her through her rain-soaked blouse and skirt reminded him again that life was more than cattle and land, rustlers and renegades. Lying in the mud beneath the wagon, he thanked God for bringing her to him. For he was finally convinced that the Lord had done exactly that.

And Cade had almost lost her.

He shuddered at the thought and kissed the top of her head cradled on his throbbing arm. He'd slept in spurts, but now dawn brightened the horizon and birds chirped from the brush as if there had been no storm at all.

Mae Ann pulled away and opened her eyes. She pushed herself up on her elbow and smiled at him, and it warmed him to his very core.

"It's over." She crawled out, leaving him profoundly empty.

He rolled out the other side and pulled himself to his feet only to be met by her hand-smothered snort across the wagon bed.

"What?"

She laughed, tried to stop, but laughed harder. "You're . . . you're . . . covered in mud!"

He cut her a squinted look as he rounded the back of the wagon. She giggled and backed away, playing like a young woman with her suitor. Turning to run, she slipped, but he caught her and lifted her off her feet.

"You're not exactly spotless yourself, Mrs. Parker."

Her mud-smeared cheeks colored like the morning breaking upon them, and he brushed his lips against the tip of her nose, her eyelids. Setting her on her feet, he cupped her face in his hands and lowered his mouth to hers, kissing her the way he'd wanted to since she'd thrown her arms around him at the old cottonwood tree.

"Glad to see you're alive and kickin'."

They both startled at the voice of the rider who'd approached unnoticed. He crossed his arms on his saddle horn and gave a quick nod. "Mornin', ma'am. Cade. I feared the two of you was washed away in that toad strangler. But I shoulda known the Almighty had it all under control."

Deacon's blue eyes snapped like firecrackers, and Cade knew he'd hear about this day the rest of his life.

Mae Ann smoothed her sodden skirt, and her chin rose in that commanding way. "You are just in time, Deacon. We need help getting the wagon back on the road. And did you happen to see Smoke anywhere nearby?"

He pushed his hat up and scratched his head. "Smoke? After that gully-washer? Not likely, ma'am."

"The mare, you old badger." Cade caught the joke in Deacon's eyes and shook his head, looking around for his own hat and finding it jammed in a juniper. Mae Ann's was gone, as was her jacket and his sling. And from the looks of her, so would be the velvet skirt that clung to her form. He ran a hand through his hair and met up with several clumps of dried mud.

251

Deacon dismounted and tied his rope to the rear axle.

Between the three of them and Deacon's horse, they rolled the buckboard out of the cedar clump and onto the road. Smoke had taken them farther afield than Cade had realized last night, and he hoped she hadn't broken a leg in her frenzy to outrun the storm.

"Any damage at the ranch?" He shoved his hat on and just as quickly pulled it off. Time for a new one. And a new suit for Mae Ann when they returned to town.

"Lightning hit somewhere on the north end," Deacon said. "Started a fire, I reckon, by the glow I seen, but it didn't last long in that downpour. Soon as I get you two back to the house, I'll ride out and look things over. Could have been a fence post or—" His voice trailed off with a shaded glance at Mae Ann.

Deacon handed him his horse's reins. "Buck don't pull, so you and the missus take him on up to the house and I'll see if I can't scare up the mare. She's probably around here close."

Cade helped Mae Ann into the saddle and looped the reins over the gelding's head. "I doubt it. She spooked pretty bad last night. I cut her loose, so we'll need a new rigging as well." He pulled Mae Ann's foot from the stirrup and climbed up behind her with a wince.

"Ain't you supposed to be harnessed up yourself?" Deacon stepped out of the way as Cade turned the horse around.

"You find it and I'll think about it." He gave his foreman a nod and headed off at a gentle walk, his right arm loose around Mae Ann's waist and her fallen hair smelling like rain. She raised a hand behind her to touch his face, and the tender act was near more than he could take. He kicked the gelding into an easy lope.

It was late morning by the time they made it to the ranch, and the sun pulled steam from the rooftops of the buildings and the backs of horses in the corral. Rivulets cut through the open yard, and Cougar and Blue came splashing up to greet them. Cade slid off first and Mae Ann climbed down and hugged the muddy dog whimpering around her skirts.

"Oh, you good boy, Cougar. Did you miss us?"

Blue held back until she called to him, and then he received her affectionate embrace too.

Cade was almost jealous. He had a mind to start a big kettle of water on the stove and fill the copper tub for a bath with his bride, but first things first, which meant harnessing another horse and riding out to help Deacon with the wagon.

Laughing, Mae Ann straightened, her face licked clean by those hounds that probably smelled better than he did. He pulled her to him, but she braced her arms against him.

"I'm sure you don't want to kiss me after those dogs did their worst." Her dark eyes sparked with laughter, luring him to do much more than that.

"I'm sure I do." And he did, kissing her until she went limp in his arms. When he pulled up for air, she tipped her head back, baring her delicate neck. He groaned and eased away, holding her arms until he was certain she could stand on her own.

"Why, Mr. Parker. You do know how to make a statement."

If he didn't leave now, Deacon would be walking home. Cade gave her a quick peck on her cheek. "I'll be back to finish what I was saying."

She blushed and picked at her sodden skirt. "Do you need my help with anything?"

He shook his head, watching Cougar, who leaned against her like a child with its ma. The idea shot his eyes to hers, and he imagined them with a houseful of babies. So many he'd have to add on a room.

He took a step back. "I don't know how long I'll be."

Her smile sank into his skin and spread clear through him. "I'll have dinner ready when the two of you get back." Then she sobered and her expression darkened, and she came to him on a whisper. "Be careful."

He brushed his lips against her forehead. "Yes, ma'am."

Catching a horse from the near pasture, throwing on the extra harness, and riding bareback to where Deacon and the wagon waited didn't cause near the pain as leaving Mae Ann behind. Tonight he'd offer her his mother's wedding band. And then he'd make sweet, fiery Mae Ann Remington Parker his wife.

~

Only three days since they'd left for Cedar City, but Mae Ann felt as if she'd died and been born anew since then. Nothing had changed at the ranch, but everything was different. Every item in the house held a luster she'd not noticed before. She was a woman loved, and it made all the difference.

Cade hadn't said he loved her in so many words, but she knew it down to her toes, and those toes squished in her wet stockings on her way upstairs. In her room she shed her ruined skirt and blouse and threw on a wrapper. If she hurried, she'd have time to scrape together what Deacon hadn't eaten—or make biscuits and gravy if nothing else—take a quick bath, wash her hair, and put on the only dress she had left.

As she rummaged through her trunk, she found a small bottle of rose water saved for an important occasion. What could be more important than a warm scented bath for a night like tonight? Her stomach fluttered as she clutched the vial against her breast and closed her eyes. *Thank you, Lord, for hearing my prayer.* Flush with anticipation, she was certain Cade had more than words on his mind.

Though it was midsummer, last night's storm had cooled the countryside, and soon the kitchen windows steamed from water she'd heated for her bath. The sweet scent of roses clung to her hair as she toweled it dry, then ran upstairs to change. Dressed and freshened, she set a pan of biscuits baking, with coffee cooking on the back of the stove and sausage gravy bubbling. She was home at last, and she'd never been happier.

By late afternoon, the biscuits and coffee were cold, the gravy had skinned over, and she'd worn a path from the stove to the front door checking to see if Cade and Deacon had returned.

Weary from the emotional ups and downs of the last three days and a fitful night's sleep beneath the buckboard, she found it harder and harder to resist the lure of her waiting bed. Climbing the stairs for a quick nap before the men returned, she assured herself that she would hear them drive into the yard, or catch the dogs' welcoming yaps. She eased onto the narrow tick with a weary sigh, relaxing for a moment—only a moment to again savor Cade's possessive kiss and the look in his eyes when he'd left.

~

The buckboard proved more of a challenge than Cade anticipated. Weakened when it crashed against the snag, the axle cracked as he drove across the swollen creek, and it was the sheer strength of the horse he'd chosen that got them up the other side at all. They stopped to wrap Deacon's rope around the splitting beam, and finally made it home as the first stars appeared. A thin ribbon of smoke teased from the kitchen chimney, signaling the home fire he longed for, but a dying one.

Deacon insisted he'd see to the animals, and Cade bolted for the house, pausing only to drag his boot soles across the scraper by the door. Inside, he pulled them off in the jack, straining his ears for sounds from the kitchen. Nothing.

And no wonder. No light from the lamps, only the greasy smell of cold sausage. The coffeepot was cool to his touch, but the fire beneath it was banked and he fed in small bits to warm up the brew. A cotton napkin covered an untouched pan of Mae Ann's mouthwatering biscuits, but it did nothing to cover the aching awareness that he had let her down.

He found her asleep on the narrow bed in his old room—not where she belonged across the hall on the feather tick. He bent close to kiss her brow and finger her dark hair splayed on the pillow. She smelled of roses, and she wore her yellow dress. She needed more dresses, as many as she wanted, and he intended to see to it when they returned to Olin Springs.

Gently, he pulled her Missouri-bought work boots from her feet, his fingers easily encircling her stockinged ankles. Then he draped a quilt over her legs and left the door open to hear if she stirred.

He was as weary as Mae Ann looked, but he still had things to put in order. He gathered clean clothes, then found his mother's ring in the box where he'd left it, atop the collection of her cherished keepsakes. He slid the ring onto his smallest finger and quietly slipped out, as certain as he'd ever been that Mae Ann would accept the thin gold band.

Each step on the stair jarred his shoulder and called for a long soak in the tub, but he wasn't finished. Darkness cloaked the great room, and he lit a lamp at his desk, took a seat in the old leather chair, and withdrew a small brass key from a hidden compartment. He pulled open the heavy bottom drawer and removed a strongbox, faltering at the dull glint of worn gold letters from where it had rested.

Five and a half years ago, he'd told himself he put the leather-bound book in the drawer for safe keeping. Even then, he'd known that was a lie.

An old ache throbbed behind his ribs as he set the strongbox aside and reached for the Bible. Its weight was greater than he remembered. Either that, or resentment had added to it. He opened the front cover and, two pages in, found his family's history that dated back to his great-grandparents in the 1700s.

The older the entry, the fancier the script listing events and dates, names and places. Births. Marriages. Deaths. The elaborate writing had intrigued him as a boy, particularly the two entries in his mother's hand marking his birth and that of his sister.

The latest entry was his own, where, beside his parents' names, he'd written *Died 20 January 1875.*

His father's bold pen dominated the page, third entry from the bottom, noting the date that he and Madeline Bennett were wed. The familiar writing burned against Cade's heart like a branding iron, and resentment fired once more toward the man who failed to practice what he preached. The man whose arrogance had cost his children both father and mother.

Cade laid the open book on the desk and drew a ragged breath. More than five years was a long time to carry a grudge, and Cade wasn't fool enough not to know that unforgiveness could shorten a man's life. Same as pride.

He pushed the thought and the Bible aside and opened the strong box. His family had owned Parker Land and Cattle outright for two generations, so a fair amount of Cade's profits from selling livestock went into the box. He'd never felt right letting the bank hold all his money—another discomfort picked up from the colonel.

A cold thought snaked through the back of his mind. If he'd taken money from the box for Betsy that day, he wouldn't have been in the bank when . . .

And where would Mae Ann be?

He scrubbed both hands down his face with a groan. He'd spent enough of his life mulling over what he couldn't change. He had to make a fresh start, leave the past in the past, and move forward with Mae Ann.

He thumbed through the bills and counted out what he figured would pay off the note on her farm and allow her to keep the funds she had in her account. A smile tugged his mouth as he recalled her bracing the bank teller about that issue and winning.

Satisfied that all was in order, he returned the money box and then reached for the open Bible. Something caught his eye. Small words penned beneath his parents' wedding date, in the colonel's hand, but with lighter strokes. Cade had missed them before.

Maybe it was the play of light that brought them off the page. Or maybe it was the press of an unseen hand that made him note the reference: Proverbs 18:22.

Closing the book soundly, he pushed it to the front of the desk. He'd read it later, when he wasn't so worn out. He made to stand and his chest seized with a sudden grip—that unseen hand squeezing until one heartbeat stumbled into the next. He grabbed the Bible and fell against the chair back, searching until he found the book of Proverbs, the eighteenth chapter, the twenty-second verse.

Yellow lamplight warmed the page, and the words seemed to come alive and sink into his soul. Words that his father had noted but never shared. Words that Cade had not read or heard . . . until Pastor Bittman spoke them the day of the wedding.

Hands trembling as he gripped the old book, he blinked against his blurring vision, tears spilling on the thin paper.

"God forgive me for not forgiving him." The prayer scratched up from Cade's throat, healing an old, deep wound. He was no more perfect than his father, maybe even less so. For the colonel had realized what Cade nearly missed: *Whoso findeth a wife findeth a good thing, and obtaineth favour of the LORD.*

His mother had definitely brought favor to the colonel's life, and Cade knew the blessing applied to Mae Ann as well. He palmed his eyes and opened the ink bottle atop the desk, then he dipped the pen and made an entry below his name:

Married Mae Ann Remington, 15 May 1880, Olin Springs, Colorado. In smaller script beneath her name, he wrote *Proverbs 18:22.*

Deacon stomped his boots on the stone porch, pulling Cade back to his current situation. He left the Bible open for the ink to dry and went to the kitchen, where he set the cold biscuits in the oven and stirred milk into the gravy. After supper, he'd heat a kettle of water and soak the mud and grime from his skin.

The front door creaked Deacon's slow entry, and he came around the wall looking as if he'd pulled the buckboard himself. Cade set hot coffee at his place, then served him up a plate. If he knew Deacon, the old man would mosey down to the creek with a bar of soap tonight or tomorrow or sometime this week. Good thing Mae Ann was sleeping or she wouldn't let him push himself up to the table in his condition.

"Appreciate your help today." Cade took his seat, uneasy with Mae Ann's empty chair to his left.

"You'da done the same for me." Deacon forked in half a biscuit, trailing gravy in the process. Quick to wipe his mouth on his sleeve, he cut the next bite smaller. Cade found where Mae Ann kept her napkins and brought two to the table.

"She sleepin'?"

Cade nodded, his mouth full.

"I reckon it weren't too cozy on the knoll last night in the mud."

"No, but we were out of the worst of it." Cade swigged his coffee. "You see any sign of Smoke?"

Deacon shook his head. "It come a-rainin' so hard, washed away all her tracks. But if she's not bogged down or broke a leg, she'll come home. Horses are bad as people, wantin' to bunch together and keep an eye on one another."

Cade wondered for the hundredth time why Deacon had never married and had a family of his own.

"All the cookies are gone."

Cade chuckled, not surprised in the least.

"I hope she's up and around to bakin' another batch sooner than later."

He eyed the man he'd known all his life, and cut into another biscuit. Deacon had never been one to come out and share his feelings. Missing Mae Ann's cookies was about as close as he'd get to saying he liked having her around.

"She's staying."

Deacon looked up with a spark in his eye. "That so?"

Cade swallowed a smile. "Judge ruled in her favor and I'm buying the farm. Soon as we get the wagon fixed, we'll ride in and sign the papers."

Deacon huffed. "Didn't see hide nor hair of MacGrath while you was gone."

"He was in Cedar City. Showed up at the hearing and made an enemy of the judge, from what I could tell."

Deacon tore a biscuit in half and swabbed his gravy. "I rode over to Reiker's under a full moon two nights ago. Not a chicken on the place." He wadded the napkin. "The missus'll be plumb upset about it."

"You kept your word."

Another huff. "Shoulda gone the last full moon."

They finished every biscuit and drop of gravy, and Deacon lumbered off to do whatever he did in the evening at his cabin.

Cade washed their dishes, added boiling water to the rosy-smelling bath already drawn, and soaked his shoulder while he washed away the dirt. Tempted to sleep right there, he forced himself out, dressed, and went upstairs to check on Mae Ann again.

Leaning close, he drank in the scent of her, lifted a strand of her hair, and thumbed its silkiness. His throat tightened with gratitude. Satisfied that she was well and resting, he went to his room and fell into bed. As grateful as he was, knowing she slept across the hall wasn't near as comforting as holding her in his muddy arms beneath the stranded wagon.

She might as well be a hundred miles away.

CHAPTER 24

Mae Ann woke with a start, worried by the pale light teasing her window rather than a setting sun. Had she really slept all that time? Cade's door stood open, and she peeked in to find him lying across his bed facedown in clean trousers—spent, no doubt, from yesterday's ordeal. In spite of his injured shoulder, he'd fought to keep them safe in the storm, and he'd succeeded.

She hurried to the kitchen, fleeing the heated blush that attended her recollection of their night beneath the wagon, and coaxed a banked coal to life for a fresh pot of coffee. Cade would be famished when he woke, and more than likely sore from all the strain on his shoulder. If Dr. Weaver learned of it, he'd have him on bed rest for a month.

The biscuits and gravy from the night before were gone and dishes had been washed and laid to dry on the sideboard. A bucket of warm milk waited nearby—Deacon's handiwork, bless his crusty ol' heart. She smiled as she took up her egg basket and headed for the barn.

Morning's cool breath was nectar to her lungs, and her heart skipped lightly at the realization that the ranch was truly her home now, and not just in her dreams. She recalled Deacon's mention of a possible fire the night of the storm, and though he'd not said as much, she knew he suspected the blaze had been at Henry's place.

Their place, soon to be part and parcel of Parker Land and Cattle Company. Containing her excitement was as futile a struggle as keeping bread dough from rising.

"Mornin', ma'am." Deacon held a ladder rung in place against the back wall, a hammer in his other hand.

"Good morning, Deacon. And it's Mae Ann, please. Isn't it a glorious day?"

He tucked the hammer under his arm and pulled a heavy nail from his pocket. "That it is."

"Have you eaten?"

He patted his stomach. "Last night. Polished off every last drop of gravy and your fine biscuits. Even let Cade have a couple."

"I'll fix you some eggs and hotcakes if you'd like. Coffee's already perking. I know it's late for you, but I overslept."

"You and Cade had quite a time of it in the storm, jamming the wagon in that juniper patch and all. I figured you'd be sleepin' a lot longer."

Feigning a sudden interest in the wall-mounted ladder, she let her eyes wander to his inscrutable face for any hint of what Cade might have shared. As always, she came up with nothing. "Well, if you're not hungry, I'd like to thank you for milking the cow and ask you a favor."

He stopped what he was doing and looked at her straight-on.

"Would you please saddle Ginger for me? After I gather the eggs, I want to go for a ride."

Deacon's mustache twitched from side to side. "Beggin' your pardon, does Cade know you're wantin' to ride off by yourself? My guess is he'd want to go with you."

Sensing a wall of fatherly concern rising in opposition, she presented her most pleasant but firmly planted posture. "I'll not wake him. He needs to rest after struggling with the wagon and not wearing his sling. I just want to get some fresh air."

She'd had more than enough fresh air in the last two days, but if she told Deacon where she was headed, he'd fight her tooth and nail. He shuffled his feet, as uncomfortable as a fox caught in the henhouse. "It's not safe, if you don't mind me sayin' so. Could be ne'er-do-wells hangin' around, not to mention MacGrath."

MacGrath. *Humph.* He'd better not be, but just in case, she'd take Cade's gun. She looked toward the tack room. "I'd attempt saddling Ginger myself, but I'm not sure I know the finer points of securing a bridle, and I'd hate for some mishap on the way." She grimaced at the overtly feminine ploy, but she wanted the horse properly saddled and ready to ride, and if using a woman's wiles was what it took, so be it.

Deacon shook his head and scratched his jaw, worry adding wrinkles to his weathered face. Why was he so hesitant?

"I doubt Cade'll be too happy when he hears about it."

She gave him her brightest smile. "I'll be home before he realizes I'm gone—in plenty of time to bake a fresh batch of cookies for dinner."

~

Stinging slightly from her blatant manipulation, Mae Ann changed into her split skirt and tall boots, slid Cade's handgun into the saddlebag, and called Cougar to accompany her. She hadn't returned to the farm since burying Henry, and now that it was to be part of the ranch, she wanted to take stock of what could be salvaged and what could not.

She cut north for Pine Hill and reined in near the crosses, pleased by the prospering rose. She felt as vigorous in her own way, sensing fully the Lord's blessing. His face did indeed shine upon her. He had given her a home, a husband, and great peace.

Continuing north with the meadowlarks' encouragement, she drank in the earth's sweet perfume after the storm. Everything was fresh and clean, and she reveled in the sense of new beginnings. She clucked Ginger into a lope, marveling at the cerulean sky and rolling grassland that spread unfettered between mountain ridges. She felt exactly the same—unfettered. Free yet belonging to someplace, to someone.

Cougar ran beside her, and soon the farm buildings came into view. She slowed to a walk, and the dog's ears perked. He lowered his head and growled.

"What is it, boy?" She reined in and listened for what could have made the dog nervous, but heard only the echoing meadowlarks in the open fields.

And bawling cattle.

Cougar growled again.

Henry had no cattle, and she'd not passed any Parker cow-calf pairs in the north pastures. Had some broken through the fence during the storm?

Distracted by the mournful cries, she rode into the yard before noticing two horses tied at the flimsy corral. Fine hairs rose on her arms as if charged by lightning. Cougar continued to growl, his eyes wary.

Deacon was right. She should not have come alone. Yet this was her land and she had every right to be here. Whoever owned the horses might have penned the calves, and she steeled herself to challenge them.

A creaking floorboard captured her attention. A man leaned against a post on the sagging porch. Another man stepped out of the barn, and a flare lit in the back of her mind.

She gathered Ginger to whirl away, but the men rushed her from each side. One grabbed her about the waist and pulled her roughly from the saddle. She slapped him and he laughed, his tobacco-fouled breath washing over her with sickening familiarity.

"I told ya this weren't over yet, missy." He pressed his grimy face into her hair. "Don't you just smell fine as a flower?"

He dragged her into the house and threw her onto a mat in the corner.

As he closed in on her, she spit in his face. "You murderer."

He raised his hand, and she screamed. "Cougar—home!"

A gunshot and a yelp, and her heart burst in grief before his fist slammed her against the wall and into darkness.

~

If Deacon was not more uncle than foreman, Cade would fire him on the spot. The man faced him, hat in hand as Cade held the coffeepot and a tin cup, forgetting that one would fill the other. "When did she leave?"

"About an hour ago."

"Why didn't you wake me?" The words churned out of Cade's gut like black bile.

"I tried to talk her out of going, but she insisted. Said you needed to rest after what you and her been through. And your shoulder—"

"Hang my shoulder!" He slammed the pot and cup down on the table, shooting knives into that very part of his body.

"She took the yella dog with her."

Cade scalded Deacon with a glare. "A lot of good that'll do her." Only partly sorry for berating the old cowboy, Cade ran both hands down his face, dumbfounded that she would do such a thing. "You could have refused to saddle her horse."

Deacon's blue eyes narrowed to slits. "And have her go off half-cocked with a loose cinch if she'd done the saddlin'? You know as well as me that she was goin' whether I helped her or not. At least she's rigged up proper."

He was right. Cade fell into a chair at the table and propped his head in his hands.

Deacon joined him. "She promised to be home 'fore you knew she was gone, in time to bake . . ."

Cade cut him a look, and Deacon's words washed out.

Holding on to Mae Ann and keeping her safe was exactly like what he'd told the sheriff—holding oil in his hand.

"Well, do you know which way she went?"

"Toward Pine Hill."

She's going to the farm. Cade shoved himself to his feet. "Saddle your horse and mine. We're going after her."

Deacon strode out and Cade followed, stopping only to grab the two Winchesters from the gun rack and his Colt— which was missing. Confounded woman. He strapped on his father's Army issue and tied down the holster.

On his way to the barn, Cougar came limping across the yard, looking back every so often with a whimper. Cade ran for the dog, and his heart slammed into his chest at its grazed and bloody shoulder.

He would kill MacGrath.

With the ground still soft from the storm, it wasn't hard to track Mae Ann and Ginger. They followed her trail uphill, to where she'd stopped near the graves. It came back to him then, the day she'd come down to the house, a pail on her arm. She was watering a rose cutting that she'd planted between the cedar crosses. Another selfless act that he'd given no notice of. Like so many other things she did for him. Fear cinched a steel band around his chest, and he turned back to her tracks that took off north across the pastureland, straight for the farm. He spurred Cricket into a run.

As they neared the farm, a familiar sound greeted them that shouldn't have. Cade reined in behind a cedar clump, far enough away to see the outbuildings but not be seen. A half dozen head bawled in the corral, and he'd bet his Winchester they all carried the Lazy-P.

He and Deacon skirted the house and dropped their horses' reins fifty yards out. He thumbed the ring on his small finger. If he'd put it on Mae Ann's finger yesterday when they first got home, maybe she wouldn't have ridden out here today.

He'd let her down again.

Ginger grazed nearby, and two other horses were tied to the flimsy corral. The smell of burned hair and hide hung in the air. If Mae Ann weren't in danger, he'd look for the running iron or cinch ring used on those steers. He signaled Deacon to cut around the other side, and then slipped through the brush toward the house, catching bits of an argument. His blood chilled and he drew his gun.

"Why'd you go and do a fool thing like that?"

"Shut up and let me think."

"Well, you better think quick. We got beeves to drive up to that Cripple Creek butcher, and we don't need a woman taggin' along."

"She's not goin' with us."

Cade cocked the hammer and inched closer.

The voice dropped. "You go check the horses. I got somethin' to take care of right now."

Cade hit the porch the same time as Deacon and kicked in the door. One man fired as Cade rolled and shot, hitting the man's gun hand. Deacon's rifle held the other fella in his tracks, hands in the air.

The bank robbers.

Cade itched for revenge, for what they'd done to Mae Ann, for what they were about to do to her, but he holstered his weapon. And smashed his fist into the gunman's face.

The cur slammed to the floor like a felled tree.

Cade and Deacon tied the pair belly-down across their saddles for a trip to town, then he slapped the shooter's hat on his saddle horn and leaned close to his swollen face, lip split and bloodied and not near as cocky as he'd been at the bank. "Appears to me it's over, mister."

Inside, Mae Ann lay against one wall, out cold but alive. She looked unharmed otherwise, but he'd soon know for certain. Lord help him if those two had so much as laid a hand on her. His throat thickened and his chest nearly cinched off his air. Thank God he'd made it to her in time.

He carried her outside to Deacon, then tethered her horse to his and swung into the saddle.

Deacon lifted her to him, his eyes shining, as grateful as Cade and apparently heartsick for his part in the near tragedy. "I'll take them two cayuses into town and leave their load with the sheriff. Come back for the cattle later."

Unable to speak, Cade nodded his thanks and cradled his bride closer for the slow ride home.

~

He carried her through the doorway to one of the wingback chairs before the hearth. Her face was pale as new canvas, and his heart threatened to break from his chest at the deep blue mark now staining her cheek. He knelt beside her and smoothed loose hair from her face, momentarily regretting that he hadn't shot the scoundrels and buried them behind Henry's barn.

When her eyes fluttered open and she raised a hand to her temple, he nearly cried out in relief.

"Mae Ann." His graveled whisper drew her focus to his face.

Her lips curved up and her expression warmed.

He took her hand and pressed it against his lips, gratitude overwhelming his ability to breathe. "I love you."

The words set him free, and he marveled at the rush. He should have said them weeks ago, for he'd known early on that she'd not just moved into his house. She'd moved into his soul.

She laid her hand against his cheek. "I love you too."

Her clear and simple declaration was all he needed to go on. To keep ranching, to keep living. "I'll be right back. Don't move."

She huffed and fingered her cheekbone. "You say that a lot."

He returned with a pillow for her head and eased it behind her.

She frowned. "Cougar. Have you seen Cougar?"

He took her left hand. "He's fine. A bullet grazed his shoulder, but I'll clean him up after I take care of you."

Her brows peaked and she winced. "He really made it home? He really did what I told him to do?"

Cade fought the urge to suggest she practice what she preached. Instead, he knelt again, pulled the ring from his finger, and dropped it in his open hand.

Her lips parted with a small gasp and her eyes glistened.

"This isn't a proper proposal because you're already my bride, Mae Ann Parker. But I'm asking you if you'll be my wife."

Such somberness filled her expression that fear jammed his throat at her hesitation.

"I have one question."

He swallowed around the mass. "What is it?"

"What were you about to tell me on our way home when lightning spooked the mare?"

He'd never met a more disconcerting woman, or one who could so easily tie a knot in his liver and leave him dangling. As gently and as calmly as he could manage, he pushed her hair back from her face. "I said, 'I'll give you that and more if—'"

"Home and security."

"Yes. And what I was about to say was"—he kissed the palm of her hand—"I'll give you that and more if you let me love you forever."

Her face lit with a smile that brightened the room as he slipped the ring on her finger and his arms around her, meeting her warm lips in a nuptial kiss. "Now that I've got you, Mrs. Parker, I'm not letting you go."

Her smile deepened. "That's perfectly fine with me, Mr. Parker. There's nowhere I'd rather be than here in your arms."

~~~

Acknowledgments

Thank you to all who aided and supported me in telling Mae Ann and Cade's story, particularly Jill Maple, Amanda, editor Christy Distler, and Old West experts Paul and Linda Scholtz.

Bestselling author and winner of the **Will Rogers Gold Medallion** for Inspirational Western Fiction, **Davalynn Spencer** writes heart-tugging romance with a Western flair. Learn more about Davalynn and her books and sign up for her free newsletter at www.davalynnspencer.com.